"We are what we pretend to be, so we must be careful about what we pretend to be."
Kurt Vonnegut

"Find out who you are and do it on purpose."
Dolly Parton

"It is not known precisely where angels dwell – whether in the air, the void, or the planets. It has not been God's pleasure that we should be informed of their abode."

Voltaire

To Deer Heart and to liberation

Matador
9 Priory Business Park,
Wistow Road, Kibworth Beauchamp,
Leicestershire. LE8 0RX
Tel: (+44) 116 279 2299
Fax: (+44) 116 279 2277
Email: books@troubador.co.uk
Web: www.troubador.co.uk/matador

ISBN 978 1784624 316

British Library Cataloguing in Publication Data.
A catalogue record for this book is available from the British Library.

Printed and bound by CPI Group (UK) Ltd, Croydon, CR0 4YY

Matador is an imprint of Troubador Publishing Ltd

The Wonder Turner

Deborah Sanderson

Edited by
Chris Bryce

Cover Design by
James Higgins

Matador
Troubador Publishing Ltd.

Chapter One

What time was it? She looked at her watch and shook her head.

Pointless toy.

Someone was hammering on a door. She perceived the insistent knocking, coming in waves through an open window to her right. There was a pause, and a voice could be heard, urgently shouting something. Then the knocking started again, but this time more furiously. The Woman paid no mind to it as she was lost in thoughts of a more serious and perplexing kind.

Steven Frayne, could he be part of this? Ridiculous notion! But, was he the catalyst?

Everything which had happened had been out of character for her, but suggesting his involvement seemed tenuous to say the least.

What other answer could there be?

There was no one she could confide in for fear of being damned as mentally disturbed, or as a freak of nature. Either way, it would surely mean incarceration of some kind, for 'the protection of the Person and the General Public' perhaps, or even, in the interest of science. The hammering on the door abruptly stopped, and she could just make out the sound of running footsteps descending stairs. It didn't concern her, so she resumed her thoughts, and checked her watch again. Television Illusionists defying the natural forces of gravity aside, she was still unable to find a way to explain her present predicament to any credible degree. Maybe it was better for the time being to keep certain facts hidden, even from herself? As she sat, she considered secrets and how they are known and kept. Everyone has their secrets, some are decadent, some are dubious, but the average eavesdropper, would mostly find them dull. If her guesses were right, her secret, as to how she was here in the first place, was difficult to believe, certainly not logical and definitely beyond the rational. From this vantage point a part of her longed so desperately to be dull again.

Some things have no reason, they just are, but in this case, an explanation was urgently called for. Here she was, sitting precariously on a bird-limed window ledge in the early morning sunshine, some forty or fifty metres up and in a town she didn't recognise.

How the hell did I get here?

Or was it more a case of not knowing how to explain being here? What seemed true involved unimaginable things, and she felt the need of a convincing story to back her up. Her sanity demanded it.

How long she had been perched there was unknown to her, but the sensation of pins and needles told her it must be a while. Her conscious mind grasped for a reason to justify being on this perch, while her sense of the ridiculous was amused by how wryly funny the need for a reason seemed.

Hopefully I look so insignificant to anyone looking this way. Knowing me, even here, I'll blend into the wall behind me.

For despite her memory loss, she felt she had surely been an extraordinarily ordinary person who might effectively disappear into wallpaper and no one would notice her gone. She took a deep breath and very slowly leaned forward to check if her position was really as it appeared. A lurch in her guts said, it is. There below, the sprinting shadows of morning were speeding across the ground, and the height at which she overlooked them made her head giddy. One part of her hoped for this to be all a dream, though if it was, it was convincingly realistic. Another part was excited by what she could see, for if she did wake up, with her feet safely on the ground, she knew she would feel disappointed, cheated even. Despite this apparent short term amnesia, the Woman had a sense this was possibly one of the most thrilling things to happen to her in recent years, making her imminent danger strangely exhilarating, or was that just vertigo?

Come on woman – figure this out!

How could anyone have predicted her being here? That was a puzzle in itself.

Certainly the prediction would not have come from Angela Bagner. She was a sensible woman, she watched her diet, voted when required, and was as 'Christian' as a non-Christian could be. She made jam for goodness sake. Granted, she had felt for some time that her life had become something like a roundabout, with the same daily routine, the same place, the same time. But, regardless of how and why she had come to be sitting here at her peril, this was not exactly the remedy she had in mind to rectify it. But would she in truth go back to how things had been?

Go back to the grinding tedium, the pain of facing another relentless day of just getting through? No, never again, I would rather ... I would rather ...

She shook her head at the passing thought. That final solution was one to only seriously consider if she was unable to find an acceptable explanation or disguise. Angela was becoming far too noticeable for her own liking, and her present position was a case in point.

Thankfully, little by little, focus and memory were coming back, as the needle-stings in her muscles were subsiding. It was strange, for as she looked at the sunlight on her skin, her flesh appeared to flicker, blurring her outline and making her definition appear modulated. At times she seemed like two bodies, not one. Most disturbing of all, one of the bodies didn't even look like her own. The double vision it created made things appear to sway.

Leaning forward one more time confirmed the absolute. She was alone and on the edge of a hotel window sill, several stories up. Opposite her ledge, across the street, a pigeon roosted on a decaying clock. The Woman's vision was oddly acute, for despite the considerable distance between her window ledge position and the building opposite, she could see the new crust forming on freshly evacuated lime made by the nesting bird which pecked, at first sight, mindlessly on the stone about it. Looking deeper, she could even see the tiny insects crawling in the cracks of the clock marking the time. The steady procession of seconds and minutes had only a small comfort to offer Angela, for although she knew what the chronological time represented in this strange sun-dusted town, what she really needed to know was;

What time am I in?

There was a square far below her, and the slightest movement made small fragments of the ledge crumble and fall, echoing with a rattle when they hit the ground moments later. The sound made Angela's head begin to swim, and she leaned further back into the frame of the ledge for safety.

"Get a grip Woman," she murmured to herself, "Think!"

She closed her eyes, allowing the bright sunlight to tingle on her skin and her mind began to submerge into memory, like reels of film running on a screen in her head. Grainy images began to take focus and charted her route to this elevated position.

Chapter Two

It was early summer when she first noticed the irritation. Angela was having yet another 'evening in', one in a succession of many dreary evenings in. It was always the same. She would leave her clerical work at the hospital at about four-thirty, walk slowly down the high street from Lossingham Station, pausing occasionally outside shop windows, sometimes to mouth 'hi, how are you?' through the glass, but only if she caught the glance of a familiar assistant.

'Oh, fine, fine.' she would mime in reply to these brief exchanges and then would hurry on apace to leave an impression that she had business elsewhere and that it was nothing at all to do with feeling awkward, or heaven forbid, lonely. Routine was her main line of defence when it came to that relentless and questionable companion and, if she kept to her rules, she could just about keep one step away from this shadow catching up. It wasn't always easy though. It would take a feat of thespian skill to disguise the inconvenient ache of not fitting in. The sheer teeth-gritting frustration of moving in the everyday world was at times intolerable. It seemed to Angela, the paper cut-out Everyman was far better equipped than she when passing the time of day. This daily challenge would on occasion fill her with dread and her eyes with angry, glistening tears. No one must know this of her.

Oh, I'd be so ashamed!

In defence of this happening, Angela would rely on her Plan B, which was largely determined by the season. In the winter months she could adopt a cold for camouflage, and in the summer, she had opportune bouts of hay fever which obliged her to wear sunglasses. At the age of forty-three, the magazines told her she was in late youth, knocking off a few years was still possible, and a careful regime of cosmetics and hair colourants saw to that. As it was sunny that particular day, Angela took advantage of the warm afternoon as an excuse to quickly nip into Raffetty's, one of her favoured off-licenses along the route home, to buy a large bottle of cheap white wine.

Raffetty Wines wasn't the only establishment she gave patronage to, there were several, as she felt it prudent to alternate her visits by rotation. This was so as to reduce any suggestion of, well, having a problem. Quiet and demure Miss Bagner, surely she didn't have problems? She was well adjusted and self-reliant, at least that was the image that she wished so desperately to project and be. There would be a time soon when Angela would crave a little more discernment when it came to wishing. She would soon find that many wishes obligingly come true, whether careless or considered. But for now, it was another normal day. A short trip to the local butchers for some steak and then on to home, though to call it home was arguable.

The main reason for her protracted daily return journey was to delay that sinking, desolate feeling that swallowed her up when she turned the key of her basement flat and closed the door behind her. Sometimes she would bitterly joke out loud to the emptiness, "It's only me darling!" Once, she had even toyed with the idea of getting a cat, for something to talk to, rather than just the air. This notion was quickly dismissed, with the realisation that she could never tolerate a cat's ease and predisposition to cruelty. Although she accepted animals may have to kill to survive, the feline love of torture made her more than uncomfortable. Surviving birds in her back garden could bear witness to many a sly intruder receiving a soaking from the contents of Angela's garden bucket, their plans for carnage quashed. Moreover, she had always been a little phobic when it came to cats, finding them too unnervingly sentient to be a domestic pet. They were always watching everything you might do.

Some things behind closed doors ought not to be observed.

Perhaps too, this was the reason why, when almost on the last leg of her way home, she altered her usual route to avoid a particularly over-friendly cat which regularly threatened to accost her from a front garden she passed on the way. Angela was one of those rare people to have animal magnetism. Creatures of all kinds would sense this and gravitate towards her. In her case the gift was an unwelcome one, especially because she seemed to have an uncanny knack of attracting the feline species, and she certainly did not return the infatuation. As soon as she spotted the animal from a distance, she crossed over the busy street to the parade of shops on the other side. Past the hairdressers called 'Drastic!' where bored spiky-haired juniors slumped on the counter and stared vacantly out the window, then on to a charity shop and the newsagents.

The last shop front on that block belonged to a new travel agents. Out of a vague curiosity and grateful for any chance to extend her journey time further, Angela stopped for a moment to ponder on places unknown. Instead of the usual postcard display of cut price bargains, she viewed an eye-catching diorama of various inviting sunny climes. Spanish, Portuguese, Italian, and Greek paradises were topped by a sign that posed the question, in bold blue letters, 'Wish You Were Here?' with a display of photographs of each chosen country, in front of which stood an appropriate bottle and glass along with its respective flag. Angela had no particular interest in what the shop had to offer, not until that is, her eye was drawn to the far right hand corner of the window that was 'France'.

"Aix-en-Provence," she read out loud from the captioned picture, "where is that?"

The scene was of a wide, tree-lined avenue, bordered by sunlit cafes, all laid out with crisp, white linen tablecloths and peopled with beauties and businessmen. At the corner of the picture, she could just make out a carousel, brightly painted and gilded. It was clearly an old town, the buildings having the slightly decaying antiquity of better times. The plaster had fallen, the fountains were overgrown, but the street was still very much alive, for it bustled.

Oh to be a foreigner, Angela thought, *to be lost and alone, but not lonely, drinking good coffee and smoking bad cigarettes, contemplating life over a cognac and watching the World and its brother go by. Ah, now that was a way to live!*

She could see herself for a moment, peaceful and content in the dappled sunlight, waiting for a friendly stranger to arrive, someone with whom there would be an immediate affinity.

In answer to the window display's question, Angela reluctantly sighed back to reality, and with her reflection replied,

"Wish I was there? Of course I do."

By the time she was back at the flat, it was almost quarter to six, and the departure and arrival of cars and residents had begun in earnest. Windows were open to the warmth and the mixed sounds of domesticity wove their way down the street. Angela had lived there for longer than she could really remember.

It was about 14 years wasn't it?

Whatever the case, she had seen the various comings and goings and soap-opera of lives as time had gone by. She had little close contact with her neighbours, bar the common courtesies of each day and an annual greeting of seasonal best wishes. These were to the few die-hards who had remained a constant in Rotherfield Street. Mr. and Mrs. Miller, an elderly retired couple who lived across the road at number 32, Janice Brinkley, a designer who worked from home at number 18, the boisterous Collins family further down at number 5, Pierre and Miss Bee, a heavily accented brother and sister (who she thought originated from Haiti), who owned number 35 next-door and, the intriguing Mr. G. Messenger.

Mr. G. Messenger was a solitary man who lived on the top floor of Angela's building. She only knew him by his formal title, and even then only because some of his post had been misdirected to her basement flat one time. Taking the trouble to hand-deliver them to their rightful owner, she had rung his doorbell from the front step, but after waiting, grew impatient to get back to her own home. After what seemed like an age, there was the sound of feet on stairs, and the door was opened by a slightly gaunt looking man, with peppered hair, a friendly smile and, Angela had not been prepared for his eyes. They were of an intense turquoise, with a depth which made Angela feel disorientated, for gazing at them was like falling into a big, big sky.

This evening however, she had only seen the Collins children, riding their bikes on the corner. Ronnie Collins, the elder of the two boys, had called out to Angela as she passed by. It was clearly something amusing as the boys then burst out laughing, only Jenny Collins, their younger sister, chided them "not to be so mean." Angela was well aware that to many of her neighbours she was perceived as a curio, an oddball, and the Collins children were no exception in this belief. Daily, the unknown story of Angela was used as an opportunity to tease and coerce younger siblings into submission. Perhaps she was a witch, a child snatcher, or just plain mad. Whatever the latest tale being told, Angela's response was simply to walk on, choosing not to listen to taunts and accusations. She had long resigned herself to not fitting in and in a way it was her protection.

Up the street Angela could smell the aroma of spices and could hear the sound of Latin music pulsing from the open first floor window of Pierre and Miss Bee. They were an old couple, and the pair could be heard to yell at each other on a regular basis, either because of the loud volume of the music, or because one or both of them were more than a little deaf due to their indeterminate age. Angela liked them, though it could not be said she could understand them much. Their accent, Pierre's in particular, was treacle thick and mostly indecipherable. However, they were kind and generous to Angela, always greeted her with warmth and offers of rum, smiling upon her as they might an honorary niece, ever since she had delivered home-made mince pies to them one Christmas. Angela always managed to find reasons to decline their hospitality.

As soon as she got in the main task was to open the first bottle of wine for the evening and tonight there was real urgency in the struggle with the screw top lid, not just because of dry thirst, but due to a particularly taxing day at the office. Her co-worker Helen Ellis, and self-appointed superior, had taken delight in belittling and undermining everything Angela did that day. Of course, Angela being Angela had just meekly accepted each humiliation without comment or curse for she generally did as she was told. Despite her quiet and studious work, Angela had been given the sorry role of dogsbody and scapegoat, and the only reason for this long-running victimisation was solely because Angela had allowed it to continue. No one had thought she might not care for it.

"That's right," she slurred into the bottom of the second glass. "I'm always such a jolly good sport".

A creature of habit, her evening meal was made as soon as she emptied the shopping out, synchronising domestic chores with the six o'clock news on the radio. However, earlier in the week the batteries had finally faded, reluctantly forcing her to use her dusty television for background noise, until memory would serve her better and she bought new ones. Angela didn't subscribe to the modern trappings of the internet, and rarely watched television. To Angela these things encroached too deeply into her privacy. Instead she busied herself with reading and various evening classes;

Woodcarving, Embroidery and Household DIY Made Easy. These were mostly wound up during the holiday periods and Angela would find herself at a loose end.

Angela's flat was cool and dark, with sparse second-hand furniture and wooden floors. Pulling back the heavy velvet curtains revealed a small set of French windows, that led out to the patio area and the south-westerly facing garden. Sunlight cascaded in through the open doors, and spiraling particles of dust fell onto her upright piano, which stood in half shadow on the left side of the room. On top of this rested an old wooden mantle clock, solidly ticking a resolute time. Next to this stood a few dusty, framed photographs, mainly of her estranged family, and alongside these exhibits, Angela had reverently arranged a museum of found souvenirs collected from people and places. There was a pebble, a well fingered piece of flint, an animal claw and a discarded tobacco pipe. With her third glass of wine in hand, she dug deep into her jacket pocket with the other and placed a new small object carefully alongside the row. It was a carved soapstone Buddha, the sort millions of tourists bring back from their Thailand holidays. Angela curled her top lip into a crooked grin, edging the little artifact nearer to the others with her forefinger.

"Ah! Phuket indeed, however you pronounce it!" flicking her hand dismissively.

It might be seen as a sad thing indeed to replace people with objects, and agreed it had been Angela's choice to separate from her family, but for this solitary woman, it was unlikely her absence had made them grow any fonder. To Angela, an owl-in-daylight which she surely was, the birds which gathered everyday around this time to wait for crumbs and scraps, were probably the nearest she could describe as close friends or relations.

Out in the Human world, Angela felt always out of place and out of time, making her self-conscious and clumsy around others. Sensing this, the Outside World would reflect the same awkwardness back, often with an unfathomable urgency to rid her from its company. This had in the course of years led Angela to avoid people altogether, choosing instead the comfort of wild things. They were far more dependable in behaviour. Each evening commune was something she looked forward to, for the birds were impartial as to what value lay in Angela's repetitive life. Surrounded by chattering and chirping creatures at her feet, Angela took their counsel as an honour. When the sun decided to descend, she and they would freely exchange the most up-to-date news from the world of the wild. On occasion, a robin would sometimes grace her by perching on an extended finger, and she would thrill at this brush with magic.

While the pan heated with olive oil, butter and garlic, an evening meal of steak was prepared. Onto a marble slab the wooden tenderizer began its pounding beat.

"Don't...smash...it...or...pound...as...hard...as...you...can," Angela happily sang, "but...you...need...to...be...firm!"

Another gulp of wine and the mallet slammed down onto the meat with a force worthy of a correctional High Court Judge. Slam! Slam! Slam! It was a thick piece of flesh and it took a little more pummeling to achieve the thinness she preferred. From a kitchen drawer the mallet was exchanged for a small headed hammer, ideal for raining down short, sharp, blows.

"Phu...ket! Phu...ket! Phu...ket!" The hammer punctuated every syllable. "Who on earth Phuket-ting cares how you say it?"

The steak spread out thinly, like cloth from battle, tenderized to such a degree that tiny sprays of steak-blood stained her apron and a few drops splashed on her mouth, but was quickly wiped away with the back of her hand. It was at times like these that the contained rage of the day would subside.

To the right of her backdoor, a wrought iron fire escape, festooned with purple wisteria, linked the two upper floors of number Thirty-Three. The flat immediately above hers was let out every six months, generally to students it seemed. At present there was a young couple in their late twenties renting it. Angela thought they perhaps worked in the arts, but only due to the flamboyant style of their dinner party guests. She quite enjoyed the noise of laughter and glasses chinking, as it would add another dimension to her cloistered comforts. They were back early tonight. The sounds and smells of yet another soiree in preparation announced them from the window above. Angela raised her second glass of wine and, in a quiet toast of approval, jokingly told the birds that one day she would invite herself upstairs because:

"It's about time I introduced myself to Society."

This however was unlikely to happen, for despite efforts to stretch herself socially, it was easier for Angela to remain a singular person; relationships of any kind could be so complicated. She knew her neighbours in Flat B to be very 'touchy-feely' judging from the animated evenings she had so far overheard. Touching was where Angela drew the line in terms of social interaction. She preferred to keep things – at arms-length.

The top floor flat was owned by Mr. G. Messenger. It seemed to Angela that her mysterious neighbour must work from home, or have some unconventional means of income, as it appeared that he rarely went out. When he did leave Rotherfield Street it would be for months at a time, often in winter, returning in the spring with sun-tanned skin. Intrigued by his travels, Angela held more than a passing interest towards the top floor of the building and, on days off, would listen with concentrated attention to the tap-tap-tap of an antiquated typewriter which could sometimes be heard from the open window of Flat C.

Around eight thirty, the young couple upstairs, together with their dinner guests, made a noisy departure to the local pub. This was marked by scrambled footsteps and a slammed front door overhead which Angela could hardly avoid hearing as it shook the window frames. Now there would be a certain peace until nearer midnight.

About this time, she ran a bath to ease her day, and briefly channel-surfed so as to find a distracting background noise. The small television glowed up from a low shelf, next to a high-backed armchair and old sewing machine. Angela distractedly watched the flickering screen but game shows and soap operas left her wanting. Stumbling across the room, the remote control was thrown onto the chair. There were chores to complete, the last being to take down washing from a line in the garden. Her routine was then to neatly fold each piece before placing them in the clothes basket that sat on top of the patio table.

Pouring another glass of wine, she sat down for a moment to enjoy the sharp chill as it descended her throat. She knew the night could not be kept at bay forever, and at some point she would be alone with her thoughts and troubled sleep, so to dull them now would make the inevitable a little less fraught. At this time in the evening, the soft warmth of the setting sun on her pale face and enough wine in her blood, Angela felt a little less strained than she had earlier in the day. The not too distant hum of life outside her walls was ebbing away. Here in this garden, Angela had created a sanctuary of a kind. A place in which she could lose herself, albeit in transient moments. This was a place with manifest seeds of potential, Angela's potential.

Towards the far end of the garden grew an old, gnarled apple tree, bending its branches over laden with fruit each and every year. That evening, it was still engulfed in a cloud of pink and white blossom which had burst forth only a few days before to announce that Summer was coming. The sweet scented blossom had already begun its bitter-sweet fall, reminding Angela she was on a turning world. Previous owners must have had children, as there were still the remains of a rope swing, long time embedded into the bark of a stout branch. Beneath its shade, there was a small wooden bench decorated with woodland plants, violets, wood anemones and celandine. These spread their path outwards to the undulating borders. Great swathes of pink phlox, purple lavender, sweet valerian, every-shade-of-blue delphinium and provocatively tipped red hot pokers gently rustled and entwined with long stemmed grasses. Bright-eyed marigolds, creamy-white comfrey, crimson-headed clover and all manner of herbs grew rampant. Angela didn't hold with too much weeding, allowing the flowers to self-seed, as she considered Nature to have a way of combining colour, scent and texture quite perfectly without any interference or supervision. This also allowed Angela a small, but significant release from her need for control in other things.

On the other side of the garden stood a wide and expansive hazel tree whose cool darkness beckoned you to enter on hot summer days. It also served to block the view of any prying eyes from the houses beyond. To the left of the hazel, Angela had built a small, oval-shaped pond against the surrounding ivy-covered wall, with the specific aim to attract wildlife of all kinds. Water boatmen and toads, mosquitoes and midges, water beetles and frogs all thrived, and amongst the chickweed and iris spears – a rare jeweled flash of a dragonfly.

The scent of jasmine and the heady perfume of a yellow tea-rose hung dreamily in the air and stillness was cast over the walled haven. All of this was Angela's oasis, her idyll, where quiet interludes of time could pass without concern for what must be done. She would stay here as long as possible in the warmer months, observing the universe of the minutiae, the population of which were oblivious to the efforts and intrigues performed on the grander, human scale.

While she slowly sipped the remaining wine in her glass, a shadow passed across her face. She could see the gathering dusk ushering in the darkness and with it, silhouettes of birds gathering in to their home trees. Angela knew it really was time to go in if she was to attempt to get any sleep tonight. Sleeping tablets would have been a more efficient way to find rest she supposed, but she held an aversion to medication of that kind. It would also require a visit to a doctor to obtain them, and then she would have to explain her need.

That would never do.

Above, the first stars were beginning to open their eyes, and a thin crescent moon sailed through the sky. A New Moon, a time for sowing seed and for new endeavours.

"Farmers used to do that didn't they? Farm by the rhythm of the Moon? At least I think I recall something like that, but everything is all industrialised and electronic these days. Things change don't they?" The birds chirruped their reply.

Pulling back her shoulder blades in a brief stretch of muscle, she craned her neck to watch the twilight return of a Blackbird, newly mated that year. The spouse was no doubt waiting back at their nest in the apple tree, impatient for her freedom. As his dark form swooped effortlessly into the cradling pink and green of the tree, birdsong, liquid and silver, filled the garden. As the lovers marked their reunion in a brief duet and in the pure joy of being, the pair lifted up into the evening sky to circle and sing.

It never ceased to amaze Angela, how a creature, with no more than what seemed to be the lightness of thought, could rise up and ride those airstreams simply with the absolute knowing they were in their true element. They belonged together, bird with bird, and bird with air. It was this more than anything she envied most of all, a real sense of belonging.

Suddenly, from inside the flat Angela heard the sound of people screaming in alarm. Quickly moving to stand by the open French windows she watched a baffling scene on television. On a pavement in some unknown city, a small group of women and men were reeling backwards in what looked like astonished disbelief, so much so, one had fallen over whilst another was running away. The reason for this commotion was equally confusing to Angela, for there in front of their startled faces, a dark-haired man appeared to be levitating about a foot above the ground. Yes, levitating. Moving closer, the rolling caption told her he was someone called Steven Frayne, and apparently he was an illusionist, though not a familiar name to Angela. There were no obvious cables or harnesses and clearly by the panic he created no one was near enough to him to explain the drama. Angela bent her head from one shoulder to the other trying to understand what it was she was actually seeing. The levitator repeated this marvel to another unsuspecting group, with similar effect, only this time, Angela watched more attentively as to how he accomplished this feat. The camera was handheld, and if Angela was to believe the apparently objective viewpoint of its lens, there were no visible supports of any kind. An expression of calm and focused concentration formed on the man's face as he quietly told the onlookers to watch him.

Then the man on screen lifted higher and hovered above the pavement.

Is it a camera trick? Group hypnosis? Could it be real? Bewilderment twisted in her brow, reflecting the astonishment of the crowd. She scratched her head, unable to comprehend what kind of hidden mechanism could achieve this act, for there had to be something to explain it, like a mirror perhaps, or a magnet.

Just as she was racking her brain for answers, she heard a sudden dull thud overhead. Angela swung round to see a small, dark object plummeting downwards, landing directly into her basket of dried washing on the patio table. Her heart leapt into her throat as she rushed to discover what had fallen, so much so she gripped her glass too tightly and it shattered into her fist. But the subsequent bloody gash across her palm seemed inconsequential in comparison to what she had just witnessed. For lying motionless in a crater of clothing, Angela found the young female Blackbird, and judging from the unnatural contortion of the neck, she had not survived her descent.

Angela gasped in horror at the dreadful sight. This little bird, this beautiful bird, flying only moments before, had just died. Here in Angela's garden, something precious had gone. Trembling she scooped up the hen, its drooping body still warm with life. Angela stood staring at the corpse. Paralysed with shock, her breathing came close to hyperventilating, as rivulets of blood trickled through her fingers. At first she couldn't see or hear anything but the dead bird she held in her hands. Even the whimpering cry that came from her own throat made no sound to her ears.

"Are you okay?"

From somewhere above her, a window had been drawn up, and Angela could hear a distant voice calling, a man's voice. She glanced up to see from where the voice came, but the last rays of the sun were reflecting on the upper window so brightly, they blinded her.

"Are you alright? Hold on, I'll be right down."

Angela was unsure of what was happening, she couldn't seem to stop shaking. From the fire escape came the rattling, metallic echo of hurrying footsteps, and from the purple and green emerged Mr. G. Messenger.

"Hmm, I'm afraid she flew into my window, quite a bad hit, she cracked the glass,"

His voice was calm and steady as he gently touched the bird's lifeless form. Angela was still trembling. It felt as if she was coming up for air after nearly drowning for she almost gulped her desperate words.

"She's gone... gone... oh sweet thing, but she's gone, oh no, no, no..."

Distraught, her grief began to choke in her throat, and tears ran down her face. This was more than an unfortunate accident to her, for it seemed she held something of herself in her hands, something which had died and only now could she see.

"It's too late," she sobbed, "she's dead, dead, dead."

Now her whole body started to shake and realising her distress Mr. Messenger took hold of her cupped hands in his to comfort her.

"Miss Bagner, please listen to me. Look at me now."

Her staring, dilated eyes looked nervously into his and despite her disclosure of more pain than could realistically equate with the death of a bird, she nodded that she understood.

"I would like you now to lift your hands up, a little nearer to me. Yes, that's right. Now, hold it just there."

Guiding her with his hands he positioned the dead bird close to his mouth. Very carefully, he removed his hands from hers, and clutching his palms together, he bowed his head slightly in what looked like a prayer. His eyelids were half closed while his lips murmured something inaudible to Angela. She was now so near to him, she could see the lines and furrows on his face; they did not match the youthfulness of his voice or his eyes. However, she was still too much in a state of shock to question what he was doing, let alone fully appreciate the closeness of this man with whom she held a long fascination. Just as she was beginning to regain composure, he took a deep breath and shaped his hands into a funnel. Then leaning forward over the bird he blew, from what seemed to be the very depth of his being. What happened next was beyond anything Angela had ever experienced before.

At first, Angela felt only warmth on her skin. She thought it must be his expelled breath that spread slowly through her fingers and wrists, but as it travelled further up her arms, the warmth became a growing heat which steadily increased, till beads of sweat broke on her forehead and made her head giddy. As it continued, the heat created a secondary sensation, a tingling. It was somewhat like bubbles popping on the tongue, except they were being carried in waves through her, and the bubbles had colour. Myriad colour, opaline and effervescent, flowing through her veins, filling every molecule of her body and mind. Time and space seemed to wash away and she felt so very far from the physical world. She was still holding the bird, Mr. Messenger was still there, but she was certainly no longer in the garden. Instead, she found that she, they, were enveloped in light, pure light, light that was almost palpable, that had substance. Most of all she felt... What was it she felt? She was unsure at first, as it had a distant familiarity she found difficult to put a name to, like trying to recollect the words to an old, old song. As the feeling began to radiate in ripples through her, she became aware of a presence, a surety, that in this place, this moment, anything was possible. Then she knew, it was joy, boundless joy which expanded in the centre of her chest until she thought she would overflow.

And in that moment, she heard herself wish so strongly in her mind, she thought she could be heard, and the thought was this,

Let her fly.

Just as instantly as the thought was there, it was gone, and with it, the light melted away and she was back in the garden, holding the young bird in her hands. Mr. Messenger was looking at her and he was smiling.

"Look now," he said, his hands roofing the bird with his fingers. Imperceptibly at first, so slight Angela thought it must be just the breeze brushing the bird's plumage, she could see tiny flickering movements which sent pulsing vibrations into her hands. She looked more closely. The flickering became stronger, and soon there was a twitch, a twitch that flexed through the entirety of the bird's body until suddenly, it moved its head – it was alive. Angela gasped out loud with wonder as the bird shook itself, looked quizzically at Mr. Messenger and, in a flurry of flapping wings, made good her escape to her true home.

"Oh my..."

Angela's voice trailed away, her mouth still slightly open as she followed the Blackbird's return to the air.

"...oh my..."

Chapter Three

It was about 3 a.m. and long before the bedroom alarm rang, when Angela awoke with an acute itching between her shoulder blades. Her waking was so abrupt, she felt as though she had just arrived in her body. The room was the same room, but somehow the shadows on the walls appeared slightly different, more animated. The luminous clock face on her bedside cabinet gave forth an almost sentient glow with its relentless stare. Across her quilted bedcover the early dawn light was creeping. She looked down at her hands.

Are these my hands? My skin?

Something had happened to change what she knew.

My name is Angela, Angela Bagner,. I live alone in a garden flat. The garden!

She had been in the garden, bringing in the washing and drinking wine. Perhaps the wine was at fault.

No, surely not. She rarely drank that much as she didn't enjoy losing control.

But I wasn't alone was I?

There had been someone else there. Now that was unusual. Even more so as it had been a man, and not just any man, the Man upstairs: Mr. Messenger.

Oh heavens! What was I doing?

Lifting her cover she realized with horror she had gone to bed naked.

Of course, I had a bath, before bedtime, but why didn't I wear my pyjamas?

Angela's heart began to speed in her chest and the agitation spurred the stinging on her spine. She twisted her arm around the back of her torso in an attempt to relieve her discomfort, but with no real success. The more she scratched the more it itched. It was a welcome distraction from her confusion, and brought her back to a semblance of consciousness, enough to scan the room for anything which might answer her. Thrown across the end of her bed was a discarded towel. It seemed to point a direction to the half open door to the hall, beyond which a light was shining.

Still scratching her back, Angela began following a trail of what must have been her wet footprints down the parquet floored hall. At least she hoped they were hers. As she passed the other room, the one which was always kept shut, she quickened her pace. Yes, the bathroom light was still on. It was shining on a pile of clothes positioned by the skirting board, dropped apparently where she had stood. The faulty extractor-fan hummed a low meditative drone, allowing condensed steam to sweat on the tiled walls and cloud the wash-basin mirror. Angela caught her breath. For a moment it looked to her like another world, jungle-like, one of brightness and abandonment to flesh – primeval.

Stepping through, her feet trod softly, as if into a forbidden place. The tap dripped a staccato into the un-emptied bath. Automatically reaching down into its depths she searched for the plug, and finding it she pulled with a firm grip. There was chaos about her feet, wet towels, flannels, a soap bar and shampoo leaking out of bottles formed glycerol pools. It was just at this moment, when the last guttural gurgling of the bathwater ran away, she saw the blood on the edge of the sink and she remembered. Mr. Messenger and the bird. The bird that lived. He had said,

"Everything will be alright now."

He had gently placed his open palm on the small of her back and told her to wash her hands. Like a sleepwalker she had dutifully obeyed. Inspecting her hands, she remembered leaving the garden and removing her clothes outside the bathroom door. She remembered too the sticky crimson wash away from her fingers and she remembered... *oh.*

Angela gasped and looked intently at her hands once more. There was no cut, a faint, pinkish scar yes, but there was no open wound, and no cut. Even the faint remains of an older scar had gone. Everything was the same but different, and the more this baffling realisation took hold in her mind, the more her back itched.

She wiped clear the wash basin mirror to find her reflection. It was her, but it had seemed such a long time since she had really looked at herself it was hard to recognise herself under the stark bathroom light. Her heart shaped face had a glow and her large eyes seemed brighter. The mirror had the function for tidying hair and adjusting clothing, not for contemplating her true face. Her mop of dark brown hair looked odd for some reason and moving some away from her face it revealed the arrival of a lock of pure white, not there the previous day. Angela gulped in astonishment. Her skin too had changed. It had brightness to it, was rosy, and warm to the touch. Angela traced her fingertips across her neck, her breasts, her belly, as if they were landmarks on a map to some unknown land. Maybe it was the steamy warmth, or maybe it was seeing herself naked, but her expression wasn't the same either. She had the same hazel brown eyes but! Angela didn't look as frightened as before. In fact, she found herself giving way to a nervous giggle, for she looked ... well, defiant, and she liked it.

A fiery spasm sprang in-between her shoulder blades, making her gasp.

This is excruciating. What is it?

Taking a small mirror from a shelf, Angela turned to angle it this way and that to find the cause of her irritation. Sure enough, perfectly parallel on either side of her spine and at the level of her heart, were two small, but quite noticeable red marks, like bee stings.

"Damn insects!" she declared out loud, surprising herself with a new clarity in her voice, and yet she continued as if in conversation with her reflection. "I've got some calamine somewhere."

Rummaging through a plastic first-aid container from under the sink she searched for some relief, only to find there was no calamine as she had hoped, just a tube of antiseptic cream.

"This will have to do," she muttered, stretching an arm to smear a little balm onto the offending spots. "I'll get something else tomorrow. Hah! It is tomorrow. I've hardly slept."

The surprising thing was, she was neither tired nor bothered with her situation, moreover, all she felt was curiosity and excitement. Change had happened, and she wanted to find its source. Somewhere in this flat there must be clues to the mystery she had found herself in, a whodunit, whatever 'it' might be.

As if in direct response to her train of thought, Angela suddenly heard a loud cheer from the adjoining room. Rushing through, she found the television was still on and now broadcasting American Football. Someone had scored, and the crowd was ecstatic. Picking up the remote from the chair, she flicked through the channels with the half-belief this box of boredom might prove helpful as to what had happened. However, the talking heads from News 24 gave no bulletins; the Open University lecturer only offered an approach to advanced mathematics, while Bette Davis lit two cigarettes, one for her and one for Charles Boyer.

"Why ask for the moon Jerry, when we have the stars," she mimicked, "I know, I..."

On the last channel to surface, end credits were rolling up the screen over lingering arial camera shots of a leafy French town. It was the town of Aix-en-Provence. She felt a twinge on her spine.

"I need some coffee."

While she waited for the kettle to boil, Angela opened the kitchen window allowing a gentle breeze to blow warmly against her skin. It filled the room with the early morning chorus of birds. It was the clearest song, with the rich sweet notes of her resident Blackbirds. A smile bloomed on her face, which in turn gave way to irrepressible laughter bubbling in her throat.

What has gotten into me?

Whatever it was, it felt good, like a holiday mood.

"A holiday with sunburn," she feigned a complaint as the itching on her back called for attention again. Despite this annoyance however, she was beginning to find this puzzling morning almost entertaining and in truth her buoyancy of spirit was a holiday of a kind. It was still only four fifty a.m., she was already up, and unlike other mornings, she was looking forward to what the rest of the day would bring.

"Quite unlike me," she commented out loud as she sipped her coffee, sitting at the patio table, "quite unlike me at all."

There she sat, musing, sipping, scratching, smiling to herself, and occasionally inspecting her wounded hand. The sun was rising, she was naked in its warmth and it was nothing short of glorious.

By about quarter to seven the street was beginning to wake up and Tina Collins was cajoling her kids into action for the school run. There were only three more weeks until the end of term – then what could she do with them? Teddy and Ivy Miller were on their second cup of tea while they listened to Radio Four. Teddy liked to keep abreast of things with 'Yesterday in Parliament', while Ivy later enjoyed 'Thought For The Day'. Jan Brinkley yawned and stretched across her big double bed, promising herself she would definitely get up in, *just another ten minutes*. She had been working late the night before and in less than five minutes, she was fully asleep. Meanwhile, the students upstairs to Angela would continue to snore on with boozy breath until much later in the day, and all of them, were totally unaware of the naked Miss Bagner taking the air.

If it hadn't been for a next-door window opening, Angela might well have forgotten she was meant to be working that day. Cuban music poured out from No 35. It curled enticingly over the windowsill, bouncing its way down the guttering pipes and made its way assuredly up the naked ankles of an unsuspecting Angela-in-the-Sun. By the time it had reached her knees, her toes were tapping out a rhythm, by the small of her back, her bottom was wriggling to the infectious beat, and as it got closer to her shoulder blades, she seemed to be taken over by something. Her arms would not, could not remain still. The joyous throbbing through her bones was delicious and the more she moved, the more she itched, and the more she itched, the livelier her dancing became, until she was up on her toes, her hips swaying across the patio floor.

"Izzat dyu Mizzabahg-nah?"

Suddenly Angela was brought to her senses. She was outside, dancing in her birthday suit, whilst her neighbour Pierre was peering out of his window, trying to focus on what exactly he was seeing. Fortunately for Angela, he had rather poor eyesight and generally did not wear his glasses until after breakfast, so it was unlikely he could have clearly seen the spectacle of a very proper lady in a state of very improper undress, gyrating aux naturelle by her back doorstep. She grabbed a toweling robe from the top of the wash basket, still out on the table from the night before.

"Oh, hello Monsieur Pierre, er, lovely day already, um, how is your sister?"

This was the first thing that came into her head, and it seemed such an incongruous pleasantry in light of nearly being literally exposed, that she clapped her hand over her mouth in an attempt at stifling her nervous laughter.

"Aw, she fine Mizzabahg-nah, and dyu? How are dyu dis fine, fine day?"

"Never better Monsieur Pierre."

She giggled again when she realised she was still jiggling to and fro on arched feet. It was rather like treading water, and it gave Angela a surprisingly agreeable sensation throughout her body. She felt – curvaceous.

"Mizzabahg-nah, dyu wonna com ron ti nite afta yo'wok farra rhom?"

Before she had time to think about what she was saying, Angela had answered with enthusiasm.

"Oh that would be wonderful Monsieur Pierre. Thank you, I will."

Pierre smiled, gave a little wave and turned to go back in and, as he did so, a little of Angela's former self returned.

"Whatever possessed me to say that?" she mumbled in self reproach, "and what the hell am I doing here like this? Perhaps I'm coming down with something."

Glancing through the kitchen door, she caught the wall clock marking fifteen minutes past eight. It would be a race now to catch the eight thirty-five train. Trouble was she was completely unprepared. Normally she would have ironed her blouse and pressed her suit the night before. Normally she would have had breakfast, and normally she would arrive at the station, with enough time to buy a paper to read. Normally.

Clearly this was by no means a 'normal' morning by any stretch of the imagination. Normally she would not find herself cavorting bare skinned about her garden and, as it was obvious she would now miss her train unless she suddenly developed Olympic athlete stature, she made an unprecedented decision – she would arrive late. As minor as this choice may have appeared to an outsider, to Angela, this was nothing short of unqualified rebellion. She was of the opinion that time keeping spoke volumes about a Person, therefore she was a strict time-keeper. Angela was never late, in fact, she would usually arrive at least twenty minutes early to open up the office reception, for although this was not an official part of her job requirement, she had simply taken on the responsibility by virtue of being there. Now her colleagues would regularly lean heavily on this assumption, leaving Angela the daily chores of an unsung hero.

But not today. Today, she would take her time and they would have to wait.

She would need to find something to wear, something loose and cool, for the day was already promising to be a hot one. Angela's usual tailored smartness would most certainly aggravate her troubling skin irritation. She rummaged through her bedroom wardrobe searching for something to suit, but as she did, she realised that she had been neatly wrapped in shades of grey and beige for years. She had been all tightness and taupe, contained and closeted. As she searched through every drawer and inspected every clothes hanger, an uncomfortable nausea began to rise in her throat. Everything looked like yesterday's left-over oatmeal, cold, insipid and very unappetising. Angela needed colour – vibrant colour, as if colour were the only draft able to quench the driest, sleep-waking thirst.

There was however one place that she hadn't searched, the other room, the room she kept shut and tried to ignore every day and every night. The room which had remained closed since the day she moved in, and before her self-control returned, she found herself turning the handle of the door, halfway down the hall. It opened and the air within seemed to sigh as its vacuum was unsealed – where have you been?

Angela's heart was beating fast, whether it was from fear or frenzy it was difficult to tell, although she did have a sudden and distinct urge to empty her bladder.

"This is ridiculous!" she barked out loud, "This is only a room, a room full of boxes."

And indeed it was true, it was just a non-descript room, with a dusty wardrobe, faded closed curtains and a pile of dilapidated boxes. At least fifteen were stacked against the boarded up fireplace. Nothing frightening here, only, it was the things inside the boxes which made Angela shudder.

Some things might be best left alone.

Turning her attention to the wardrobe, where a small key sat in its lock waiting for her fingers to change its world – open me! And just like Alice, she did. Inside hung about a dozen dresses, protected by dry-cleaning plastic bags. Beneath these stood three pairs of lightly heeled shoes, purple suede, red kid-leather, black patent and all with the thinnest of ankle straps. Her hand brushed across the tops of the hangers and at random, she plucked one from the rail. In a moment its cover was stripped, revealing a dress out of time, a dress of colour, and such colour! Peonies of ruby and plum-pink plumped their petals against the softest sage and leaf-green. It was a late nineteen thirties dress. She remembered now, she used to collect them. Without hesitation, she slipped it over her head and shoulders. Oh how light the crepe material felt against her skin. It was almost like wearing nothing at all, and when she turned around – swish! It accentuated her movements in waves of cloth. It anointed her. Swish! Swish! On went the red shoes. She was beginning to feel a little giddy, Swish! Swish! Swish!

Grabbing bag and keys, she rushed to meet the waiting world outside with a strange sense of mischief.

Chapter Four

"It really isn't on you know," Helen Ellis muttered in a stage whisper to Sandra and Jeanette, the two other clerical assistants working alongside her. "She's supposed to be here to open up. The look I got from Mr. Lockhart this morning, well! I said to him, Mr. Lockhart, I said, Miss Bagner usually opens up and she hasn't arrived yet and do you know what he said?"

Sandra and Jeanette shook their heads blankly, which was the silliest thing really as they quite obviously knew what had been said, considering the pair had been there at the time. However, they had also long realised there really was no point in voicing any contrary viewpoints to Helen, as she was always right and everybody else was always wrong. Helen Ellis was unconcerned as to whether or not her colleagues had witnessed the conversation. She continued on, her sneer stretching her vowels.

"He said, 'and until today, in the six years since I have been manager here Mrs. Ellis, Miss Bagner has not been late once, nor has she had one day sick-leave, whereas your good self'... The cheek! It's all very well him singing her praises, always willing to work indeed! Miss Perfect indeed! Nobody is that good! Well, it's not as if she's got anything better to do with her life, has she? Shrivelled old baggage! Who would have her? Some of us have busy social schedules."

Helen Ellis was not used to being contradicted, let alone reprimanded. It didn't feel easy on her ears. Her manner to any superiors she might aspire to impress was always an ingratiating one. There were times when she would lean into their personal space, her face too near to theirs, which resulted in most managers agreeing with her just to avoid any further physical closeness. Unfortunately this had led to a mistaken belief held by Helen Ellis that she was somehow higher in rank than all others. In her mind she was clearly meant for greater things. Mr. Lockhart however had not responded in the way Helen was familiar with. There had to be someone to blame, and Helen Ellis was adamant that someone was Angela.

Just behind the staffroom door, Angela stood and listened. She had finally arrived one hour and forty-five minutes late. The journey to the next town of Beaconshill had been horrendous, as her newly found confidence was short-lived. As soon as she had boarded the train, those feelings of exuberance had quickly subsided into nothing, leaving her stranded with her old timorous Miss Mouse persona. Feeling desperately exposed she clutched her bag closer to her chest, but it did little to regain her dignity. People were looking at her. A woman with her two children had tried to chat to her, and a man in a suit had smiled at her in a very forward manner. Angela had blushed inside out, for she had lost her armour of the anonymity of the unseen woman.

The only change to remain was the constant itching on her back, adding physical discomfort to her mental unease and causing her to wriggle further.

Arriving at work she sought some reprieve from her embarrassment in the coolness of the hospital corridors. She had hoped to quietly slip into the Finance office without anyone noticing, but now standing behind the office door, she was at last hearing firsthand what she had long suspected. The barbed remarks and catty innuendoes were not a product of her imagination. Helen Ellis was simply a bitch.

She was a little younger than Angela and modelled herself on the lifestyles of stylish coffee-table magazines. Her husband worked in television, both her children were of course gifted, and she and all of her friends were on the up and colour coordinated. Everything was perfect in her world, and she held no qualms in crushing the efforts of anyone that got in the way of her rise up the social ladder, for Helen Ellis climbed with manicured talons. Listening to the acerbic character assassination she was receiving Angela began to shake. This time not from her usual cowardice concerning the much opinionated Mrs. Ellis, but from a seething rage which was burning in her chest. Oblivious to the eavesdropper, Helen Ellis persisted in sharing judgments with her office audience, with affected indignation.

"I mean, you've got to admit, there's something a bit peculiar about Baggie. She hasn't got the necessary rapport for this kind of work you know. There's times when she just stares straight at you sometimes, like you're not really there. Brainless bint! It's a good job she never comes to the staff outings. She'd make a wet Sunday out of any occasion. Does she realise what she looks like? And what is it with her fifty shades of beige? Dull in the head too I think. Doesn't mix well with people, unlike myself."

At this point the staffroom door swung open like a western saloon's, and Angela stood there, guns blazing, or at least her eyes were. This was not the staid spinster Helen talked of.

"With not mixing well, would that be not having an implement to hand such as your own spoon and cauldron Mrs. Ellis?" Angela glared defiantly, but answer came there none. Angela further explained. "You're an overbearing witch without any power other than leeching off the good nature of those around you. You know, the poor unfortunates who only cover up your misgivings for the sake of a quiet life!"

The room fell silent, but for the hum and whirr of computers and fax machines, and somewhere in another room a telephone sounded but rang out unanswered. The wide-eyed Sandra and Jeanette submerged behind their computer screens, both with their hands clamped tightly over their mouths, waiting for fireworks. Helen Ellis was dumbstruck.

"What's the matter Helen? Cat got your tongue? It seems to me you do an awful lot of talking without actually saying anything, don't you?" Angela leant nearer and tapped out words onto Helen's forehead. "That's ... because ... you ... are ... an ... empty ... vessel!"

Sandra and Jeanette looked at each other and began to laugh nervously. Helen Ellis continued to stare wide-eyed, her mouth gaping open and shut, rather like a landed cod.

"I don't have to answer to you as to why I am late. Never once have you offered an apology for any of the many times I have covered for you. In fact, considering my length of service to this department and to this hospital, anyone might suggest I already have seniority over all of you, but particularly you Mrs. Ellis, you manipulative, self-serving, duplicitous parasite!"

Angela slammed her hands onto her target's desk with a sudden thrust. Helen Ellis visibly shrank into her swivel chair.

"I shall now be taking an early lunch. I do not know when or if I shall return today, for I have things to do and...and people to meet!" Angela turned to make a grand exit. "By the way, thank you Mrs. Ellis, you have reminded me – I need to buy some disinfectant."

And with a final swish of her dress, Angela left the building.

At a corner table of the Rendezvous Cafe, in the middle of The Azure Heights Shopping Centre, Angela sat with her head in her hands and quietly groaned to herself. Between groans, she lowered her left hand to scratch the incessant itching by her spine. This was not the day she had hoped for, not that she held any specific hopes in mind. Perhaps this was the reason she was feeling so frustrated and confused, because, unlike the other endless days of her life, earlier this morning she had welcomed the thought of something different happening. Now, amidst the potted palms and the clatter of crockery, Angela sat alone, convinced the incidents of today were only symptoms of menopausal onset. The mood swings, the sudden rush in body temperature, the terrible skin irritation, it all added up, she was going through The Change. Despite this, she had to admit how thoroughly she had enjoyed letting rip at the malicious Helen Ellis. She felt cleansed, but how could she go back there now? She couldn't bear the thought of saying sorry to the woman. One, she wasn't sorry in the slightest, and two, if she retracted everything she had said, Helen would never let her forget it, and her life would be truly intolerable. There was only one thing for it; she would have to resign, but then what?

What was I thinking? They'll probably fire me for walking out.

She groaned again, her head dropped and her hair dangled into the remains of her cappuccino. How she had arrived here was a mystery in itself, for Angela usually avoided crowded places as much as possible. The ant-like collision of the people as they rushed to embrace the religion of spend, spend, spend was something to avoid. She hated the synthetic seduction which took place here, and she hated too the sterilised light from the high-vaulted glass ceilings which poured down to bless the heads of young and old, acolytes all in a temple of consumerism. Angela's reason for being here was an equally embarrassing one in light of the other events of the day. In her enthusiasm and hurry to dress earlier in the morning, she had forgotten to include a vital part of her ensemble, her underwear. Contemplating the coffee, her mind recoiled with appalled dismay when the sudden vivid memory of the overly friendly man from the train jumped into her mind.

Oh my God! The sudden recollection of how she must have been sitting made her visibly cringe and she groaned in embarrassment again. In search of a solution to her predicament, she found herself wandering the echoing halls of The Azure Heights shopping centre. From a shop called, 'Yes Tonight Josephine' she hurriedly bought a matching set in a somewhat racy pink.

"Would Madam like them gift-wrapped?"

Angela just quickly mumbled, "I'll wear them now," and had dashed into the dressing room to put them on. Now in the noisy café she sat alone, lost and utterly miserable.

Meanwhile a small team of very corporate looking personnel were making busy preparations in the entrance area of the Rendezvous. Brightly costumed young women adjusted their skirts and ruched blouses. Banners were hung, emblazoned with the title 'Viva!'. Scott McKenny, an ambitious new area sales manager, eager to impress the bosses at head office, saw fit to not only offer free samples to the lunchtime customers, but also add that certain extra something. To get customers into a carnival mood he had hired the musical talents of a live Salsa band.

The Rendezvous Café management were pleased with the planned publicity, for sales had been taking a down turn recently. Scott McKenny had assured Carolyn the cafe manageress there would be maximum coverage by local press and radio, all of whom had been invited to the event with a flimflam promise of a surprise celebrity guest. Scott's efforts to attract a local footballer and his daytime soapstar girlfriend had fallen through but he still thought this event could nab him salesman of the year at the firm's autumn conference.

Los Diablos de las Cantinas were also pleased, as being hired for this lunchtime gig was a much needed piece of exposure towards their aspirations for fame and fortune. There wasn't much call it seemed for Latin American music in this rather conservative part of the country. And so to maximise their chances of future concerts, Eduardo Perez, known as Eddie to his friends, had also contacted the local regional television station that morning in the hope they might send a reporter to cover their show.

"Yes," he urged, "there may well be a surprise celebrity appearance."

Jackie Brent, the junior reporter on call at the news desk when Eddie rang, was pleased as well. She had been eagerly looking for a reporting break, and here it was. The senior reporter had fallen sick with laryngitis and was unable to speak, plus, the newsroom was one item down on broadcast copy. When the Editor said "Go!" she grabbed the chance.

"We'll get some on-the-spot interviews with the punters," she told her cameraman on the way, "so keep a sharp eye out for any interesting looking characters."

Everyone was pleased. Everyone was happy, everyone that was except Angela. Poor Angela was too busy chastising herself for her various indiscretions while she absentmindedly tore at a promotional napkin. She didn't notice the special efforts Carolyn the manageress had made in decorating her coffee-bar. The chrome was sparkling, the pristine counters shone like new and the added detail of a single red rosebud on each table suggested romance. Forlorn and forgotten, Angela however didn't notice the arrival of the press, radio and television reporter. She didn't notice the ruffles and maracas of Los Diablos, nor the small crowd which was gathering, fuelled with curiosity as to whom the surprise celebrity might be. Neither did she notice Paul Hollingsworth, the managing director of 'Viva!' coffee, arrive with his personal assistant and quietly position themselves in a corner almost opposite to where Angela sat.

Eddie Perez stepped up to the microphone with certain trepidation. There were more press people here than he had anticipated.

We'd better make this a good one, he thought. *Think big Eddie, think Stadium.*

"Hello Beaconshill! We are Los Diablos de las Cantinas, and we play for you, en su drama y su alegria, with drama and joy, y el Espiritu Vivo, with a live spirit...Viva!"

With a raunchy punch, the horn section brought everyone's attention to the Rendezvous Cafe. The percussion, the congas, the bass and guitars, all were in perfect syncopation.

Good thing we hired the practice room last night, thought Eddie, *but why aren't they dancing?*

Sure enough, despite all the best laid plans of cafe and corporation, the straight-laced people of Beaconshill were hard to move into the spirit of anything. In fact, there was a stiff awkwardness amongst them, too many coughs, too many dead-pan faces. But just then, unbeknownst to the waiting audience, Angela's toe began to tap. Followed by her foot, then her leg, then suddenly...

Angela leapt up from her chair, tossing back her hair with an arching of her back. Her arms stretched upwards with a flamboyant flourish and snatching the rose from its vase, she clenched it between her teeth. Weaving her gyrating hips in and out of the cafe tables, her dress swirling, she found herself presenting the rose to an unsuspecting gentleman customer.

"Viva!" she mouthed, and then moved on again, fingers clicking in time.

Cups of coffee were poised in mid-air, lips half open gasped in delighted surprise. Who was she? Angela limboed up to another table, grabbing the hand of a young man, fresh out of the office, and with her other hand, she seized a pretty shop girl who had stopped for sandwiches. Pulling them together, she paused for a moment to whoop "Viva!" once more. En route, her shoulder bag hit the back of the head of a Lady-Who-Did-Lunch, causing her to impact with the cream horn she was holding.

"I'm sure I've seen her on the telly," whispered one housewife into the ear of her friend.

"MTV, mum," interrupted a surly teenager by her side.

"No, no," corrected a bespeckled man, "it was that T.V. Arts show. Don't you remember Alexia? They've been doing a big revival of her stuff up in Town. Now, what was her name again?"

And so the rumour grew and grew. Angela was so confident, so brazen, no-one had the least suspicion she could be anything other than a Star. "Yes, of course, it's you know, thingy. She's just flown in from a tour." Someone had definitely seen her arrive in a limousine, she had a new album out, a new film out. "Isn't she the new owner of the big estate outside Beaconshill?"

Eddie Perez eyed the changing mood of the crowd with a relieved smile, his mind working overtime.

So this is the surprise celebrity. Everyone seems to recognise her except me. What'll I do? This has to be seamless Eddie. You've got to be ready for anything if you want the Big Time!

By now Angela had coaxed at least two-thirds of the cafe audience to get up from their seats to dance with each other. Angela herself now had the commanding position on top of one of the tables, having seemingly leapt there with balletic ease. She looked wildly about her at the customers below, and began clapping to the infectious rhythm. Soon everyone had joined in, whooping and yelling. She jumped down to join the throbbing crowd and Eddie saw his chance, "Take it down boys!" he yelled to the band. Angela was near the stage area, shimmying to the pulsating beat. Eddie lent over to her ear,

"What do you want to sing? What do they call you?"

"Call me?" Angela was caught off guard, "Angela, my name is Angela."

Eddie swung back to the band, nodded and with the smile of a man who thought he knew what he was doing, Eddie Perez uttered what he hoped would be career-changing words,

"Ladies and Gentlemen, Señores y Señoras! Our special guest today, Angeliquita! Angeliquita y Los Diablos!"

A huge cheer went up from the crowd as Los Diablos struck up the music of a Latinesque version of 'Call Me', an easy-listening track to which Angela was not very familiar. Not wishing to appear phased by her slowness to perform, Eddie began to serenade her, and as he did, he placed a rose in her hair, much to the crowd's approval. Then Angela began to sing.

Eddie could hardly believe what he was hearing. What an amazing voice! She glided through her notes like an un-caged bird, soaring and curling into the very hearts of every listening, awestruck café customer, lodging there and imbedding within the very pulse in their veins, pulling them up and up, until in their minds they flew with her. With a doe-eyed and sultry gaze, directly focused into Eddie's eyes, she sang with an allure which was bewitching and beguiling. Both the audience and Eddie were now her willing playthings, all mesmerized with the sheer mystique this woman oozed. Given the rare exposure to anything extraordinary in the backwater of Lossingham, the Diva before them seemed a veritable goddess who danced with her voice. For some it had an almost explosive impact, and caused change to every person there.

What a natural comedienne. Eddie felt he was in the presence of Greatness. *Look how she fakes stage fright. Brilliant!*

Her former sense of self was beginning to come back, where was she?

"Call me!"

She dueted nervously with Eddie. *What am I doing?*

"Call me!"

A sea of faces focused only on her and she felt as if the entire world had shifted on its axis.

"...Call me!"

Angela knew she had to get away, and in a wild panic, picked up a whole bouquet of flowers lying on the counter, and threw them into the cheering crowd. In this brief moment of distraction, Angela had enough time to slip hurriedly away, around a corner, through an exit door and out into a quiet street backing onto the rear of the shopping centre. She could hear the music still playing and the sound of approaching footsteps. Glancing both ways to find some escape, a bookshop across the road caught her eye and, heart pounding through her chest, she made a dash for sanctuary.

Chadwick's Bookshop was cool and calm compared to the rising heat Angela had been generating only moments before. Low-lit table lamps sat on small mahogany cabinets, nestling against large and sprawling sofas and armchairs. Dark green carpet muffled any sounds bar that of a slowly swinging pendulum clock, and everywhere, the soothing smell of leather and beeswax. Angela, still panting for breath from her trauma, collapsed into a welcoming wing-backed chair. There were a few customers engrossed in reading. The sales assistant looked up briefly, only to return to his book which held far more interest for him. For the time being Angela felt safe in this refuge. She could rest here while she waited for the excitement to die down.

Outside the window, about a dozen people ran past, heading towards the high street. Angela wasn't sure as to whether or not they were looking for her, but she wasn't prepared to take that chance, so she sank further into the upholstery in the hope she might become the furniture itself. The tall clock swung its pendulum, back and forth, back and forth, like a hypnotist, marking the seconds and hours between the pages of time spent here. With a deep sigh she looked about her. Although Chadwick's was an unknown place to Angela, there was something quite familiar in its air, and it eased her aching head towards a more peaceful sanity.

From floor to ceiling, stood shelves bulging with book upon book, all of them an entrance into another world, any of which Angela would have gladly stepped into at that moment if she had known the way. As she glanced across the room, she noticed a walnut desk, stacked with a newly published work. For some inexplicable reason, she found herself drawn towards it, and as she got closer, she did a double take. Angela couldn't quite believe what she was reading or seeing, for below a grainy black and white portrait of a rather gaunt, slightly greying man, read the words,

'From the writer of 'Where We Stand' and, 'Higher Ground',
Ad Astra Publications is proud to present,
'Everything Still To Come'
by Gabe Messenger.'

It was Mr. Messenger, her Mr. Messenger, the man who had been in her garden only the night before, the man who… Angela held her breath. She was making connections which didn't make sense.

But how could he have anything to do with my behaviour today?

This was all too farfetched for her to fathom. She continued to read,

'Gabe Messenger, a relatively new writer for our times, has already earned for himself
the reputation as highly respected travel-writer with a difference.
Leaving his previous career as a professional free-style climber,
Gabe Messenger has chosen to ascend the pathways of the forgotten tribespeople of the world, in search for the treasures of ancient wisdom once believed lost.
His adventures leave us breathless with wonder and

inspire us with the eternal endurance and courage of the Human Spirit.'

The startled sales assistant looked up from the counter. A twenty pound note had been pressed into his hand and he could just see through the glass door, a woman in a floral dress just leaving. She was clutching a book.

Turning the corner near her flat, Angela heard a voice call her name from up the street. It was Pierre from the top step of his open front door. He was beckoning to her with one hand, whilst the other held an open bottle of dark rum. She felt too tired to resist any changes which came her way now, and to be perfectly honest, she thought she could use a drink in the company of someone who she knew liked her without any question, and with whom intelligible conversation was unnecessary.

Pierre and Miss Bee's front room hadn't been decorated since the early fifties, although the vagaries of fashion made their presence known through the photographs of the many generations of relatives lining the walls, as bonnie babies turned into brawny men, and tottering infants soon teetered on high heels.

"Mi farmillee," Pierre oozed with pride and poured Angela another rum, "dey all fly de nest whun day, but dey all cum home agin, we iz buds ova fedda!"

"Must be nice, having close family I mean."

"Awwh, itz joosta marta o' fined'n yo' own kyne Mizzabahg-nah."

Angela sighed wistfully, probably due to the effects of the rum, which for some reason was making it easier for her to understand her smiling neighbour. She felt happily fuzzy-headed. Soft reggae was playing on a dated hi-fi, and reassuringly, only Angela's feet were moving in time.

Perhaps the storm has passed. Relaxing a little more, she gazed about the room. Between the clan pictures, she noticed there were at least three peculiar paintings on the four walls. On each, strange symbols encircled a single eye.

"What are they Monsieur Pierre?"

"Awh Mizzabahg-nah, dey from de ol contree. Dey protect." Pierre tapped his nose, "I av de ol waze, dyu no?" He leaned closer. "If evva dyu in trubbow, dyu cum ti Monsieur Pierre, okay Mizzabahg-nah? I make de ol waze moove."

Angela nodded her head, without a clue as to what old ways he was talking about. She had an odd sense he was telling her something important to remember.

"I'd best go now Monsieur Pierre. Thank you so much for the rum."

As she got up to leave, she felt the room spin a little and, stumbled slightly. As she closed her own front door she laughed out loud at the bizarreness of it all. Passing the open door of the previously closed box room, she blurted out with a drunken bravado,

"You don't scare me! I've been dancin'!"

Striding in with a swagger, she ripped open a small dusty box resting on top of the others. It was full of old books and papers, including a small collection of handwritten letters tied with twine, which after some inspection, gave Angela an unpleasant twinge in her chest.

"I know you alright!" she slurred scornfully, and threw them back in the box with disdain.

The rest of the evening was spent in a bumbling fog. She had a bath, ate a little food, drank a little coffee and scratched her itching back, finally collapsing onto her unmade bed. For a time, her mind was blank from the madness of her day, and how long she had lain there listening to the evening sounds was hard to say, for in her stumbling she had accidentally knocked the clock to the floor. Only the changing shadows on her bedroom walls now marked the time. It must have been towards late evening when she heard her upstairs neighbours come in. They were alone for a change and they too had been drinking, for their laughter was loud again tonight. Angela listened, following their journey from the front door to their bedroom, below which, Angela lay.

At first she didn't notice nor recognise the noises from above, little murmurs and groans, gentle creaking as the bed shifted position. A rhythmic thudding began, the ceiling light was swinging above, an urgent cry of approval rang out, then the whole cycle would begin again, this time with an increased volume and a more robust thudding. They were making love.

When was the last time for me? Angela wondered as she watched the swing of the ceiling light gain momentum,

It seems so long ago, it might as well be fiction. I never knew when it was going to be the last time, but then, who could know when the last time is the last time – or the last time for anything come to that?

Two muffled voices called out from somewhere above. They seemed to go on forever, until everything went quiet. Angela lay in the enveloping silence for a long while, until she drifted into a deep sleep and began to dream.

She was outside. It was a beautiful night. The sun had just set, leaving a trace of fuchsia-pink on the lip of the horizon. Myriad stars hung in a deep violet-blue sky, and a sliver of a crescent moon gently steered its silver rudder up through the heavens. The air was warm and there was a sense of expectancy all around her.

She could not help but look up, for it seemed the stars were welcoming her. One sparkling eye after another opened, and as they did, dulcet notes sounded in the velvet air, sensual and yearning. She could see these far off suns swell and blossom with their own unique song, and awestruck by this spectacle, she reached out a hand to touch each one. As she did so, a luminescent image gently exploded into being, like fireworks embroidering the sky with pictures – real pictures, a cow, a goat, a bouquet of flowers, a violin. She turned around and found herself watching Mr. Messenger as he worked at his typewriter. He was seated at a desk, lit by an angle-poised lamp, a cup of something hot at his side. As he typed, she realised his typing was in perfect synchronisation with the rhythm of the sky orchestra, and it made her smile. Then, without any apparent surprise, he looked up from his writing to return her gaze. All this time, the music made manifest living pictures around her, till Mr. Messenger raised his arm and gestured for her to follow his direction.

The whole sky was brimming with life and colour as luscious flowers bloomed in vases as vast as planets. A donkey brayed and a pair of coupling lovers flew in close embrace. They waltzed and whirled, and for a moment, she felt as if she were one of the lovers herself, her heart pounding like a visiting circus parade. As they moved, she felt a surge of lightness lifting her higher. Now as she rose she could see far into the distance, and cascading light falling from her limbs illuminated the ground. Below was a landscape of all things which had happened and all things that could be. Gazing with wonderment at this wide and endless panorama, she felt herself lifting to an even higher position than before. In one pool of light, she could clearly see a hilltop near a sea, where a naked couple were wrapped in pleasure amongst tall grasses. They had picked blackberries, their young flesh streaked with sweet purple juices. A salt wind blew across their entwined hair. All this beauty left Angela breathless. She could see and feel everything. She could even taste the lapping water from the shoreline. It was Elysium. Down on the rooftops, moonlight glistened and a flame red cockerel heralded the dawn on a church steeple below...below...*oh!*

Her descent from dreaming was fast. She awoke in the crumpled white sheeting of her bed, with a delicious aching between her legs and a scent of brine on her fingers.

Chapter Five

"Martin..." Tina yelled up the stairs of Number 5, "come and have a look at this!"

Her bleary-eyed husband leant over her shoulder where she sat at the kitchen table watching a morning television show.

"Where's my tea?" he grunted.

"I'll make some fresh in a minute. Now, who-d'ya think this is?" She pointed to the screen. An item was running about dancers and a band.

"I dunno, ask me again in a minute." He stumbled over to switch on the kettle. He knew he would have to make his own.

"It's her, you know? Her down the road, the odd one."

The young female news reporter continued with her commentary.

"Yesterday, The Azure Heights Shopping Centre saw the surprise debut of a new sensation known as Angeliquita. Little is known about this brand new artiste, but clearly from the scene at the Viva! promotion, her appearance has already created quite a stir. Shoppers at the centre later inundated local radio stations and the Avante Records Store with requests for any of her singles, but found themselves disappointed as none were in stock. A spokesman for the record chain said he would be contacting all available outlets to satisfy the sudden huge demand. ' I just wish whatever record company she is signed to would let us in on the secret. They're sitting on a goldmine, and we'd like to get our share.' This regional station is now on the hunt for the scoop on this enigmatic performer. To anyone with inside information, please contact us on the number scrolling on the bottom of your screen. This is Jackie Brent, toe-tapping and dance crazy in Beaconshill, signing off for Breakfast News."

Martin slurped his tea, finally coming to after his traditional Friday night. His wife stared at him, expecting his reply.

"Well?"

"Well what?"

"It's her, at least it looks like her, from number 33, seems a nice enough woman though. She helped me out with the shopping when I was pregnant with our Jenny. You know, the one the kids are always making up stories about."

Martin scrutinised the dancer on the screen. There was a vague resemblance.

"Nah," he replied at last, "don't be daft, that one's at least ten years younger."

"Would you like another slice of toast Teddy dear?"

"Sorry my Love, what did you say?"

"Toast, Teddy, toast – goodness, you are distracted this morning. What are you reading?"

"Oh it's a photograph of that nice young woman across the road, at least it looks like her. Jolly well hope it is. Terrible waste, fine looking woman like her."

Ivy placed the warm buttered toast onto Teddy's plate, and bent over a little to see his newspaper.

"Oh yes, good to see her getting out at last. She looks as though she's enjoying herself doesn't she? Remember when we used to go dancing, up the Palais? You were so nimble on your feet."

"Where we first met my Love. How could I forget? You were the loveliest girl I had ever seen. You wore a dress which seemed to swirl about you. I couldn't keep my eyes off you – I still can't." He gazed up at her lovingly and squeezed her hand. "I am a very lucky man, a very lucky man indeed."

"We are very lucky Teddy dear. You know, it might all have turned out so differently if it hadn't been for missing my bus home that evening." She smiled at her husband, as the years rolled away with the memory. "Life's is a bit like dancing isn't it? Much of it has to do with good timing."

Jan yawned and stretched her arms above her head. She had gone to her French Conversation Club the previous night, and then had worked at home to finish a design brief to make its deadline. She didn't sleep until gone two a.m. and now shuffled into her kitchen on automatic pilot, switching on the radio, then the kettle. She made her way down the two flights of stairs to check the post, and saw the local paper had arrived. Back upstairs, a lively radio DJ was bellowing something about everyone at the station being 'Latin Looney' and 'Salsa Psycho'. Jan liked this kind of music, but not quite so loud first thing in the morning. She turned down the volume and opened her paper to find an article which made her sit up with surprise. It was her, the Woman across the road. Jan had seen her a few times last term around the local college evening classes. Jan had a feeling this neighbour might have something in common with herself and had long wanted to break the ice with a friendly conversation. However, Jan struggled with shyness and bouts of low self-esteem, whilst her neighbour,

Miss Bagner wasn't it? Well, she always walks with such poise and grace. Jan was more than a little in awe of her, but it all made sense now. *She must be a trained dancer of some kind.*

"I wonder if she might give lessons?" she thought out loud, "Next time I see her, I'll buck up courage and ask her."

After her long sleep, Angela awoke with what felt like cotton wool in her mouth and a distant and repetitive buzzing and ringing in her ears. Despite this, she was feeling surprisingly energised. Her back was itching furiously now, far worse than the previous day. The buzzing continued.

A little too much rum. I've developed hangover tinnitus.

Halfway down the hall, she stopped in her tracks. The door to the other room was open. She was sure she had closed it the night before.

Come on Girl, you were a bit tipsy.

Over on the living room shelf, a dust-laden phone was ringing. Fumbling with the handset, she held it to her ear as if it were the first time she had ever heard it ring. She paused to hear the caller. After less than a minute of listening she growled in a lower register.

"Listen whoever you are, you have the wrong... fucking... number. No one goes by the name Valerie here! Don't ever fucking call here again. Do you understand?"

She slammed down the receiver. *Wrong number again!* Angela rarely received phone calls, but when she did, they always seemed to be wrong numbers, always asking for someone she didn't recognize. She had decided it must be due to the phone line she had inherited from the previous owner. But that bizarre outburst of expletives had startled her, shocked her even. It was like a switch had been turned on and off and she had suddenly become someone else.

Where did that come from? It must be the rum talking. And yet the buzzing continued. It wasn't coming from her pounding head after all. It was coming from the front doorbell. Clutching the collar of her dressing-gown tightly, she slowly opened the door by a crack. Her heart thumped when she recognised her visitor. It was Mr. Lockhart, her manager.

"Miss Bagner, I... I do apologise for appearing on your doorstep like this. I was trying to call you all yesterday afternoon, but there wasn't any reply. I was concerned you might be unwell after, ahem, after the... the unfortunate incident with Mrs. Ellis."

That's it then, he's come to sack me.

Angela was blushing crimson, better to leave with some dignity she thought.

"I'm sorry for the disturbance Mr. Lockhart, but I cannot possibly work in such an atmosphere any longer. I will forward you my formal resignation this week."

"No... no...no, please Miss Bagner, please reconsider. You are my, I mean, you are our most valued member of staff."

He thrust a small bouquet of flowers towards her.

"Take some time off. I know you have plenty of holiday leave. No, how thoughtless of me, never mind that, just take a few days off, a week off, as long as you want, just please Miss Bagner, dear Miss Bagner, please don't be too hasty in your decision."

He smiled nervously. Angela was a woman whom he had grown to respect, and her sudden absence had brought him abruptly to admitting to himself he felt more for her than he had previously realised, and he didn't want her to go.

Unaware of the internal turmoil she was engendering in her boss, Angela grabbed the flowers and quickly mumbled,

"Very well. I shall think about it. Good day Mr. Lockhart."

A brief expression of relief could be seen on Mr. Lockhart's face as Angela pushed the door shut. A muffled reply could just be heard as she leant in shock against the latch. She waited till his footsteps receded before she breathed again. When she did, she found herself laughing out loud. Her back was tingling, she felt as if she were a little straighter in her spine, taller even, and as she looked down, she realised this was in fact the case, for she was standing on her toes, like a ballerina, and quite elegantly balanced, as if she were floating just ever so slightly off the ground.

"Almost like wearing high heels," she heard herself say, "Invisible high heels."

She minced through to the bathroom to begin dressing and she smiled to herself at how different things were without any real outward change. This observation was short-lived, for when she checked the state of her back in the mirror the reflection made her gasp. The two bee-stings had changed and had now increased into a size and shape quite similar to a pair of child's fists. The other somewhat worrying development was the apparent swelling which appeared to radiate outwards in a spiral shape from the centre of each crimson mark, each a mirror image of the other. There was no getting around it, she would have to visit a chemist without any further delay.

Out in the sunshine everyone she passed appeared to smile at her, even her neighbours seemed to be friendlier than usual, with some waving as she sauntered past. That morning she had taken a cinnamon orange dress from the spare room wardrobe; creamy lilies with pulsating crimson stamens trumpeted their wearer's coming. Perhaps it was merely the good weather, but she had a new spring in her step which made her hips sway with a confidence found only in a feeling of content in one's body. This was not the entire reason for the approving glances she was receiving, for Angela was as yet blissfully unaware of any impact or interest she had made in the world outside from her choreographic antics the previous day.

On the more fashionable side of Beaconshill, Helen Ellis smiled to herself as she jotted down the number shown on the rolling local television news. The children were at their Saturday clubs, and her husband was away filming – again. Her life bordered on frenetic at times, what with violin and horse riding lessons for the children and health spas and wine bars for herself and her friends. On those rare occasions he was home and not playing golf or in the gym she and her husband would do theatre and restaurants so as to catch up on their separate diaries.

"Well, well, well Baggie, you're a bit of a dark horse aren't you? I bet old Lockhart doesn't know this side of you. Hitting the bottle perhaps? Everyone thinks you're sooo sweet don't they? Well one day you're going to get found out, and that day is coming sooner than you realise. Looks like you're really losing it now – Angeliquita indeed! I wonder what Lockhart might say? Not quite so upstanding now are you?"

She had been on the receiving end of a second dressing down the day before. Mr. Lockhart had heard everything Helen said, through his open office door. He had also heard Angela's response to the verbal bile, and blankly said Helen deserved it. To further rile her, he had virtually ordered her to make friends to Angela.

Unbelievable! How dare he suggest I mix with the likes of her!

It had simply ruined her evening at the restaurant.

Oh but now, oh this was going to be too easy, she thought, as she licked the corner of her mouth. Here was an opportunity to demonstrate how she was a woman of an incisive ruthlessness. It was certainly true that the paralyzing look of abject fear which had passed over Angela Bagner's face in the breakfast programme footage had not passed Helen by. Fear was something Helen could work with. It had seen her through boarding school and found her a suitable husband. Life was dog-eat-dog, and Helen considered herself as Alpha, while Angela, well, she was clearly an Omega. Flicking through the telephone directory, she traced a column of numbers with her red polished fingertip under the heading 'Musical Agents'. She lifted the phone receiver and dialed.

"Oh, hello, do you represent the Latin band I've just seen on the television this morning? The ones who were playing at the Azure Heights? You do? How marvellous! I would like to book them for a fundraising event I'm organising. Yes, it's for the local hospital..."

I'll be nice to her alright. I'll give her a night to remember. Helen purred to herself, for a plan was forming.

Chapter Six

On the kitchen counter, Angela surveyed the mountainous range of pharmaceutical goods she had purchased from every chemist in Lossingham High Street. It had been an excursion met with raised eyebrows and scrutinizing stares, and at one particular shop counter, an overly suspicious assistant had virtually interrogated the agitated Angela as to why she was in need of so many different products.

"Has Madam travelled to any foreign countries recently? Or have you been in the company of any – colonial visitors?" she quizzed, eyeing the warning posters near the wall telephone over the horn rim of her glasses. "Has Madam been experiencing a high temperature?"

To which Angela had tersely replied:

"Of course I've been feeling hot, its bloody summer isn't it?"

Slamming the shop door behind her, she sought out another chemist on the other end of the town. On the way, she harangued herself over what she considered to be a rude and appalling outburst.

"The woman was only trying to help you Angela," she reasoned. "Well," came the tetchy reply, "she ought to have minded her own damn business! Was she a trained doctor? No! She was just a nosy cow!"

Something was definitely up. Talking aloud to herself was not a habit she had engaged with so publically before.

"What on earth is going on with me?"

Her paltry groceries paled into insignificance when compared to mighty peaks of bottles and jars and tubes of every ointment, lotion and cream. There were salves and liniments, balms and emollients and pots of preparations. From antihistamine to aqueous cream, from Benadryl to burn spray, from calamine to calendula, and all the way through to a small jar of Zirtex. Angela lined them up in rough alphabetical order, but despite her expertise at office filing, she was little concerned over such details right now. She had more pressing thoughts, such as the rasping inflammation between her shoulder blades which was increasing by the hour.

"Which one of you shall be first?" She considered as she inspected her troops, "I suppose I'll just have to work my way through from A to Z."

Smearing a little antihistamine cream onto her swollen back, she suddenly noticed how unkempt the bathroom was. The sink was unwashed, the bath had a tidemark of scum, and that annoying fan was still unfixed.

Come to think of it, she thought to herself as she wandered from room to room, wiping finger trails through the dust, *it all needs cleaning. I've probably got some allergic reaction to the dust. How did I allow it to get in this state?*

But she knew really it was simply years of holding her breath for fear of change, and the layers of silent neglect had fossilised her internal world like the last hours of Pompeii.

"Right!" she announced loudly to her adversary as she pulled on her Marigolds with a twang, "You've had this coming a long while now!" And picking up a cloth and a can of polish, battle commenced.

The campaign took most of the day, as floors were swept, and shelves dusted, both interspersed by a compulsion to wash everything from doormats to door handles. By late afternoon, she stood victorious, like some domestic Valkyrie, with a dripping mop in one rubber gauntlet, and a murky bucket of suds in the other.

"There!" she exclaimed with satisfaction, "Only the box room to go!" However, the box room was the shrine to her creeping fears, and like an aging concierge, it goaded Angela to dare cross it. She did not have the energy yet to overcome her loathing.

She needed a cooling bath. The bumps on her back were growing in size and colour, and the burning sensation was increasing. Despite this, Angela was strangely in buoyant mood. She had worked up quite an appetite and the thought of food genuinely enticed her, instead of her usual 'eating out of duty.'

"I shall dress for dinner I think," she giggled, "one has one's standards."

Stepping into the box room with a strange new confidence which seemed to pulse in her arched feet, she pulled another dress from its wrappings. Bright orchids of violet-blue immodestly poked out their tiger stripe lips against a soft blue-grey, and between the flowers, hovering hummingbirds penetrated every flowery orifice with their pencil thin beaks, some teasing a flower's column with a long pink tongue. It was a dress to be admired and to draw attention to the wearer's sex. She eyed the boxes and calmly lifted another from the pile. Much like the first, it was full of old papers and dog-eared paperbacks.

"Well, this can all go in the bin," she tutted, scooping out the contents, stopping only when she found a lone C.D. of Latin music at the bottom. Later, as she skipped around her kitchen, cooking pasta and chopping vegetables it occurred to her that singing and dancing was something she used to do all the time when she was young, sometimes with her Father too.

"But only when no one else could see me," she declared with a spin. "Hah! Not much has changed then!"

After making her bed with fresh sheets, she laid the patio table for her evening meal. Mr. Lockhart's bouquet in a glass vase took centre stage. It had been a roasting day, leaving the evening warm and sultry. She sipped her glass of wine, its vanilla buttery taste courted her mouth as she swallowed.

"It's been an odd sort of day," she concluded to the birds as they pecked at her feet. "I don't have a clue as to what is going on, but do you know? I don't care."

A golden hued evening lay before her, and retrieving Mr. Messenger's book from her bag, she opened its cover to read in the preface;

> 'There are shadows in the darkness, but people cannot discern them. There are trails in the sky where birds fly, but people cannot recognize them. There are paths in the sea along which fish swim, but people cannot perceive them. All people and things of the four continents are reflected in the moon without a single exception, but people cannot see them. But they are visible to the Divine Eye.'
>
> I found this extract while travelling through the upper mountainous regions of rural India.
>
> Its message of our unique life purpose has a resonance today, countering the growing malaise within Humanity's collective spirit, and begging the question,
>
> 'Where do I belong?'
>
> I hope you will now join me in a journey beyond Life's blind bend. A journey in which, in order to understand where we are, and as to where we are going, the Pilgrim must accept his or her past for all it is. The Far Pavilions of our Future await and promise us:
>
> Everything Still to Come.'

"What absolute twaddle!" she exclaimed with contempt.

Begrudgingly she read on. Despite Angela's initial urge to bin the book due to the distinct smell of festival patchouli about it, and against her previously linear, better judgment, she relaxed her internal set of rules and decided to read. It was a different sort of writing to what Angela usually accepted as literature of merit, but she persevered and by nightfall had already invested her attention into several chapters.

The following day Angela left a message on Mr. Lockhart's voicemail to the effect she would be taking five weeks leave owed to her. She didn't want to run the risk of speaking to him in person. He seemed so odd in his manner, a little nervous perhaps, instead of his usual quiet command. What was he doing turning up on her doorstep? How inappropriate! *On a Saturday no less, with flowers, and he begged me to stay!* She blushed at the thought and covered her mouth to hide her broadening smile.

Oh for goodness sake, don't be so ridiculous, he was only acting as any conscientious manager should. He is a professional.

As much as she tried to convince herself that Mr. Lockhart was only concerned for her well-being as a member of staff, for several days later, her smile and pinked cheeks would return to say otherwise. This was almost the last straw for Angela. She had put her job in a precarious position, she had made a public spectacle of herself by dancing on tabletops and now, now she was entertaining the ludicrous idea that her boss was harbouring an infatuation towards her! Every time her humiliation made itself known, she found herself scratching between the shoulder blades in agitation.

Oh yes, she observed cynically, *I can add two lumps on my back as well, I'll be a female Quasimodo before too long, either that or a camel.*

Clearly the various ointments she had so far tried had not made an iota of difference to her strange affliction. The growths were steadily changing in colour and size, the itching more urgent and inflamed than ever before. Reluctantly she resigned herself to see her doctor, a visit she would most certainly not relish due to the inevitable physical contact it would necessitate. After booking an appointment for the latter part of the next week, she decided to create some kind of distraction in two ways. The first was to read Mr.

Messenger's book from cover to cover and the second would be to clear the contents from the boxes in the other room.

In the ensuing days, she very quickly established a routine of cleaning in the morning and reading in the afternoon. The morning was for cleaning and clearing, as the rising heat of the summer afternoons made any kind of strenuous work almost unbearable. As to the boxes, they had to be cleared. She and they had travelled together since she had left home at sixteen. Many things had been added, but nothing had been thrown away. They were like a museum vault of her past and that was not something she cared to contemplate. As soon as anything was added to the archive, it was to be forgotten. Indeed, much of what she found in the boxes were papers and oddments which meant little or nothing to Angela, for they had been packed hurriedly when she had moved years before.

Now for the first time in years they were open to the light of day, and for some unfathomable reason, since her first dream of night flying, it was easier to throw them out, as she had a new perspective. The only items which made her literally pause for thought were ones which held memory, found in innocuous objects hidden underneath; a ragged childhood toy, a souvenir from some foreign travel, or a random photograph of someone she could not put a name to. When these appeared, the itching on her back came more acutely into focus. Often her understanding of what an old watch or discarded toy might mean was at first lost upon her, however, each article from her clouded past would herald a corresponding dream. Every night she would find herself exploring the skies above the seemingly endless landscape of her dreaming nocturnal world. Within the patchwork below appeared to be a fragment of her past, of everything which had happened, late for school, cooking in the kitchen, walking in the woods. The inconsequential events of the day-to-day. Things which were so mundane, it seemed odd how much they were treasured.

She soon discovered she was developing an ability to direct what she did within her nocturnal excursions, whereby although her aerial self might be floating aloft, she could extend her thoughts and feelings into the possibilities being played out below. She could influence them. One by one, she began to understand how these places and times were connected to the treasures found in the boxes. For at each meeting of these moments, the aerial Angela would swoop with joy, dipping down closer so as to relish them all in the finest detail, all her senses were heightened into one. With this came a new discovery. In her dream world she could slip down into the moment and memory and she could smell the varnish of a schoolroom desk, she could taste the orange from a Christmas stocking, she could feel the thorns from a blackberry bush.

One morning she found an old bone china teapot. It had a willow pattern and a bamboo handle, much the worse for wear. Having cleaned it, she placed it on the box room window ledge then thought no more of it. That night she flew in her dream to a sunny garden. Hovering there for awhile she caught a glimpse of a small girl of about four years old and she felt herself being pulled down. The experience was not too dissimilar to diving into a depth of water, or the sudden pull of gravity felt in a lift. When a sense of equilibrium had returned she found herself looking out through her younger self's eyes. She was playing alone in a pink, scrap-wood hut. Her father had made something similar to this, with a faded rug on the floor and a wooden orange-box to act as a cupboard. The small girl poured a water tea from a bamboo-handled teapot for a company of friends who could not be seen. As Angela became more aware, she could hear the thoughts of the small girl at play.

Mummy isn't very well. It makes Mummy sad and it makes Mummy cross. Daddy doesn't know what's wrong. Daddy doesn't know what Mummy does when he goes to work. I wish he'd come back soon so I can go back in. He tries his best but Mummy is still cross and shouting. Everyone is hiding now, 'coz the shouting is too loud. I'll stay here 'til it's quiet.

It was quite shocking to hear these familiar sounding thoughts, for Angela had forgotten how solitary much of her own childhood had been, despite having four brothers. She found herself murmuring piteous words to her little self,

You sad little thing...

"Who's that?" the little girl said out loud. Angela felt herself lurch, as the girl swivelled around looking for the voice.

She can hear me!

"Of course I can hear you. Where are you?" came the wide-eyed response. "Have you come to play? What's your name?"

I'm... I'm Angela.

"That's funny, that's my name too, but everyone calls me Little Angie," then she paused for a moment and whispered, "everyone except Mummy. Would you like some tea?"

It was some time before Angela returned to her body in the sky. A woman's strident command had broken their tender play, and it sent an alarm through the old and young Angela in unison. In the process, Angela felt herself rising rapidly out of the quivering child, and try as she might, she knew she couldn't remain there much longer.

"I've got to go," said the small girl trembling.

So have I.

"Will you come back?" she asked anxiously. Angela could feel the little girl's heart thumping in her chest.

Angie, listen. Whenever you need me, just talk to me.

The girl began to calm a little.

"But you will come back, won't you?"

It was only after she had awoken from her dream Angela remembered the invisible friend to whom she used to speak to as a child, in times when her Mother's anger became too much to bear. The Matriarch had been ill for most of Angela's remembered childhood. It was manifest in angry disappointment with everyone and everything around her. Mother had found fault particularly in where they lived. It was a rural backwater where she had no friends. Of course in her mind, her husband was sadly lacking in any drive or ambition, settling happily as he did to being a family man. And then there was Angela.

The truth behind her animosity towards her daughter was simply she reminded her too much of herself, for the child was a younger mirror image. It was tragic, for internally, Angela was more like her Father, being creative, funny and, like him, longing for approval from her Mother, only to find it rejected. The subsequent mental cruelty metered out would in turn teach the siblings to copy their Mother's example, because to them Angela was the reason why their Mother was always angry. It began just after Angela was born had it not? Without Angela to bear the brunt they too might be next in line to become a target. Children will do any manner of unexpected things in order to survive. As time went on, the girl called Little Angie retreated further into herself, talking more and more to her imaginary friend and calling her to return. The siblings' behaviour compounded her isolation. After some years the hope of her brief companion's return faded, and the girl had no one. Here in her adult self, Angela could not help but baffle at the strange coincidence of her dream. Nevertheless, spreading her hand over her heart she made a silent vow never to forget her younger self.

From then on, Angela sorted and sifted through the forgotten archives of the box room with the hope she might somehow recall their past. She grew to know her dream world as if it was her own reflection, and she began to look forward to sleep. Yet always, far off in the distance, there was always another place and memory to explore. This dream world was not just a collection of memories, it was one in which lay possible futures. It was as if all these possibilities somehow simultaneously co-existed in the same moment of Now, each one different but as equally real in themselves. It was a landscape of multiple outcomes: a multiverse.

Layer upon layer, these worlds resided not just side by side but in the same place, all of their expressions decided by a different decision, a different choice, a right turn or a left, a greeting or farewell, a mistaken purchase of ill fitting shoes might lead to an unfortunate step onto an unsafe pavement stone or; to a fortunate chance meeting with a stranger at a station. As Angela became familiar with these layered worlds, their pavilions gathered clarity and focus. Tenderly, as she began to trust their possibilities, these layered worlds began to open up to her like flower buds blossoming into being. Layered worlds of different choices which might be taken would create different timelines of outcomes, and Angela's acceptance of each one gave way to waking others, and fortune of all kinds flowed through them all. There were timelines she could not fathom, some which she steered away from, like one in which an approaching shadowy figure made her shudder. But then she would turn her attention to others, somewhat like changing a television channel, leaving those uncomfortable timelines to run their own course without her direct attention. In one Angela lived a life as a demented recluse, stuck in a moment of barely existing. It was a sorry scene in which this other self sat alone by the light of an open refrigerator door, surviving on only white bread and milk and talking only to herself and the birds in her garden. This had left Angela nauseous, as the comparisons of her present life felt too close for comfort. However, there would appear a more balancing choice of more pleasant future outcomes presented to her as well. One in particular beckoned her with a golden glow.

Angela could just make out a sunny street where she was sitting at a linen clothed table, waiting but not knowing what or who the wait was for. The anticipation made her tremble with excitement. She had to see more. Pushing more strongly through the air currents she flew to gain a clearer view, but just as she thought she was near enough, a huge darkness expanded in front of her, and an oppressive tightening grabbed her throat. It was barring her way to the sunny street. The darkness was palpable, thick and congealed. Just beyond its border Angela could see something else, a distant spiral of colourful light. A closer view showed a carousel whose faint melody rose and fell as it circled. It looked gentle and peaceful, a place to rest, and how Angela yearned to rest there too. But its mirage image fluttered, like a transparent sheet in the wind, and the dark border was too powerful to cross over. It imprisoned all within. There in the midst of the darkness was a lone figure of a girl. It was Angela again, only this time she was a little older than the first encounter. Angela the Girl was playing in a garden, but as to why this made her floating self recoil in horror, she didn't know. All she did know was the terror with which it filled her was beyond anything she could bear.

On waking there was an unshakeable feeling that at some point she would have to return to the place of Darkness if she truly wanted to reach the place of the Carousel and find a place of rest. Revisiting the dream sky and its starry firework display, Angela hovered at first over places she knew in the now. Little by little, she began to venture further into the lands she could see way off in the horizon-less distance. In each night time excursion, she would explore a new possibility Each different choice she might have made in her life, created a different life.

In one possibility, she was living in a house with children and dogs. The house was cramped and shambolic. A whoop of children of different ages and origins happily wrestled, teasing each other into jovial submission. Dogs barked and bounced, tails wagging and tongues slobbering. The playmates jostled and rolled in and out of house and garden, while Angela patiently guided them with firm cautions and kind words, as their benevolent matriarch. She stood watching them at all times, splashes of paint on their beaming faces. Kettles boiled, toast popped, baths were hot and bubbly and the towels were warm and fluffy. She sighed with satisfaction when the last child had been tucked into bed and she could finally sit down in relative peace, only to be called once more for a cup of water and just one more story. In this place and time, this other Angela laughed.

In another possibility, Angela saw herself in a company of friends she had never met in her waking life, but here seemed so familiar. They were in a kitchen at a large wooden table, filling glasses and nibbling bread. There was a tangible generosity and appreciation which passed between everyone in the party, Angela included. One woman kissed her briefly on her cheek while topping up her glass. Angela kissed her back, only turning away to stir a huge pot of vegetable curry while her affectionate party giggled and joked. Every now and again this other Angela would join in with the animated chatter. The gang were dissecting their last hilarious excursion to a Zumba class, and were beginning an outrageous plan for another jaunt, away to somewhere warm, with Angela. In this place and time this other Angela was smiling.

And in another possibility, Angela was standing majestically tall, with an entourage of fellow musicians. She was singing an aria, 'The Nightingale's Song', in a great domed theatre, with tiered balconies all the way up to the Gods. Her sweet notes slowly rose and spiralled on what felt like a current of pure joy. Rising higher, she was no longer terra bound for her voice effortlessly began to soar to one sustained note, ending with a thrumming trill of violins. For a moment there was silence, then a sudden eruption of mass applause.

"Bravo! Bravo! Encore! Encore!"

The painted Chagall angels on the auditorium ceiling were dancing over the standing ovation below them. Angela was being presented with a voluminous bouquet of velvet-like, ruby-rich roses. A buxom Angela pulled the blooms close to her bosom in a Lover's embrace. She bowed, she laughed, she smiled and, in this place and time, Angela felt proud.

In each and every one of these reveries, she shimmered above the tableau, an unseen witness to the drama below. However, one night's dream haunted her long after her waking.

One morning after breakfast, she decided to press ahead clearing what she now considered a spare room and no longer, that room. It was now quite an exciting prospect to transform it, perhaps into a sewing room.

Wasn't I once an excellent seamstress?

It was about time she woke up her sewing machine. Why she had left that skill to neglect she couldn't remember. Lifting off a newspaper cover, she found an old box in which lay a pink angora cardigan. Too small for any adult, but Angela couldn't tell the age. Some yellowing magazines curled underneath it, and what looked like an old wooden skipping rope. Picking up the faded garment, something wrapped inside fell to the floor. Retrieving it, Angela turned it around in her hand, trying to focus her eyes and memory as to what it was. A glass necklace, cut to shine rainbows. A cheaply bought trinket from a seaside town, but a priceless treasure to a child. Angela choked a little, as a stabbing pain seared through her heart and a small shift in time rose up like bubbles in her chest.

I felt like a princess wearing this, a princess off to the ball, but then came midnight.

With a look of ragged disgust, she tenderly replaced the necklace back into the box. Then the door to the room was closed once more, but that night she dreamt again.

Angela was standing in a garden as the sun descended on the late evening. A golden glow lit the trees and borders with warmth that seemed to kiss everything it touched. The crystal glass necklace sparked rainbow colours around her milky skin. She looked at her hands. They were much smaller, much younger than before. She was a child of about nine years old dancing in her childhood garden. Dancing with her shadow. Her shadow was her giant self and she could make it do anything! Around and around she danced, laughing and jumping. She could make her shadow take to the air. She could make her fly! As she leapt with joy, she became lighter and lighter – she sparkled. Then her body began to change. Her legs became taller, her breasts grew like flower buds, and she was now thirteen. Then, from somewhere, she heard a voice calling, a man's voice, dark and gravelly. It was blowing on the wind about her night-gown and filling her lungs with a thick malodorous stench of pipe smoke. At first the voice seemed soothing,

my girl, my girl,

But then its intonation changed. It was cold now, so cold, it seemed to cling to her, whipping about her ankles, lifting up her hem. The shadows of the trees grew longer and stretched across the lawn towards her, getting nearer and nearer. The branches were changing form. They were fingers, dark, dark fingers, cold and clawing. Her heart began to beat in her throat. She was trying to call out loud, towards the house at the top of the garden.

They will help me won't they?

But no sound came from her mouth and the last light had gone out. They hadn't noticed she was missing. The wind voice continued to blow about her. It was now tearing at the cloth of her dress. She wrapped her arms about her waist, fear rising as the shadow fingers climbed her legs. *Help me!* She mutely screamed, *help me!* But no help came. She looked down beneath her feet, a fissure of blackness was being ripped open by the shadow fingers. *My girl, my girl,* menaced the wind voice. The torn ground churned and shook as its attacker dug deeper and deeper into its earthy flesh. A chasm was widening, and losing all balance, she fell down and down, deep into its gaping abyss.

Angela sat up with a start, cold sweat trickling over her body. A slight breeze was blowing through the open window and she could hear a blackbird singing in the early dawn. Wrapping the quilt tightly about her quivering body, she curled foetal, her face buried into her pillow and she began to cry. Inconsolable tears for a little lost child, until at last, she fell into a dreamless sleep, from which she would not wake until much later in the morning.

Strange to have remembered her dream now, after years had gone by without any solid memory of what haunted her. All that remained was an uneasy gnawing in the pit of her stomach and a dull ache in the area of her heart. Abuse wasn't an easy memory. The shock of it had launched her into a premature adulthood and fossilised her willingness to feel.

It was too soon. I didn't have the words to describe it, or even to know what had actually happened to me. All I knew then were teenage dolls and party dresses. How could I tell anyone, when I didn't have the words?

Now she could remember something. Not all, but something nonetheless. It was a piece of a jigsaw puzzle, the picture of which she had long since mislaid, was now in the light of her adult self and she could observe it safely from the distance of time. Indeed, she found herself conversing internally to the understandably distraught child imprisoned in a state of shock. Angela resolutely promised she would now be Little Angie's Protector, albeit in retrospect. Little Angie was a child, with all the hopeful potential and anticipation children bring into Life. These childhood events of predatory men and mad mothers had cracked her like a broken cup and clipped her flight like a soiled dove.

It was strange to recollect too in waking, of the strange demise of that particular predatory man some years later that had involved some kind of wild animal attack. Memory of this was indeed foggy as the only details she could recall had been drawn from a newspaper sometime after she had left home.

The police at the time had drawn a blank, and the case of the predatory man was literally buried. She did remember her satisfaction when finding the brute to be dead.

There are such things as happy accidents after all.

Up in the air of her night travels and as a witness to the terrible assault upon the Little Angie's body and soul, Angela the Woman swore that somehow she would make things right from that moment on. She would defend her life, and was prepared to do anything to make sure of this. The turbulent waters she navigated through in the workaday world were nothing in comparison to the untold things she had experienced but kept secret. Things no one must ever know and not all for shame. She had always known she was damaged as a person but as to how deeply this had altered her psyche remained a mystery, as much to herself as to others. It was almost as if she had deliberately built a deep shafted well within. A dark prison sheltered her from facing the terrible pain that that lay deep down. To own the pain would mean awakening. The internal prison belonged to someone else. Admittedly it was worrying there were still too many blanks when it came to her memory of past events. Intuitively, she knew the changes occurring so rapidly were surely a herald calling her to something better.

"It is our fragility which marks us, not our perfection," she murmured to her internal self.

In her waking hours, and in the balmy afternoons, she sat outside in an easy chair and read. Pierre and Miss Bee appeared to be away, as their music was silent for the first time in a long time. Her student neighbours were also absent, having apparently left for the summer and no new tenants had appeared. There was nothing to disturb her from immersing herself in the book, nothing except the relentless heat. The smell of salt baked on her sunny skin, leaving her feeling drugged and not quite in the world. The days continued to pass, and like the breath of a deep sleeper, Angela grew to revel in the rhythm. She now had time on her hands, and delighted in her own decadent dalliance with every warming sunrise.

Despite the growing irritation on either side of her spine, she was becoming inured to its presence and would, after scratching, momentarily stretch like a satiated nubile. With a languid smile and half-closed eyes she would sigh, with the tip of her tongue at the corner of her mouth as if licking the last of a delicious ice-cream.

Under the circumstances it was fortunate that Pierre was not there to witness the emerging worshipper of Dionysus, for she was quite unlike the quiet recluse who had previously inhabited her skin. And though the tapping of a typewriter from the top floor flat was gone, there were recurring moments when Angela's gaze towards the top flat lingered a little longer than usual, curious for turquoise eyes.

As the days went on, the temperature rose even higher, lending a curious quality of sound to everything around her, almost as if sound existed in a different pace of time. As if, hanging in the air like descending helium balloons, time was slowing down. Beyond an echo, time was changing into an audible stillness. It was an absorption which unconsciously became a meditation to Angela, for the stillness emanated from her. Angela was becoming lighter.

Yet still she persevered with Mr. Messenger's book. At first glance it could be read as a slightly New Age travelogue, merely listing amazing accounts of travel adventures. Narrow mountain paths which led to obscure shrines, swollen rivers through which a lost tribe was to be re-found and of a strange and avenging demoness named Lilith, winged and taloned, re-discovered in a carving on the rock of a hidden temple hidden thousands of years before. Most strangely of all, he spoke of internal travel, in which, from what she could vaguely comprehend, he described worlds within worlds. It was hard to glean the meaning of this, and was lost in significance to

Angela. She began to wonder why it had felt so vital she read it the first place when, on the last two pages something in her understanding began to shift. Writing of a steep treacherous climb to the summit of a high mountain, the author said;

"I got there, and I could see all around me, and I thought, 'I really am a lucky man.' As I gazed at the clouded mountain peaks below me I watched how the sun painted every part with the most vivid and yet subtle colours and how it touched the feathers of a gliding eagle, a realization came into focus in my mind. I thought how insignificant we all are in comparison to everything around and beyond us. But by the same token, how equally immense our lives are. Here I am, I thought, sitting on a mountain and gazing at the stars beyond and I am made from the same stuff as they. We all are. In fact, taken from that view, we share more in common with every stranger on the street than we had previously dared hope or dread. We are of the same blood and bones, the same mountain and stars. We are not so far apart. I felt the distance of things shrink and melt – the joy was boundless! Mountaineering and trekking has given me a fortunate perspective, one which has accumulated from a culmination of small truths and mysteries. It has helped me to perceive a much bigger picture; a much bigger family to which we all belong. All I had to do was to remember there are no borders in the Universe; only the borders we create for ourselves. We are already home."

Angela scratched her back in agreement, for her skin now had an almost litmus reaction to what was true. As she scratched, she felt an unnerving change. The intense inflammation had certainly subsided in the last couple of weeks. The bumps had become bigger and scalier and she had noticed a hardening under the skin. Perhaps the brittle flaking was due to too much sun. It irritated her to distraction, but the hardening... The hardening was solid and had a patterned structure. Two spiralled mounds, about the size of a pair of large butternut squash, stood out from her flesh like skeletal tumuli and, well, *they moved.*

Chapter Seven

In Surgical Outpatients Angela slid further down into the waiting room seat, whilst tightly gripping a well-thumbed copy of 'The Lady' shield-like in front of her nerve-wracked face. Her confused and concerned GP was obviously troubled by the growths, and even more so by the mobility of her afflictions. It had left the kindly doctor ashen-faced and trembling when under examination, the bumps had quivered in his hands. Immediately he had begun making urgent phone calls to a colleague in the local hospital to ensure there was no delay. In truth, he had never encountered anything like this before and thought perhaps the stress of a heavy workload was getting the better of him. While she sat outside in the waiting room, Angela could hear the doctor plead on her behalf.

"No Julian, I'm not pranking you because of the last squash game! I'm telling you this woman has something moving in there. She needs emergency tests at once!"

The emergency referral was arranged for first thing the next day – at the very same hospital where Angela worked. The possibility she might be seen terrified her, even though the Outpatients department was situated at the other end of the hospital building to her own office. This of course did not prevent her agonising as to what would happen if she were recognised by staff. She had little concern as to what the Doctors might find.

All I need now is for Helen Ellis to walk through that door. Angela peeped over the top of her magazine to check. *Of course she's not there. I'm being paranoid.*

"Miss Bagner? Would you please come this way?"

By the end of the afternoon Angela was absolutely exhausted. All day she had been prodded and poked. She had endured umpteen blood tests, x-rays, an MRI scan and, "Oh, could you give us a small urine sample as well?"

Back in the consulting room, the number of Doctors attending appeared to have tripled since the morning. They were excitedly talking amongst themselves when she returned, and on her arrival they rushed to offer chairs and cups of tea as if she was a visiting dignitary and they were nervous schoolboys.

"Tell us more about your family history," one of them asked.

"Any relatives with birth defects?" asked another.

Then an older member of the team rose and invited Angela to look at her x-rays on the light box. The red threaded veins on his nose gave him a certain authority akin to W.C. Fields.

"You see Miss Bagner, we are unsure what to make of this, for this is quite unlike anything we have ever seen before," he conspiratorially confided, pointing to the screen and tracing an outline of the shadowy shapes, "The perfect symmetry of the two structures and intricate articulation of their makeup."

"It might be dermoid cysts from an embryonic source?" suggested an enthusiastic young bespeckled doctor from behind.

"Or it might be a brachial cyst revealing a fistula?" added another.

"Yes, yes, yes, quite right, quite right. It might be a fistula, or rather a genetic throwback. However, the test results will take some time before we can rule any of these things out, but still, it is very curious, for seems as if ..." He coughed hesitantly, averted his eyes with a little embarrassment as to what he was about to say. "It appears Miss Bagner, you are growing, erm, wings."

The collective withheld breath lasted for some time. There was indeed no denying the images presented to her. Three x-rays told the undeniable truth. In the first the shapes enfolded towards each other. In the second, the shapes changed slightly, disclosing bony extensions, and in the third, the third showed distinctly, small but unmistakable feathers. The band of doctors returned their gaze to the dumbstruck Angela, waiting in baited breath for her reply.

"There is one last test we must carry out today." The rosacea-nosed consultant was already directing his subordinates away from the side of the examination table. A nurse entered the room pushing a rattling trolley of various surgical instruments, sharp instruments. Angela gulped.

"If you wouldn't mind undressing down to your waist behind the screen."

The nurse was prepping a syringe, and a small arc of liquid jetted from the spike. Angela felt a panic rising in her chest.

The red nosed doctor continued. "... then we will take a small biopsy of these anomalies. Just to get it out of the way."

He patted Angela's visibly trembling hand to reassure her.

"There'll be no pain under local anesthetic."

Whatever else was said next to calm her, Angela couldn't tell. All she could think of was:

GET AWAY! GET AWAY!

The growths on her back were thrashing up and down, faster and faster. Her heart was racing and the only reply to come from her throat was a high pitched and loudly piping note of alarm, which sounded remarkably like this:

"Peenk! Peenk! Peenk!"

Before they could get any closer, she had somehow managed to run from their grasp.

Down the corridors, avoiding wheelchairs and trolleys, Angela fled. She had not been prepared for this news...*Wings! Knives!* They were going to cut her! Visions of formaldehyde and specimen jars swam in front of her mind. Despite the shock of her rise to Queen of the Freak Show, she felt incredibly defensive and protective towards her new self.

Like when the hen Blackbird crashed into Mr. Messenger's window and...

"Peenk!" she exclaimed out loud.

She pulled herself to a stop. She was outside in the car park.

"It was then! Peenk! That's when this started, wasn't it? Peenk! Wasn't it? Peenk! Peenk! Peenk!"

The bystanders she addressed this to decided to walk on, thinking perhaps she was from the psychiatric department around the corner. Angela was too distressed to notice. She had to get back. She had to find Mr. Messenger.

It was however unfortunate for Angela that she had left the Outpatients in such a noticeable manner. Her flapping arms and wild-eyed look, with the addition of the constantly repeating alarm call emitting from her throat, had created a striking spectacle. This drew attention from patients, staff and visitors alike, and most especially – Helen Ellis. She had been taking a roundabout way back to her office as she felt her afternoon break was never quite long enough, when a commotion from up a side hallway drew her interest. Angela Bagner was running zigzag through the busy corridor, a dose of doctors were calling her to stop as onlookers stared at her disappearing through an exit door.

"My, my, we do get them don't we?" Helen commented to the reception secretary, making sure she could clearly see her Hospital I.D. badge. "And you on your own as well! Anything I can do? Filing or anything?"

"Oh thank you, I'm totally swamped. That one," the girl at the desk nodded in the general direction of the disappeared Angela, "she's been here pretty much all day. I've missed my lunch, I've got a backlog of files to get back to the medical library, and I need the loo!"

Helen was seamless in seizing the opportunity in front of her.

"Look, tell you what, you nip over to the canteen and get a sandwich etc, and I'll hold the fort here until you come back, okay?"

"Are you sure? Oh you are an angel. See you in ten minutes."

"You take your time."

Helen seated herself behind the desk, with a large pile of patient files in front of her. The clearly harassed nurse thought nothing of the changeover of reception staff. She had too many other things to do. And so, into the welcoming hands of Helen Ellis was delivered the medical file of Angela Bagner.

"Take care of that would you?" the nurse curtly asked.

"I certainly will," Helen replied with a smile. She switched on the office answer machine. She did not want to be disturbed.

Chapter Eight

She had been hammering on the outside door to the flats above for what seemed like an age, every now and then ringing the doorbell. There was no answer. How Angela had managed to get back to Lossingham without completely losing her decorum was a small miracle. She had jumped into a waiting mini-cab, willing the traffic out of her path all the way home. Her head was reeling with careering thoughts banging and clanging like a trapped animal in a cage. *Wings! Am I going insane?* The only possible clue was her strange meeting with the mysterious Mr. G. Messenger. Something had happened, something beyond her ken. Something so anomalous and peculiar it required an extreme suspension of disbelief to attempt conceding its very existence. Angela rang his bell again.

"He's not in."

Angela, startled by a girl's voice swung around, nearly stumbling down the front steps she teetered on.

"He's not in." repeated the girl, her voice rising up from the pavement. "I saw him leave this morning in a taxi."

Angela rubbed her brow frantically. "Who left?" She was speaking to Jenny Collins, one of the brood from further up the street. Jenny was playing with a Cat's Cradle in her hands and she continued talking as she wove.

"Mr. Gabriel. He's gone again," she added proudly as if this was clearly something impressive. "He waved to me from the car."

"When will he be back?"

"Don't know. He was gone for ever such a long time before."

The small girl looked sad for a moment and seemed to drift somewhere else in her gaze. Angela noticed then how skinny the child was, with lank hair which clung to her face, only just shading her large dark eyes. Jenny abruptly snapped into brightness, as if cheering herself.

"Not to worry. He'll be back. He brought me back a lovely thing last time. Here, do you want to see?"

Plunging her hand into the pink plastic shoulder bag she was always seen to wear across her clothes, the girl pulled out from it a small object. She thrust her hand forward towards Angela, urging her to look. Slowly stepping down to the pavement, Angela stood over the waif-like girl who was looking up at her with eyes as big as saucers, an eager smile stretching across her freckled face. She pushed her hand nearer for Angela to have a closer view. In her palm lay a charcoal gray, terracotta bird, crudely carved, and with indentations of the artisan's fingers still visible on the surface. A hand painted red flower decorated each wing.

"It's a whistle. It came all the way from Russia!" Jenny happily exclaimed. "Do you want me to show you how it works?"

Without waiting for Angela to answer, she lifted the tail end to her mouth and blew.

"Peenk!"

Angela, recoiling in shock at the high-pitched note, stumbled and scrabbled, reaching out a hand to find a railing to cling to. Jenny however was totally immersed in her demonstration, oblivious to the power she was wielding over this horrified grown-up.

"Peenk! Peenk! Peenk!"

She glanced up to Angela's open mouthed expression and suddenly stopped, taking the bird-whistle from her pursed lips.

"Would you like a go?" Jenny chirruped, offering the plaything up to the astounded Angela.

"What on earth is that noise?" Angela was shaking her head in disbelief. The sound was almost identical to the cry from her throat earlier in the day.

Jenny of course, was delighted to impart her knowledge. Rarely was she asked her opinion at home as her brothers would always overshadow her in noise. She mostly kept herself to herself in the family and at school, not letting on her thoughts or feelings to adults. But Miss Bagner, she seemed lovely – exotic even! And she knew Mr. M! Somehow the faint connection opened a gate of trust for the child.

"It's the noise blackbirds make to frighten off cats from their babies," she continued with authority. "I don't like cats. Do you like cats? They kill baby birds, but they don't eat them. Anyway, Gabriel said it was for me to warn off bad things, or…" she lowered her voice and leant nearer, "….or bad people. My Uncle ran away from my Dad after my Dad heard it. My Dad was telling him off. He called him a perv. I don't know what a perv is, but my Dad said Uncle was. We haven't seen him for a while. I hope he doesn't come back when Mum and Dad are out."

Angela paused in her panic and observed the child in front of her with curiosity. Jenny had pricked her concern and it humbled her how trusting the child was to her.

"Why, what would happen if he did?" She brushed a string of hair from across Jenny's furrowed brow.

"Can't say, I'll get in trouble if I do. Uncle said so." She looked down at her cotton shoes, avoiding Angela's gaze. Later Angela would marvel at her own response.

"Jenny isn't it?" Angela asked, gently lifting the girl's chin up with her hand, "Don't keep secrets from your Mum and Dad. And if your Uncle comes round and you're on your own, run 'round to me, okay?"

Jenny nodded and without any prompting launched herself against Angela, skinny arms wrapping tightly around her legs.

"Thank you," Jenny gasped.

Angela tentatively stroked her hair. Then just as suddenly, Jenny released her hold and ran away down the dusty street.

In the seclusion of her garden, Angela resigned herself to the absence of any answers from Mr. Messenger...Gabriel Messenger. An intriguing picture of this enigmatic man was beginning to materialize like a face emerging from fog, but always with those intense turquoise eyes.

Chapter Nine

"Come in."

The frosted glass door to Mr. Lockhart's office opened and Helen Ellis stood waiting expectantly with a bundle of papers and files.

"Well?" Mr. Lockhart grunted, returning to his computer screen, having briefly given only a cursory glance up to see Mrs. Ellis. He was busy with the urgent financial annual audit report. It was overdue because, for some time, James had noticed an unexplained pattern of inaccuracies. As he certainly didn't wish any of the staff to be aware of this, should an internal inquiry be needed, he was keeping his unofficial investigation hush-hush.

The atmosphere since the incident with Miss Bagner had become painfully fraught. As much as he would like to, he was in an impossible position to further approach Angela. After all, he was her line manager, and overseer of the smooth running of the whole department. Miss Bagner was an invaluable and dependable member of staff, that was true, but he had only recently admitted to himself she was also an attractive, intelligent and honourable lady. And, as Mr. Lockhart was an old-fashioned gentleman from the Old School of courtship, he believed she would be a perfect match for him, but only if he followed his personal code of courteous protocol. Until the air in the office was cleared of the Mrs. Ellis dictatorship, James Lockhart felt it totally inappropriate to venture forward for Angela's consideration.

Without any definitive evidence of negligence on the part of Helen Ellis, there was little he could do to rectify the problem. He had given a verbal reprimand as to inter personal relationships and had logged this in the office staff diary. The ridiculous woman had then entered a counter complaint, claiming that there was a petty thief in the department as a precious holiday memento had recently disappeared from her desk. Whenever Helen Ellis was late, or gave an excuse for shoddy completion of work which she had foisted onto another member of staff, Mr. Lockhart watched and took note. He was compiling a dossier.

"Here are the reports you requested Mr. Lockhart," Helen announced with terse over-politeness. "I have the itinerary for the department's Charity Summer Ball as well." She placed the files on his desk, then personally handed him a listed sheet. He began to read aloud,

"Las Estellas des Verano. The Summer Stars Ball ... hmm, a Latin themed night eh? With live music, tapas and tortillas," he mused, "Sounds different. When is this?"

"In twelve days time. I know it seems short notice, but the venue was available due to a cancellation. It's the perfect place, with a starlit roof garden," Helen simpered with an ingratiating smile. "A chauffeured car will be at your disposal as well. The whole department appreciates how much you love quality presentation in all things Mr. Lockhart."

"Quite right Mrs. Ellis. Right you are, just make sure all staff have been made aware of the dates and times. That will include Miss Bagner who is on holiday leave presently. Is that understood?"

"But of course Mr. Lockhart! I hope you don't mind, but I took it upon myself to design the invitations which will be sent out to everyone. All the publicity is ready to press send. We just need your signature on the Master copy before they're printed."

She thrust another sheet towards him. Mr. Lockhart in his urgency to remove the obsequious Helen Ellis as soon as possible from his breathing space, duly signed his name with a flourish and paid little attention to any written detail, most especially the small print.

Closing the door behind her, Helen chuckled to herself.

"This is all too, too easy – God! These people are so stupid."

Helen was almost delirious with her plan for revenge. The indignation which sprang from Angela Bagner daring to challenge her was fuelling a highly detailed and exquisitely elaborate enterprise for Bagner's retribution. The last time Helen had felt this alive was when she had risen through the ranks of the Parents Association, so as to become Head Governor of her children's school. With that came the superficial subservience of fellow parents and reluctant teachers. To Helen's credit, that particular ambition was in part to ensure her children were given premier attention throughout their schooling. Mostly though it was to bolster her ego with a stupefying sense of importance. It also acted as a mask to the unspoken cavities in her marriage. Her husband had a prestigious position as a freelance art director in television production, most recently in a popular soap opera series. This had the added kudos of weekly credits to his name, and vicariously graced Helen as well. It was due to this she accepted his regular trips away, for with them she could utter such high status phrases as,

"Nick? Oh he's away at the mo, Prague you know – wonderful architecture."

Or,

"Nick? No, he's at an Awards ceremony in Barcelona with his production team."

Or,

"Nick? Tricky, he's on location in Italy for a new pilot series...I can only contact him via his Personal Assistant."

The Lossingham Hospital Annual Summer Charity Ball was a timely occasion. Traditionally, every department took turns in its organisation, heavily competing with each other for the highest fundraising yearly total. The proceeds generated were a valuable income for their overstretched medical budgets and so the perennial event was allowed ever more fanciful extravaganzas so as to attract the wealthiest of patrons to attend. Fortunately for Helen Ellis, it was the Finance Department's turn this year, and she had volunteered to be in charge. As self-titled 'Principal Programme Producer' or 'PPP', Helen was contriving a spectacle which would mark her as an outstanding events promoter, and just perfect for her CV. No longer interested in promotion she felt her skills were entirely beyond the limitations of the Finance Department's daily grind, which was relentless, soul-destroying and of course, completely beneath her. Helen had taken the job just as a stop gap while husband Nick was pursuing his career. With no real desire for an ordinary job, Helen did however desire the charms of status and celebrity. And of course, the joy of bossing others also had its attraction. She intended to create a spectacular leaving note her colleagues would be telling their offspring of for years to come, and one which would launch her into a far more salubrious setting – PR.

The cherry on top of this particular cold and vengeful cake was the chance to publicly humiliate Bagner. It seemed the Gods were smiling upon her when Angela's medical notes came into Helen's possession. It was too good to be true, but there was the hard evidence, Angela Bagner was some kind of mutated creature. The World would want to know about this, and who was she to begrudge The World? It would be her public duty to reveal the identity of the mysterious woman who had caused such a stir recently. Why, they were begging for news as to her whereabouts, and Helen felt it would churlish to deny them.

Acting as 'an insider friend', Helen leaked an email which disclosed the personal appearance of 'Angeliquita' at a forthcoming show. Delivered in her most innocent of voices, hints about its nature were given to pique media interest. She followed up the email campaign with phone calls to Radio, T.V. and Press, all about the Latin themed Charity Ball. It didn't take a great deal of skill to join the dots. Local newspapers couldn't resist, for good copy articles were few and far between in the backwater of the Lossingham area.

Reading of this, at the counter of the Rendezvous Café, Caroline, the manageress, passed the page to visiting Area Manager, Scott McKenny, who rang the mobile of Executive Managing Director of 'Viva!' coffee, Paul Hollingsworth. Viva's Chief then persuaded Helen Ellis to send him a dozen tickets, while instructing Scott McKenny to ensure a personal photographer for their group, as well as suitable, but of course tasteful, 'Viva!' badges for each of their party to wear.

Scott McKenny, now basking in the glow of his new-found distinction in the eyes of his superior, garnered the confidence to impress Caroline with an invitation to join their exclusive table, with the thinly disguised proposition of an after show 'lift home.' Caroline was glad for a break from the monotonous foam and steam. Scott McKenny was glad for this sudden leverage into a more fast-paced and, possibly racier life. While Paul Hollingsworth was glad because this was potentially a promotion for his business that present funds definitely couldn't buy. If he could secure 'Angeliquita' to represent 'Viva!' coffee, he was sure sales would go through the roof. This became such a burning hunger for him that it became his main occupation in thought. Eager not to miss this unique stroke of luck, Paul Hollingsworth decided he would design such an imaginative offer 'Angeliquita' could not possibly refuse. This enterprise would be Top Secret in its invention. No one must know, for fear his competitors might replicate it. He told only his secretary and his driver, both of whom he trusted implicitly. Helen Ellis would of course be totally in the dark as to what he was planning.

Meanwhile, Mrs. Ellis had already booked the marvelous Los Diablos de las Cantinas and assumed the position of Personal Manager to 'Angeliquita', who was very choosy as to where, when and with whom she played. 'Angeliquita' had apparently been scouting for a suitable quality backing band for a forthcoming tour and television appearances. Los Diablos were on her shortlist of would-be contenders, so of course Eddie offered to play at the Las Estellas des Verano Summer Ball for free.

"It would be our pleasure to give something to such a worthwhile cause," he told Helen. "We will give you a show to amaze you. No charge!"

"Oh what a refreshing attitude," Helen affected flattery. "Nevertheless, you must invoice me for your trouble, for the appearance of our books of course." She was not going to be out of pocket for this scheme, far from it. The expenses for such an event would appear on paper.

She used the publicity bribe in every meeting she made for her contrivance.

The lucky chosen venue was a newly refurbished restaurant situated on the roof above the Beaconshill Country Conference Centre.

"Think of this as a showcase presentation of what your future clients will desire. All the best people of importance will be there you know."

The management of Beaconshill Country Conference Centre were then practically falling over themselves to accommodate Helen's every need, whim and suggestion.

"A Complimentary Margarita to welcome each of the guests? No problem," they said, "we have a fully equipped cocktail bar."

"The Roof Garden will have a Starlight canopy in case of inclement weather?" they said, "We've just had one installed!"

"You want hanging Piñatas over each table?" they said, "Please feel free to decorate in whatever way you wish, Health and Safety withstanding of course."

"Sombrero-serving-dishes of tasty tapas served by Salsa-clad waiting staff?" they said, "Okay, that's fine.'

"A live burro carrying baskets of party farewell gifts in the foyer?" they hesitated, "Erm, we'll look into it."

It is extraordinary how much people will believe, and accept if they are directed with a firm, confident tone. Helen was certainly adept in this aspect of her character, and she swept aside any voices of doubting dissent purely by the assertive nature of her delivery. She was not a person to be trifled with. So with venue, live band and a lavish Spanish-style dinner secured, Helen then concentrated on the finer details. Local trades-people were equally excited at the mention of the possible media attention, and offered all kinds of services gratis, from inflatable cacti to chilli pepper lighting, from fireworks to prestige cars. Naturally all the contributing businesses would be mentioned for their charitable generosity on the evening's programme. These invitations would be sent to a select list of the Great and the Good, and to anyone with Celebrity status, major or minor. Most importantly, Helen kept everything, especially those things for her nemesis Angela, as secret as possible. Not even her husband knew. Helen had convinced him that he would be missing a golden opportunity if he were not involved in this exclusive night. After all, it was to be the most coveted occasion of the year. No, not even husband Nick knew of the machinations driving his wife Helen forward.

It is a fact indeed, that a person can live a long time with someone, and yet never truly know them.

Chapter Ten

Carefully adjusting the straps, Angela regarded her creation in the mirror from over either shoulder. She had spent the whole day customising a medium sized rucksack using the old sewing machine which had sat neglected in her living room since the day she had arrived. It had taken a while to set up as the needle was still entangled with the last thread and a jagged strip of black leather jammed there.

Too many years had passed, and it did irk her to have left such a mess. It had taken ages and several bouts of swearing to unknot, but eventually it was resolved with the slice of a sharp thread cutter. Strangely, Angela was no longer shocked with the torrents of vulgar obscenities she launched at the offending machine. It seemed natural to her now. Angela usually took pride in her meticulous nature in both organization and manners. It was evident in her clerical work at the hospital. Things had obviously changed for disheveled sewing machines to be as acceptable as "fuck". While she took apart and rebuilt the machine, she occasionally scratched her back.

The ever growing wings could now be clearly seen just under the thinly stretched flesh of her back. They were dark in shade, but as yet, indeterminate in colour, the blood vessels having increased in number over that area of skin. Perhaps this was her body's response to the new structures. Much like a foetus which demands sustenance, her circulation was providing a fine, threadlike net. The wings moved quite regularly now, and always in response Angela's thoughts. Moments of stress and fear brought an agitated and thrashing movement, while at times when she had put aside these internal agonies, she experienced a sensation of stretching and relaxing. When she was focused on a task, such as the final clearing of the last few boxes, it seemed her unconscious mind set a rhythmic beat into the young bones and feathers. They gently but firmly moved with the pulse of the heart they backed on to.

It was when she became aware of this, she found the rucksack. It was a piece of her history as a younger woman. Back then she hill walked, in all weathers, sometimes with company, sometimes alone. It had carried essential items on all her travels.

Rifling inside, she discarded most of its contents, until she found at the bottom an old photo in a frame. Sitting back on her haunches, with the afternoon sun spilling across her lap, she released a weighted sigh. It was nothing extraordinary. A group photograph of distant friends, one of whom was her then-partner. They had met a short while after she had separated herself abruptly from her family, when she had left for college. There had been too many family disruptions, and her chaotic family life had caused Angela's resolve to up and leave without a forwarding address if opportunity knocked.

Sometimes you just have to cut people out of your life, she had thought.

In the last year of her college, she met the man she was to live with. He was an attractive and harmlessly likeable man, and reminded her a little of her father. He gently courted her over some years, until she agreed to move in with him. He brought a ready-made group of friends in tow, who welcomed her into their company. No one suspected anything eschew in her character in the time they were together, only perhaps that his partner could be a little shy and retiring. It appeared to all that there was love of some kind between the couple. She had loved him as best she was able, for as long as she was able, but he had loved her better. Her own demonstrations of affection were mainly closed and limited.

Then out of the blue, she had fallen in love, in real love, with someone she considered entirely inappropriate and completely unobtainable. Her Grand Passion was to remain undisclosed and unfulfilled. It wasn't simply because she found she loved a woman, the gender was beside the point. It was a question of trust, for fear that undisclosed things might become known. Her unfortunate early history, and the methods she had used to survive them, she carried secretly at all times with a necessary and strict code of conduct. The survival skills required objectivity, making her feelings and subsequent emotional turmoil frankly – irrelevant. Intimacy would cause alarm bells to clang through her carefully choreographed interactions with others. She could not afford to allow anyone to suspect how damaged she truly was, how soiled. However, try as she might to seal her authentic feelings inside, by being just a good friend, the tension it induced eventually became too unbearable for her to manage or contain.

Her internal code considered it to be entirely selfish to confess her emotions, most especially as the woman she loved was happily with another, and the man who loved Angela most certainly deserved better. To remain and play a part would ultimately treat him less than he was worthy. For the depth of love he had given was tragically something she could not conjure nor return. So, in a sincere wish for his greater happiness, she had left. No clandestine affairs, no cruel turn of fate. Her personal sentiments were inconsequential in the great scheme of things. It was just how it was. Though devastating to Angela, it was an unremarkable moment in history with no enormous impact on the wider world. You love who you love and unfortunately, you don't always love the right person. Added to which, the emotional seismic waves caused by the inconvenience of Love had left her feeling unstable and unsafe, fractures on the surface of her life would surely show if unaddressed. The answer was to leave. At least by her leaving he had a better chance for happiness, and in this she was sure she had loved him in the best way she could.

When the taxi had arrived, she had grabbed her luggage and quickly thrown together boxes which, in Lossingham, had remained undisturbed until the evening of the fallen bird and Mr. Messenger. On reflection, it seemed that she was always arriving and disappearing, not just from the fear of too much familiarity, but also from herself and all the knotted threads which held her in tangled place. But knowing the possibilities her dreams had now shown, perhaps there was somewhere a possible life being lived alongside hers, one in which she and the Man who loved her, loved each other and lived happily ever after. Wasn't that how it was supposed to be? Were these not the outcomes everyone was taught from their earliest beginnings? Apparently not in the lifetime Angela occupied. Looking at the Man who had loved her from the distance of time, she sighed again. There he was in the picture, smiling for the camera with his long lost group of friends. Dusting the edge affectionately with the corner of her skirt, she placed the photograph on the windowsill. Angela's beloved was not in the frame, but Angela didn't need a photograph to remember that face.

Under their taut translucent membrane of skin, the wings pushed up and down with firmer movements. She would have to go out soon. The post had arrived early morning delivering a personal invitation from Mr. Lockhart to the hospital charity ball, the Saturday after her due date back from leave. The prospect of crowds of people and Helen Ellis caused her feathers to be unsettled, jittery even. The wings were sending a message, an indefinable, but instinctual urgency that she must attend. To prepare for this, she would have to venture outside of her flat for various supplies. On the brink of a complete alteration of her rooms, she felt she needed to add flowers, as beautiful as those in her dream skies. Angela yearned for food with flavour and wine with taste. She wanted to find perfume with a scent of freedom which matched her transformation. The risk of public discovery of her altered self begged the necessity to re-model the rucksack. With a combination of cutting and gluing and her old sewing machine, Angela removed the panel which ordinarily rested on her back, and constructed a quite convincing covering to her emerging wings.

"Quite a good fit," she murmured aloud, pleased with her handiwork. "Not bad at all."

To face the outside world, she felt it wise to subdue her now somewhat striking appearance. Her skin was nut brown, her eyes were bright, and the lock of white hair had thickened and spread into a mane of white. Angela was feeling confident in herself now and no longer cared for the arduous trial of dyeing the roots. So to create a hair disguise, and to avoid stares and unwanted comments, an old silk scarf tied behind her head. This new woman stepping out into the world was not fully aware of what had changed in her neighbours' attitudes, though she sensed a change of some kind. They would wave to her from across the street, and surprisingly, even to Angela, she would automatically return their greeting with genuine pleasure.

Carefully placing her sunglasses onto her nose, she stepped out the front door into the blazing sunshine. The drone of lawnmowers buzzed over and under the back garden fences of the surrounding street. Barbecues were being lit, sending wafts of charcoaled smoke through the fences and hedges. Nobody was about except for Pierre and Miss Bee. Pierre was sitting on his front step, sipping a glass of cold beer. Miss Bee was leaning out of their front room window, resting her chin on folded arms. Her eyes were half closed and her head was gently nodding to the reggae which pulsed from inside.

"Hey dare Mizzabahg-nah, how you doin'?" Pierre lifted his glass in a toast. "We joost cum back fram the Ol'Countree farra faamilee gettee-gedda." He beckoned Angela to him. "Ah gat youze som ting."

Angela lowered her glasses to inspect the gift the old man had placed in her hand.

"Izzah gris-gris Mizzabahg-nah. Itza fram de Ol'Contree. It will protect youze."

Angela turned the small, stringed leather pouch over in her hands. It was etched with what looked like Arabic lettering, over which was a faint red-brown stain, a dried splash. There were objects inside. She looked curiously at Pierre as she held the strange trinket.

"Ah made it joost fa youze. You can look inside, but youze must neva show annudda, okay? Youze been dreaming. Big Dreamings. But youze nat de onlee wun. Dare are oudaz. Dis," he pointed at the gris-gris, "Dis will protect youze, fa wat eva cums."

"Thank you Monsieur Pierre. Your kindness means a lot to me."

"Youse a gud woman Mizzabahg-nah." smiled the Old Man. "Youze remembas dat, okay?"

"Okay."

Pierre placed the loop of thread over her head, then letting the weight of the pouch hang around her neck he gently kissed her on her forehead. The kiss tingled on her brow.

Quite speechless at this blessing, Angela shyly smiled and waved goodbye to both him and his sleepy sister, mouthing 'thank you' again as she turned away. The kiss never left her. Its presence remained on her forehead all the way through her journey to the busy market and back again. When she did finally return, she was hauling several heavy carrier bags full of foodstuffs and pleasantries. The afternoon was leaning into evening, and the dry heat was becoming humid. Trickles of sweat ran down the back of her neck and across her encased wings. She sensed the wings were struggling to be released, and in truth, she wanted them to be freed too. Stopping on the corner of the street to relieve the itching by rubbing her rucksack against a wall, she looked about her in case anyone might see, unsure the covering was totally discreet. Her wings were growing at an incredible rate and beginning to fill its space.

From her position on the corner she suddenly noticed Jenny Collins standing in a side alley close to her house at Number Five. A tall, scrawny man was leaning over a nearby gate, his greasy face looming into hers. She was backing away and struggling to find something in her pink bag. The tall man was looking around him, then back to Jenny who was clearly frightened. Jenny started scrabbling over the fence opposite to him. Angela dropped her bags and began to run towards the girl just as Jenny pulled out her bird whistle.

"Peenk!"

A man's voice yelled from the side alley, and suddenly Jenny's father and two other men came dashing out and gave chase. The tall man ran, only just escaping by bolting across an adjacent lane, with shouts and violent threats thrown behind him. Jenny was being comforted by her mother who led her away to their garden. The men returned, then all was quiet again, and no one noticed Angela watching aghast.

Closing the door behind her, Angela shuddered. The brief drama she had witnessed had drawn such anxiety from her. Jenny was safe, for now, and in that she was greatly relieved. In the quiet of her patio, Angela rested after her evening meal. The air was warm and moist and the rising heat held the scent of expectant rain. It made coherent thought a strained task. Angela nibbled distractedly on a piece of apple and gazed absentmindedly across the garden. As she stroked her neck, she remembered the leather pouch placed there by Pierre. She carefully opened the small bag and looked inside. It smelled of sandalwood and there were markings of strange script and symbols on the interior surface. Splashes of what looked liked drops of wax overlaid the alien words. Inside was a bundle of thin oiled cloth, holding something else. Slowly she un-wrapped the cloth and placed it open in her hand. There were thirteen beads of lapis lazuli, nine tiny, but indeterminate bones, possibly phalanges, seven white hairs bound in a cigarette paper, on which were five crudely drawn eyes, and three burnt matches. There was one last item which was perhaps the most peculiar of all. Angela held it close to her eyes to scrutinize its detail. She was amazed to realise she was holding a miniature figurine, delicately made from plastic-covered fine electrical wire. It was about the size of one of the matchsticks, and at its back, tied with a crimson thread around the figure's waist, was a feather. It was a soft brown in colour, with flecks of cream running through the length. Clearly the talisman had been constructed with some care, most especially the tiny doll and Angela felt baffled and humbled at the same time. She truly had no concrete idea as to the significance of the bundle, but she did have a sense of reverence as she returned the items to the pouch. Pierre had made this for her with care and with love – how extraordinary!

Slipping the loop of string back around her neck, she patted it against her breastbone. Her thoughts wandered this way and that. There were angry thoughts towards the tall man who threatened the girl down the street. She thought about Jenny Collins, and the family who looked out for her and protected her. She thought about Little Angie, the small girl in the playhouse and the family who left her alone, left her to be swallowed in on herself. She thought about whether there was a point to Love, or if it was better to just assume a mantle of numbness. In answering the latter question, she knew that emotional arctic climes were not places she wanted to live in anymore. She thought it was time for her frozen feelings to melt, whatever they may be – love, sadness or anger. For some reason unknown to her, she felt a little safer now, a little more present in her skin, a little more balanced in her light-footed step and, a little more at home with her hidden wings.

The night was coming nearer, but the increasing sticky heat crackled with iron. A storm was coming. The static prickled her skin making the hairs on her flesh rise. Across the many back gardens, came the laughing voices of nightjar neighbours enjoying a temporary Mediterranean evening. She decided to shower, taking care to remove the gris-gris before washing. It commanded a strange sensation of majesty when she placed it over her head after drying. She felt taller. As the temperature became cloying, she worked in the inside cool, clearing the last of the box room debris and relics. Angela was beginning to imagine what use the room might be. Perhaps a study to house her many books. Perhaps a workroom just to potter in or, perhaps it could be a spare bedroom should she invite someone to stay. She smiled at the very notion of inviting a guest. What a change she had seen, not just in her body, but in her mind as well. Here she was, with the last box. She might have expected something slightly grander in appearance for such a momentous occasion.

The last box however was brown cardboard and parcel-taped tight. Cutting this open, she found an old, tin cashbox inside. Tightly bound with twine, it had the look of the forbidden. Time had dried the binding into brittleness, and it seemed to fall away into dust when touched. There was something inside, for it rattled when she shook it, but the tin was locked and there was no key to be found. With scissors and some impressive brute force, she began to prise open the casement on the side. The tin itself buckled under pressure until the lock gave way and it was at last open.

Now what was inside, she had not expected. It caused her heart to beat faster in her chest, and her eyes to widen. A sudden heave of nausea overwhelmed her as she stared. What was inside made her break into a sweat with an unpleasant familiarity, and when it trickled into her mouth, it tasted bitter. She began to shake, for she knew the repellent treasure within.

Inside lay a roughly wrapped package. The paper itself was covered with hundreds of the same hand written signature, Angela Bagner, Angela Bagner, Angela Bagner, over and over again like punitive lines. And beneath this wrapping was a doll. A pocket doll bought from Woolworths when she was very young. It was a doll to keep her quiet and a doll to talk to. It was also a doll which she had changed when she was sixteen, which she had locked away, and had chosen to forget, until now.

The small plastic doll was a disturbing sight. Blind with hollow sockets, it wore a tiny necklace of thirteen blue beads. Sprouting from it's all but bald head were a few sprigs of white hair. A paper skirt was glued on and decorated with five little eyes which watched in a row. It had nine little fingers, the tenth having been sharply severed. A burnt match was taped to each of the hands, like swords, and a third was held at the waist with a thin red ribbon and...she dropped the doll in shock.

Around the back of the doll, the crimson ribbon held a brown feather close to its back.

She sat for a long while, staring at the effigy. She suddenly remembered a time when she was sixteen, longing to be released from dreadful and terrible, relentless dreams, which tortured her in sleep and in wake. Crying out to the night all those years ago, there had been some kind of answer. It came in a dream of rescue by a creature who wore an amulet around its neck.

It was another constant dusk. A petrol bruised sky hung heavily over the garden. There was the Chasm, dark and gaping like a sliced mouth. The Girl couldn't get away. Her waist was tied by a sentient, serpentine length of rope, the end of which slithered from the edge of the Hole, tongue-like and lascivious. What Lay Below was sleeping for now, snoring the sleep of the satiated, and the Girl would have to be careful not to wake it. She remembered she once danced in this place, in sunlight, but now she had to tread with care, so as not to shake the earth. Any breath or vibration would do it, for What Lay Below to rise up and pull her under again. Each time it would strip her of strength to go on. Tonight the

Girl had plaintively called to the stars for release, but had expected no reply.

Crawling to the edge of her world, she could just make out glimmers of light far away from the wall of darkness. There, she could see a carousel turning in the place beyond. It looked like joy. It looked like peace. The gentle melody of the calliope brought a tear to the Girl's eye. The tear hit the ground where she lay with a resonating drop. She held her breath: nothing. Then to her horror, there was a sudden tug at her belly, then another. It was beginning again. What Lay Below was waking. She began to run, scrabbling to escape, this way and that, desperately trying to find a way through the dark wall, scooping at the shadowed perimeter with her terrified hands. She was being sucked into the Chasm, and she grabbed at the earth to slow her descent.

Then, suddenly from overhead there came a shrieking scream, one so piercing it split through the air like a shaft of metal. For a moment the dragging of the Girl ceased, as if What Lay Below was listening, then it pulled again. The Girl was screaming, a hollow scream without a sound as the rope tightened around her, ripping the breath from her lungs. Blood stained rope and silent screaming.

The shriek came again, this time saturating the air around her. She was being lifted and thrown to one side, from where she turned to watch in terror. A beautiful, winged Creature, with vicious, vengeful eyes, focused on the quarry beneath her. The Creature plunged down into the Chasm, its claws and talons razor-sharp. Its intent was on carnage and blood and it was screaming with an archaic pleasure. Again and again, the avenging angel slashed and tore at the ground, all the time sending out a shrill, merciless screech of bloodied retribution. The unholy umbilical cord was sliced from the Girl's waist and What Lay Below shrivelled and withered and died as the earth around it tumbled into the Chasm, filling the Hole.

Silence.

Then the Creature arose, replete with visceral satisfaction, its smiling mouth dripping with crimson, and its claws with a sticky darkness. The Girl cowered in fear, but the Creature was oblivious. Hovering lightly over the child, it took the Girl into its muscular arms and lifted her up. Up. They flew up. The Girl at last able to breathe, without thinking held on to the Creature's strange scaly flesh for dear life. The amulet around its neck smelled of sandalwood and lulled her. Across the wall of darkness, the Creature took the Girl away, gently landing in the place of the Carousel. Before it left her, it quietly said in a deep, toneless voice:

"Play."

All those years ago, the young Angela had woken in a semi-trancelike state, and had naively invoked this charm in the hope of connecting again with her Saviour, but the effect from that time on, was she walked through life in an anesthetized torpor. She had to forget the person she had been. This had protected her through the years from the burden of emotions, and the fear of letting go. Though the night-time dream assaults continued to dog her, she would wake with amnesia and a weighted heart, but she could at least function. Now, a functioning life is sadly not necessarily a life well lived. Merely functioning was only to exist and this could no longer continue if happiness was to be sought.

No longer imprisoned, the older Angela sat clasping the talisman around her neck, whilst her body rocked to and fro. The doll seemed as new as the time she had made it, and the departed years and memories from then rushed to sit beside her. Her mind was spinning with an old pain and a newly awoken rage. It seared through her chest and throat until all she could do was wail, with a sound of all the caged hurt and desolation she had carried for so long.

And as if the World were howling in sympathy, a low growl of thunder began to roll somewhere in the distant, outside night.

Chapter Eleven

Despite the jagged experience of the unveiled effigy, one which had left her feeling raw like an open wound, that night she fell into a deep sleep. She only dreamt once, but what she dreamt was of profound import.

She could see herself, above the Girl, who slept peacefully on a carousel horse far below. As Angela rose, she saw the claws and talons on her hands and feet withdraw, and she became her former self again. Only now from this height she could see the shadow of wings, her wings. They were spread across the land below, so wide and so broad, they seemed to become the land. The marvel of them was breathtaking, for they undulated with the curve of the endless horizon. She felt a freedom flow through her feathers, as she swooped and darted through the warm dark air, skimming on thermal currents. Her agility matched the elation swelling in her chest, for she thought her heart would break with the joy of her release. Across the darkened lands, thunder rolled nearer.

Suddenly beneath her came a lightning flash, then another and another, bringing stark light to the ground below. Whirling up, her all-encompassing wings seemed to wake the stars to watch her display as she brushed through the airstreams. She glided through galaxies, sending sparks of stardust trail in her wake, giving birth to more constellations and worlds. Thunder filled the sky around her, bellowing an announcement everywhere: Angela lives!

She soared, she spun, and she played in the air, as tears of joy ran down her cheeks, for she knew at last she was where she belonged. It was then in this peak of flight, when the first drops of rain began to fall, she felt a presence of absolute acceptance. All the infinite stars seemed to be smiling and reaching out towards her hand, coming together and forming into the shape of another flying Being like herself. The Star Being had eyes which were kind and deep, the lines on her face were from countless lives lived, and because of them she was beautiful. There in mid air, in the thundering stormy sky, hand in hand, Angela and the Star Being danced. They danced and laughed and sang in a torrent of emancipating rain, soaking them both to the skin. Soft, warm rain, cleansed Angela from all the remains of What Lay Below. When the rain subsided, the two friends embraced goodbye. Angela watched from her garden, as the Star Being disappeared into the colours of the morning sunrise.

When she woke to see the doll of her past self, sitting by the bedside clock, it no longer concerned her, although Angela couldn't be certain she had placed it there herself. She had awoken with a sensation of being fully in her body; all the broken pieces of what she had been were somehow returned and mended. Whatever had happened in her past was now past, and was not going to fill her future. It was perhaps like Japanese Kintsugi, in which a broken pot, mended with care, becomes a thing of greater beauty than before its damage. She also knew one very important thing. She was now driven by a promise to eradicate any trace of the victim, which she as survivor had allowed herself to become. Swearing to never be afraid again, she internally made an oath to fight tooth and nail to make this so.

Heading towards the kitchen, she brushed past the piano and noticed its lid was open and the framed photographs and collection of objet trouvés had changed position. The photograph of her late Father had been moved to front of stage, causing her to look at his face with fresh eyes. The picture had been taken in her childhood garden which had backed onto the farmlands beyond, and she felt a sudden rush of rolling memory in her mind like the tides on a coastal shore. There he stood, with his shy, gentle smile against a backdrop of field upon field, disappearing into the horizon. A lone seagull hung in the air above his head, and the familiar lighthouse stood tall in the distance. How dark her Father's skin had been, and she wondered at how the memory of a face could fade as much as a photograph. Yes, his skin had been dark, which explained the nut brown tan she was now enjoying. His past was dark as well, for he had rarely spoken of the land where he had come from.

Only in the stories he would tell her did she glimpse anything of the country from his early past. He had always been a man of few words. He always kept himself to himself, especially around his children, with the exception of Angela perhaps, because she was the only daughter. Sometimes in the evening, when her Mother had fallen into a sedative-induced sleep, her Father would come to tell her secret stories, told to him by his Grandmother from warmer climes. Angela remembered how he would hold her hand and draw into the tales elements of their real world outside. The crying of the seabirds above their rural home would become guardian angels, warning not of storms, but of trouble ahead, and the distant surge of the sea became the sigh of a princess falling under a spell. The stories were magical and full of hope and always eased the day's torment. All were told in secret, for fear of Mother's wrath, as all attention had to be Hers. Even now, as his monochrome image gazed meekly back at his daughter, his expression gave nothing away in terms of posthumous wisdom. He had been trained that way. It was the way Mother liked it. Everyone, including Father, had to do exactly as they were told. Rebellions which had transpired were mostly quiet and insignificant, but the quiet defiance Father and Daughter shared over his bedtime tales, reached beyond his passing. She had never told another. His death had closed the book.

Ah well, we all have our secrets.

However, these present small, but significant changes to her photograph arrangements were met with a matter of fact non plus. She must have simply moved them in her sleep, and she was as equally untroubled to see muddy footprints leading to her bed all the way from the French windows, and the garden. Nothing seemed to have any logical answers, but what end would questioning serve? Angela had gone beyond questions, hoping only that living in acceptance would provide the best answer for now.

The outside air was fresh and the ground wet. It had apparently been raining in the night, and her garden smelled of turned earth and green. As she sipped her coffee, she could already hear the early rise of her neighbours. Pierre and Miss Bee were cooking bacon to the sound of gentle reggae. The upstairs sash window above Angela's was suddenly drawn up and a young woman's voice called down,

"What a storm we had last night eh?" The young woman was joined by a shirtless male companion.

"Yeah, awesome!" he added.

Angela nodded and smiled, not wishing to point out she had slept right through it. At least, she thought she had. There were those muddy footprints after all.

"You've got an amazing voice!" the young woman continued, "Have you been trained in opera?"

Angela was a little bemused at this and regarded them both quizzically.

"Your singing ... it was so powerful! We heard you last night, it was amazing, wasn't it Georgie?"

"Yeah, awesome!" the sleep befuddled head of Georgie nodded in agreement.

"Listen, we haven't been introduced, my name's Lucy. We're music students at the college. We're having a get-together soon. Would you like to come? I'll let you know the date. No big deal, curry and some good talk. Bring a bottle. What's your name?"

"I'd love to," Angela replied with a smile. "My name's Angie."

Chapter Twelve

There was a week to go before the Big Night, and Helen Ellis was nearly delirious with anticipation. The careful planning she had undertaken was extraordinary, worthy of a military campaign and equally commendable. It was the attention to the tiniest details which was so admirable. The decorations, floor plan and seating arrangements were meticulous, designed to create the perfect mix of creative conversation amongst the guests; doctors and musicians, lawyers and yogis, innumerable businesspeople and artists, even some minor politicians and popular entertainers, all of whom had been competitively donating the most extravagant of prizes. Amongst them, a shopping spree, a rally driving experience, spa weekends, a holiday in the South of France, theatre tickets, dinners out, balloon rides, and even a helicopter flight. Every donation was printed on the programme to highlight the generosity of each benefactor.

Then of course there was the Press. Helen was effectively fighting them off, as a media feeding frenzy had been brewing, due to the interest of a certain coffee company which had clumsily been making 'discreet enquiries.' It was an incredible response to her little enterprise, winning for Helen some well deserved admiration from the many skeptics around her and some surprised respect from husband Nick. He hadn't fully appreciated how capable his wife truly was, and he was seeing her in a different light. How she managed to captain such a venture was certainly impressive, and it suggested to him he might be wise to pay more attention to her in terms of his own career. Whatever the outcome of the forthcoming night's event, it would be without a doubt useful for his networking contacts.

To be fair to Helen, though Nick knew Helen was indeed a manipulative, self-serving, duplicitous parasite, she was *his* manipulative, self-serving, duplicitous parasite. He knew where he stood with Helen. It was like looking in a mirror.

Helen was unaware of her husband's approval. The cherry for her, apart from her burgeoning career as Events Director, would be to put Angela in what Helen deemed, her rightful place. Her plot against her work colleague had become completely out of proportion. Helen's very foundation had been shaken, never had she known anyone who had the audacity to confront her. Helen Ellis had always trodden the Higher Path, one which involved treading over the weak. She had prided herself in being assertive throughout schooling and adult life, while those on the receiving end would see her simply as a bully.

The final threads of her stratagem were secured when the confirmation came that certain guests would definitely be attending, in particular, the Senior Consultant and his Registrar, who had examined poor Angela concerning her apparent bone mutations. They were extremely keen for their most unusual patient to contact them, and with visions of papers in The Lancet, they had sent Angela several letters. However, they were unaware Helen had arranged for communications relating to Miss A. Bagner, were to be sent first to Helen. On receipt, they would of course go no further than the shredder. It would be reasonable to think that any uninvited medical attention would be enough to put the fear of God into Angela, but there was worse. Helen did have a tendency to go one step too far.

She had found it necessary to contact an old school friend of a similar disposition to her, Mackenzie Davis, an Old School boarder hailing from a moneyed family, who had gained their wealth through pharmaceutical research, and whose methods attracted journalists investigating the controversial and morally questionable. Based in Zurich with Research Laboratories all over the Western and Third World, the latter being a prime location for willing volunteers in genetic experiments for the global Magnadavistock International.

Helen hoped this invitation would rekindle their acquaintance and open up opportunities far wider than Lossingham Hospital. Mackenzie had always thought Ellis to be a 'Little-Jumped-Up-Piece-of-Poison' who had no place in her circle. While Mackenzie often found poison quite agreeable, her higher echelon thought of Helen as vulgar. Despite this, it had taken just one email and the attachment of a scanned x-ray for Mackenzie to bite Helen's bait.

Los Diablos de las Cantinas had also been planning for the Big Night. Since Helen Ellis had more than heavily hinted that they were in a shortlist of three possible backing bands for 'Angeliquita's' upcoming tour, they were determined not to miss but to maximize this rare opportunity. Eddie and his fellow band members had been rehearsing every night, until they were tight as a drum. As well as the version of 'Call Me!' which they had previously performed at the Rendezvous Café, Helen had advised them to find a selection of songs which they felt best reflected their talents and repertoire, but with an emphasis on the Singer. These, she assured them, she would then forward onto the artiste, for her to rehearse in private before the show. Not wishing to appear unimaginative, Eddie and the band decided to have a serious brain-storming session at his house one evening after they finished their day jobs. There they were on his front steps, drinking beers and soaking up the sun. Most of the neighbouring children were running in and out through the adjoining houses, including Eddie's sons, whilst a small group of girls sat playing under the shade of a tree.

"She had what you'd call a sultry voice," remarked Andy.

"Not just that mate, she sounded sweet," added Joey, "You know? Innocent like."

"I thought she was a woman who knows what she wants," their drummer leered. "Bit of a siren, know what I mean?"

For that remark he received a ribald shove. They were men of basic needs and bawdy desires after all. Refinement was not readily theirs to understand, nor demonstrate. As for subtlety, Eddie realised he had his work cut out to rein them in. They were two packs of beer in, and they still had no musical ideas between them. They paused and slurped as one.

"So we're looking for numbers which will suit a woman who is sweet, and innocent, but who has a sultry, siren voice," Eddie thought out loud.

"And knows what she wants!" the drummer grinned.

Eddie blankly regarded his band of boys and sighed. 'Los Diablos de las Cantinas' indeed. He had come up with the name when he was down the market with his wife. There was a stallholder selling a new range of kitchenware and Eddie had thought at the time he rather liked the logo of a little devil. The name sounded 'exotic' and had stuck. He needed a similar stroke of genius now. He turned his gaze to the children playing up and down the street, and chuckled to himself as the image of his band of devils, wearing bright red horns and dangling tails drifted into his mind. He thought of what had possessed him in the first place to start this band. Though he loved everything the band did, it hadn't been turning out quite as he had hoped in the beginning. The bookings they were able to get were largely for weddings and parties, so they were obliged to play music which was more middle-of-the-road than he liked. 'Una Paloma Blanca' was not his idea of Latin, let alone Spanish. He wasn't even really Spanish.

His real name was Eddie Bush, and though he was an intelligent man, at school he always seemed to play the fool while his classmates were studying. Later, in his teens, he had seen a television documentary about Cuban music which had transformed his life. While his peers were out at parties, he was practising his guitar in his bedroom. While they were off to college, he strummed in every and any band that would have him, playing the dirtiest dives for a pittance, getting dead end jobs in-between to make ends meet, and only just getting by on his comic charm. Thing was, he loved playing, but what drove him on was a true love of Cuban music. Eddie was completely hooked, to the extent that as soon as possible changing his name by deed poll made him Eduardo Perez, and Los Diablos was born. For, from the day he fell in love with Cuban music, dreams of Cuba surrounded him. The sounds, the colours, the smells, were all conjured by his mind. Eddie had never had a Cuban cigar before, but he saw himself smoking one there. In his dreams he was driving a Cadillac like the ones he had seen all those years ago. The dreams never left him and it was where he had the feeling he belonged.

Lately now, it felt as if he was running out of time to make his ambition come true. He had neglected his dream, and the longer it was left to gather dust, the less it seemed likely he would realise it. It was, he thought, like the thing his Grandfather used to say to him, "anything you love is like a fire, you have to tend it to keep it alive".

Suddenly, his fellow beer drinkers stopped between gulps to nudge each other. Eddie's eyes and mouth had opened wide, he held his beer bottle paused just before his lips.

"What is it Ed?" asked one nervously.

"Look! There's our answer!" he exclaimed, pointing to the girls playing dress-up in the shade.

"We're the Diablos right ... devils?" Eddie drew out the words slowly, hoping the penny would drop into their collective brains.

They nodded vacantly in agreement, but without fully comprehending what he was trying to say.

"Well, she is Angeliquita...which means Little Angel!" Again, the Boys continued to stare inanely.

He pointed again and they followed his gaze. The girls under the tree were laughing and getting up to dance, in the middle of their circle, a small smiling girl was turning around and around to show off her elasticated white feather wings to her admiring playmates.

"Angeliquita and Los Diablos! Angel and the Devils! It's a sign I tell you!"

The band from then on were filled with a new inspiration and motivation, for the morning after, despite their hungover heads, they began rehearsing what Eddie was to name their 'Divine Intervention' set, a collection of his favourite Cuban songs. Later that day, during a break, they spared no expense in purchasing individual devil horns and tails complete with battery lights for their stage costumes. Angeliquita deserved pure class.

"... not at all Mrs. Ellis, or may I call you Helen? It's my pleasure to donate to such a good cause."

Paul Hollingsworth slipped the phone back into his pocket. Sitting at his desk he smiled to himself. If truth be told, Paul Hollingsworth was a somewhat obsessive person, unable as he was to take any 'No' as an answer. This mysterious woman who had danced on the cafe table was just what he had been looking for, and had sparked a flame in his mind, a vision for the future of 'Viva!' Once lit, his energy was unstoppable; it raised the bar as to the professional lengths he was willing to stretch to, and the personal favours he decided to call in. His chauffeur had put him in touch with a helicopter pilot, which was the final piece. This Angeliquita would be seduced with offers of film and travel, and who could then resist? On the night, after the schmoozing of all who could be schmoozed, his carefully secreted dancing girls would assist in commandeering the whole show. It would become 'Viva!' night, with a Grande-Finale of a petal showering helicopter hovering over the roof garden restaurant to take the Artiste away.

Always leave them wanting more, thought Paul, congratulating himself on his originality. To this end, he had pursued the Media by suggesting several fragments of 'Angeliquita's' intriguing background story to whet their appetite. The Artiste in question was in fact an heiress to a vast fortune, she was secretly in a romantic tryst with a rather famous but as yet undisclosed film star, and she was to be the next Face for a major International company. All of these stories were deliberately crafted to have enough 'carrot' to pique interest, but vague enough to provide mystery. For Paul Hollingsworth, it was like the Good Old Days when he was *ducking and diving from the back of my van*. Each newspaper, television station and internet hub were told as though they alone had the exclusive tip off. They each then filled in the gaps to the story with their own imagination. Of course, each of them would need Paul Hollingsworth to be their 'Man on the Inside', as he had only means by which to identify and unmask her. A satisfied Paul Hollingsworth reclined into his leather chair.

"God, how I've missed the cut and thrust!"

In the days leading up to the Summer Ball, the soles of Angela's feet were hot and tingling. At first she had considered it was possibly anxiety, due to the impending meeting between herself and the odorous Helen Ellis who, she felt more and more, was quite capable of senseless unkindness. As to why Angela felt this was she could not qualify, but the more she was mindful of how her wings responded to her thoughts and feelings, the more she trusted herself and her internal voice. *Helen Ellis is a nasty piece of work.*

Angela had a notion of somehow slipping into a greater rhythm, one which seemed to link to a vastness far beyond more than just uncomfortable irritations of daily life. Her footsteps tingled everywhere she stepped and she decided it was because she was connected to everything. It was as if there was a cushion of buoyant air between her and the ground which gave her a sensation of floating, like treading in water. There was a slip stream flowing through her body and her mind, everything seemed syncopated and laughably so. From the percussion of making tea, to the beat of scrubbing the bath, Angela enjoyed it all as she had now a constant thought.

I'm here at last!

A wide smile now graced her face with the sheer appreciation of being alive. She supposed it must be something akin to how someone might feel if they were given the all clear news as to a terminal illness, for in truth, she had been affectively living a terminal life, an existence of just getting through, and that was no life at all.

In the last few days she had taken to playing the piano again, to accompany herself in song, and it was wonderful to be completely absorbed in something just for her. It became something of a ritual to place fresh garden flowers beside the audience of her framed photographs on the piano shelf above her. At the end of each recital of opera, ballads or torch songs, she would laugh again, applauding herself, feigning a bow while receiving the bouquet in the vase. She had just finished one such concert, the morning before the Summer ball, and decided to rest in the sunshine outside. A voice called down from the flat above,

"Hi Angie! You're sounding good!" It was Lucy, the student from upstairs, leaning over her balcony. "I like the one about the Blackbird, that's a Beatles song isn't it?"

Angela nodded.

"What was that opera song called? It sounded like a …"

Before Lucy could finish her question, Angela had spun round to see what was happening in the back of her garden. A sharp, pointed note of alarm was repeatedly stabbing the air. One of the nesting Blackbirds was angrily flapping its wings.

"Peenk! Peenk! Peenk!"

"Excuse me!" Angela yelled an apology, then grabbing the handles of a half-filled rain barrel, rushed to witness a stalking cat creeping too close to the fledglings. Their father, fiercely protective and brave, with no heed for his own safety, was ready for the fight, and was diving over and over again to distract the hunter. Black feathers were lost in the skirmish, but he battled on, despite the flailing claws of the cat. Angela took aim, and a gush of water hit the murderous target and drenched it into defeat. The cat slunk away hissing at its human assailant. Yet still the alarm continued, but this time, Angela realised it was no longer the defending Blackbird.

"Peenk! Peenk! Peenk!"

There was something desperate and urgent in the length of each note. It came from beyond the garden wall which backed onto an alley.

Jenny! Angela knew Jenny was in danger, but there was no time to run to the front of the building. She pushed the barrel close to where the wall grew heavy with ivy and began to clamber up. Still the piping alarm continued to sound. From strength somewhere inside her, Angela climbed the wall, scrabbling up through the ivy and stone, arriving at the top. There was Jenny Collins, ashen faced and wide-eyed with stricken terror, blowing furiously her little bird-whistle, while her tall and scrawny uncle had his arms around her waist from behind her. He was slavering over her neck.

My Girl!

Fiery anger seared in Angela's eyes. She certainly was a formidable sight, with now white Medusa-like hair, writhed with ivy tendrils, her hands were cut and bleeding, her heart was pumping and ready for her wings to burst from her skin. She leapt, screeching,

"Let her go!"

As she leapt, there was a strange surge through Angela's veins, then, a slowing down of time until everything and everyone around her were floating in suspended animation, like flotsam and jetsam rolling in a wave or a fly in liquid amber. Around her leaping figure was a kind of skin of light, almost like a caul membrane. It stretched away from the wall, and to her consternation she could see her physical body still standing there, caught in the moment just before she had leapt, she was freeze-framed shouting to the man to let

Jenny go. The unsettling aspect of this new way of seeing was her ability to turn her neck almost completely around to see what was behind, it was most disorientating. Her heart was beating steadily but so slowly, it thrummed in her ears with a heavy boom, it filled her head. With each beat her muscles throughout her body were more sinuous and powerful as she could feel herself lift higher from the ground. Her shoulders were rising and falling in the beat of her booming heart, slow and steady, Boom! Boom! Boom! On her back was a weight which she hadn't noticed before, it made her windswept as she tried to gain balance in this bubble of slowed time. Outside of this ball of light, everything was still, like the dimmed, submerged hues of an eclipse, all caught in the moment before she leapt. Jenny was caught in the moment of running away and her Uncle caught in an expression of sheer horror.

Horror?

She began by closing her eyelids, seeking through her senses what was different in her body. She could smell an earthiness in her nostrils, the blood on her tongue and hands ... hands? Now there was a difference, the joints of her fingers spread wide, in a position of attack and, tapping her fingernails now produced staccato clicks. Then there was the acute sense of hearing she now possessed, she could hear the suspended chime of the distant town clock, the burring rustle of the wind outside the ball of light, the sustained intake of breath as Jenny ran, the hanging, gasping scream of the man beneath her sights, and even the scuttling woodlice beneath him. Each living being with a different heartbeat of its own, and each one the leaping Angela heard. She had such strength now, in her pumping heart and throbbing muscles awash with adrenaline. It was clear she was no longer caged by the old self. Her eyes flashed open awake. There was a slight ripping sound as her shoulders stretched further.

My wings!

At last her wings were spread free from imprisonment, silent and splendid, such glorious wings! Stretching proudly wide above her, the outside feathers were of rich apricot, with scatterings of silvery blue mottling, and deep underneath, the softest white down. She knew who she was here. Any remains of Angela were more like those of a kidnapped hitch hiker. Now Angela was Lilith, an ancient wild power from Another Place. Surveying this fresh vehicle in which she hovered, she could also see a dark fissure within the sphere which was unseen outside in the suspended time. Rotating her neck two hundred degrees, there, like a pulled curtain, was a place of stars, floating in a sea of darkness. Her old home of night, where she was who she was, and no one could claim her in any way wrong. It was a place she longed for, and it made the rising and falling of her shoulders ache to go, to leave this shallow, paper-thin world. So much hurt and so many thoughtless actions here, smouldering in her breastbone was an instinctual desire to destroy all What Lay Below.

What Lay Below!

Suddenly a resounding screech, loud and low-pitched was released from her throat and her head spun round to scrutinise her prey. It was a snivelling wretch of a being, the stench of its sweat, vile and soured, hardly worthy of her majesty, but nonetheless, It had to be taught with the Old Wisdom, the Old Ways. Descending with heavy deliberation, she plunged silently over the petrified man and grabbed him by the shoulders, sucking him into the ball of slowed time. As soon as he entered, he regained consciousness again, or at least partially. The fearsome spectacle he was now part of was searing into his brain with the shocking absurdity of it all. Struggle as he did, he was being pulled up. Up, and into the fissure of the place of stars, the cleft closing like a zip when they both were through.

It was a sea of darkness, hung with stars, beautiful and eternal. It made the man cry out, and still the Creature Lilith flew.

Apart from the stars, the only light now came from the lands which lay far in the distance. The Creature Lilith paid no heed to the thrashing limbs she held tightly in her grasp. It soon collapsed in submission, flapping like a rag in the wind, while the Creature Lilith flew on. Over fields of time and possibility she travelled, with a world-old compass guiding her silent flight. The Rag in her talons fell into a stupor, pleading in its mind to be freed. The Creature Lilith ignored the Rag's pleas, able as she was to hear all thoughts and perceive all things. She flew on. After some time, the Rag looked down and again began to scream, but it seemed here no sound could be heard in the endless space around them.

What are you?

And at last the Rag's mute words were answered,

There are many kinds of Angels.

Then, when it seemed that years had sped by, the Creature Lilith drew near to her destination and suddenly changed course. Now she flew down, with a speed that threatened to tear skin from bone, landing at last just above an expanse of ground somewhat like an old garden. Surrounding the space was a strange hedgerow which appeared to writhe with a thick and congealed blackness. The Rag began to kick and fight, for there was something down there which chilled breath. Paying no heed to the Rag, The Creature Lilith placed her distraught passenger firmly on the shadowed ground. Her razor outer toe swivelled to the rear so as to clutch the ragged worm in her claw, whilst with a taloned finger, she bent over and cut deeply into the air. As she did so, a gash split in the ground and at last the silence was broken, but by something so hideous it would have curdled blood. A groan wallowing deep beneath the earth bellowed up, causing the Rag to spew yellow bile from abject fear. Then, without any compunction, The Creature Lilith suddenly pushed the snivelling Rag down headfirst into the chasm, only just holding the Rag's feet above ground.

To be truthful, at this point, the whole ritual was beginning to be a little tiresome. The Creature Lilith had better things to do with her time, places to go, Beings to meet, but this had to be done. She knew well What Lay Below, for the Creature Lilith had entombed It there for good reason. It was an abomination which ought not to be allowed, well, certainly for as long a time as possible. However, everything can have its uses, including What Lay Below. In this case, the subterranean was to serve as a 'cautionary tale'. Clicking her talons on the ground she waited for a while, until at last the suffocating cries for mercy had stopped, and a subdued, pathetic sobbing had commenced.

Then, just as abruptly as she had buried the Rag thing, she extracted it from the pit like the pulling of a badly decayed tooth. The sucking air from the closing earth pulled back the fissure once more, and the Creature Lilith slipped through with her cargo, into the alley behind Angela's garden wall. Everything was as it was, although now there was a sensation of time tumbling forward and speeding up, for in seconds ...

The shocking vision of this dread demoness gave Jenny the chance to break free from the man's grip and run. The Creature Lilith landed on Jenny's attacker who now lay groaning, spread-eagled and concussed, face down in the alley filth. The hitch-hiking Angela was re-surfacing in her consciousness, though her human aspect had at last caught up with the unfolding scene by clambering down the wall, she was still in a mythical form. She could hear the approach of running feet and raised male voices. In the last moments while she was alone with the whimpering man, she wrenched up his neck with a clawed hand, and gripping his throat, she seethed an icy curse into the man's ear.

"Never again...do you hear me? Never again! Not to anyone! Not in this world, or another. For I will hunt you down and I will slice you up into pieces so small, your soul, if you have one, will never be stitched together again! You will never be safe, for I will find you in your dreams, in sleep or in wake!"

The man's eyes blinked open, and seeing a frenzied creature snarling down on him he started screaming. Its lips were curled back to its blackened gums and venomous fangs, its ferocious eyes were merciless and it wore a talisman of animal skin around its neck. Just before the men reached the alley, she spat into the man's face, and then cracked his head down hard onto the concrete in utter disgust, a trickle of blood flowing from his temple.

When they arrived, a quietly composed Angela was standing away from his fallen body with her back towards the wall. The man was struggling to stand up and run, but this time he was outrun and outnumbered. She retraced their steps, leaving them to express their own disappointment with his behaviour. She wryly noticed how the deadened punches into crunching bone and smashing flesh had a certain quality of an operatic crescendo, his screams posing a striking counter-point.

"A different kind of music yes, but no less satisfying," she hummed to herself. "Ah well, there are such things as happy accidents after all."

Sometime later, Tina Collins rang her doorbell to thank her for her rescue of Jenny. Jenny was with her, clutching her mother's hand but staring up at Angela. Her mother then told Angela, the 'uncle' was now with the police, charged with indecent assault on a child, and not for the first time.

"Anytime you want to come round to ours, you'll always be welcome. We're always having barbecues. You'll have to take us as you find us mind, I mean, our house is a bit of a mess, and it might be a bit noisy, what with the children and the dogs, but our family is more important than being tidy we think. Please come, we'd be so happy if you did." At this, Tina pressed her hand onto Angela's. She lowered her voice.

"You know, what's really weird is when they took him away, he was raving he'd seen you before in his nightmares ... attacking him! Nutter!" she half whispered, "I wish I could descend on his nightmares."

Just as they were about to leave, the small girl rushed back to stretch up her arms and fling them around her rescuer's neck to kiss her. Angela flushed with pleasure as she waved them goodbye. She was ready for anything now, including Helen Ellis. In fact, she was quite looking forward to meeting her again.

Chapter Thirteen

In the early morning light, Angela stretched and yawned. She lay on her side in a pool of sunlight which rolled across the sheets half covering her naked body. It was six a.m. and the birds outside were finishing their chorus. This made Angela smile and open her eyes. It was time to get up, for today was to be an important one. Of course, she wasn't entirely sure how or why, but knew she would discover later that evening. In the last few nights, her dreaming had taken her on a tour across other people's dreams, including those of the neighbours in her street, the band which had played at the Rendezvous Café that strange afternoon, Jenny and her family, her colleagues at work, especially Mr. Lockhart and Helen Ellis and, a very disturbing figure whom she didn't recognise called Mackenzie Davis. That particular dream was very unpleasant, but as the changed person she was now, it was not something she feared. She knew she would meet Mackenzie Davis tonight because her feet tingled and her wings twitched when thinking of the name. Indeed, she was a changed woman, exuding confidence and self-assurance now.

Standing in front of the bedroom mirror Angela looked admiringly at the plumage pressed tightly up against the inside surface of her skin.

After the incident in the alley, her metaphysical wings had seemingly withdrawn, but flakes of skin which had been gently tearing away, were leaving feathers of apricot and brown protruding outwards. They would soon reveal themselves in their physical form.

She tentatively touched one. This created sensations like delicious electricity shooting through her spine, making her eyes dilate and the soles of her feet tingle with heat, lifting her whole body just a few centimetres off the bedroom carpet.

"Like invisible high heels!" she laughed aloud, "though I might need to wear a little more than just a grin!"

The last dress in the box room wardrobe was one which Angela had always longed to wear. Clearly for a dress like this, only a very special occasion was suitable, and so far, as her previous self, Angela had succeeded in living a wallpaper existence, in which she had remained unnoticed, but not anymore. The invitation's small print read,

'For this wonderful, once-in-a-lifetime occasion, please dress to impress in high-class festival style. Your invitation might be to 'The Lucky Seat', whereby you will win the auspicious opportunity to perform with Los Diablos and have your very own film of the event as a prize.'

Unzipping the cover, she gently eased out two garments. The first, was a 1940s evening gown in a rich, deep blue crepe, heavy with diamante which formed a sparkling Milky Way falling from the off the shoulder neckline and trimming the low cut back. The second was a matching shoulder cape, draped with iridescent blue-black feathers, dotted from the satin collar with more diamante stars set amongst the plumes.

"How on earth did I forget about you?" gasped Angela, addressing the pair like long-lost friends. Holding them close to her skin, she carried them lovingly out to the French windows, hanging them from the lintel to air in the morning breeze. Sunlight struck the glittering stones sending rainbows dancing across the floor and walls of the room, some shining on Angela's skin. She laughed out loud again as if the colours had tickled her.

"Your Majesty, you shall go to the ball!"

While the day unwound, she pottered in what some might consider was pure indulgence, her old self especially. Over the time she had spent away from work, she had eaten well, drank less and slept whenever she wanted. Her dyed hair had somehow grown out at speed, leaving thick and shiny silver-white locks which fell just below her neckline. Her heart-shaped face glowed with a golden brown tan, framing her large, dark eyes, bright now, always bright.

Her figure had become not only more curvaceous, but muscular, because she supposed, she had been enjoying the pleasure of good food without restriction, breathing fresh air and basking in the sunlight. Perhaps this physical change might even be due to her love of dancing on occasion, whether in day or by night. However, the talisman around her neck spoke of an altogether different reason for her newfound strength. This whispered of nocturnal excursions as a great, fearsome winged goddess.

Clutching her clipboard and mobile, Helen paced the floor of the Roof Garden Restaurant. There was just forty minutes to go before the Ball would begin and already early arrivals were appearing at the door. Thankfully it was a hot night, so it was easy to steer them to the cocktail bar, with the promise of sipping Margaritas to placate them. It had become the event to be seen at, this area of the country being thought of as somewhat provincial, a status which the indigenous country set were keen to shed.

The whole occasion had attracted notable and wealthy people from far and wide. Many were eager to encourage fresh investments and business to come their way. That and the chance to appear on nationwide television in opulent surroundings as the affluent class above all others was making the night unmissable. Helen had drummed up such interest in the night, word had spread (via husband Nick) to the ears of a major television station, persuading them to finance a pilot programme in the style of a fly-on-the-wall documentary, charting the production of a fundraising ball. It had everything they were looking for, tensions rising, overcoming difficulties, arguments, intrigues, and of course, local characters to shine a wry spotlight upon. Unfortunately for Helen, communication with her spouse being as it was, at best strained, at worse absent altogether, she was completely unaware of this production. Nick had rationalised to himself that he didn't want to upset any of her arrangements, so failed to tell her he wasn't just making a commemorative film of the night, he was in fact collecting 'candid footage of the highs and lows of an amateur Events Director'. At least, that was the essence of his programme pitch to the Executive Commissioning Producer for the television station. In Nick's mind, Helen would in the end get what she wanted, that being, having her high maintenance ego boosted at the high profile expense of others. In his scheme of career building, everybody had their price, and Nick's was easily dispensing with any loyalty to his wife. So, in the weeks before the Big Night, Helen thought Nick was home at last to demonstrate his support for her endeavour. She had no idea that while she was arranging catering and cars, or carefully writing invoices to herself, his surprise impromptu mini-cam films were not at all playful, they were to become important links for edit cuts for his bigger picture. Nick had no idea either of the sub-plot Helen was in the process of devising. They were both as bad as each other.

Her mobile rang. Helen barked a reply.

"Well it's about time. What do you mean it won't go in the lift? Pull it Man!... Well okay, but a donkey carrying small gifts is what I ordered, so a donkey carrying small gifts is what I shall have. You'll just have to wait at the downstairs door for the duration of the night."

Obviously this curt directive was not happily accepted at the other end. Helen had to hold her phone at some distance from the voice of dissent, which suggested in loud terms what she might do with the donkey should it meet her.

"Just remember your Activity Farm is on the programme. Bad publicity is not something you should invite, and I can make sure it will land on your doorstep!... Manure?... No you really haven't see the size of the pile I can promise you... Shall we agree to disagree?... Very well, I'll get some refreshments sent down for you and your donkey. Carrots for both of you?"

Nick was there with his camera crew, catching yet another comical gem, and Helen was beginning to feel the ever present lens was more than a little intrusive. She had arrived in the morning to oversee the setting up of the show. After at least three hours of elaborately decorating the main dining and dance area with every kind of chilli light, inflatable cactus, sombrero and piñata she could find, Nick finally arrived to bleakly observe,

'Los Diablos plays South American and Cuban music, what has sombreros got to do with that?' Helen's defence was, it didn't matter, Latin music was all the same wasn't it? And apart from that, she was sure they spoke Spanish, so that was good enough, and where did he find that out from anyway?

Nick didn't bother to argue his point, this was just another example of Helen believing she knew better than everyone else, but he still couldn't resist just one barbed retort,

"It was in an interview with them in the local paper, I read it Helen. You do you remember how to read don't you?"

Nick knew too well how to push Helen's buttons, and with the deliberate intention of finding entertaining footage, a small but targeted prod was all that was required to shake her cage. From that point on, the carefully choreographed timetable rapidly seemed to come apart from its joints and screws.

Helen began to scream instructions, with the stalwart attitude that the Show must go on. Restaurant staff were inspected like a line of troops on manoeuvres, piñatas were lowered, then heightened, then lowered again. Despite Nick's suggestion that her clash of Latino cultures was not entirely well thought out, those novelty castanets were not to be wasted and so were added to the welcoming gratuities on each table. Spanish flags and matching red and yellow balloons were strung in any and every available nook and cranny.

In the kitchen, resident Chef Trevor was having a minor breakdown, as Helen had, throughout the lead up to the event, continually changed the menu. Only the night before she had chosen to alter the type of tortillas, then added paella to the list. The management had given him a tight budget, seeing as this was a charity showcase. Experienced as he was, Spanish cuisine was a little outside his comfort zone, plus sourcing specialist ingredients at such a late hour had proved especially difficult, so a certain degree of improvisation was called for. Would anyone really notice the difference between plain sausage and chorizo once they had drunk a glass or two of wine? A dash more chilli would mask it surely? He had some in the stock room a sales rep had brought in, who described it as, a "chilli pepper so outrageously hot it'll knock your socks off and raise the bar takings by 90%!" Chef Trevor was of the opinion it was a rare customer around here who would like squid anyway. Cockles he thought would be an original alternative. Just to add definition to the dish, he had phoned a supplier who was delivering some unusual sea bream called Sarpa salpa later that day. At least he knew how to cook fish. However, when he discovered that morning, with only hours to go, that a well-known food critic was to be one of the guests, he was nearly apoplectic. A lifetime ambition for recognition of his culinary prowess now appeared to have been flaunted in his face, and then flushed down the waste disposal by the "bitch-baggage-in-Louboutin".

Cursing the caterwauling chatalaine who thought she was running the show Chef Trevor paced the floor. It was like a warzone in the kitchen as squid was cremated, rice was burnt dry, pans were flung and people got hurt. Scuttling out of the swing doors from kitchen to restaurant, the waiting staff had a sense of foreboding. It truly was like the old saying, 'out of the frying pan and into the fire', for just as they left the mayhem of Chef Trevor's rage, they were met by the glare of Helen Ellis who was rapidly losing any remnants of humanity, second by second. The film cameras were rolling, the guests were already arriving, the clock was ticking, and Helen was a trifle fraught as Los Diablos had only just finished their sound check while the lighting crew were beginning a practice run of the audience floor plan.

"So where is this 'Special Guest' going to be sitting?" shouted one technician from the boom spotlight.

"Just here," Helen pointed to the seat and table directly with her hand. "Keep an eye on the band, and as soon as Mr. Perez announces the winning guest performer, swing the spot around to look as if you're searching, then stop here."

She slammed her hand firmly on the back of the chair. It was a table midway from the front, towards the centre, making sure whoever walked towards the stage would have maximum audience attention. No one would be able to miss him, or her. For Helen's plan, hinted at in the small print and unnoticed by James Lockhart, was this. Under the ruse of a lottery-style seating number, whoever was found sitting in the chair-number selected, would be serenaded onto the stage by Los Diablos and, filmed for a television audience of millions. Helen had remembered the look of sheer terror on Angela's face and decided a more public event would kill or cure her, but Helen had no idea or understanding of the profound change of heart which Angela had recently undergone. Helen was, as they say, in ignorant bliss, unable to foresee what might unravel later that night.

Helen was uber-maitresse, screaming out orders like an ambitious Third Reich gruppenführer, for, she believed, this was what she was born to do. Her time had come and she would at last be seen for who she truly was.

Paul Hollingsworth leant on the bar of the cocktail lounge, sipping at the salted edge of a glass of Margarita. He preferred a good single malt, but that could wait until later, after his plan had been revealed. For now, he was 'undercover', save for his secretary Elaine Beattie and his chauffer Bill King, both of whom he had known back in the day. In gratitude for their long service and confidential contribution, to both his career and to tonight, he had invited them along as his dinner guests. It was of course, vital they were there to make sure certain key things were to happen. They, in turn, had invited guests themselves, Bill brought his sister Tina, and Elaine, a long-time career woman, had invited a friend she had met at an evening class, Janice Brinkley. How they had all laughed at the coincidence when their limousines had each arrived at the same street to pick up Tina and Janice, and how Tina and Janice knew each other as neighbours! By the second Margarita, both Tina and Janice were unwinding happily into their new company. Tina being naturally gregarious, even confided the dreadful tale of her husband's one-time friend, known previously as 'Uncle' to her children, who now was awaiting Her Majesty's Displeasure for being a 'pervie nonce'. Bill had brought her along to cheer her up.

"Complete and utter maniac nutcase, he even said one of my neighbours was a giant harpy attacking him in his dreams! She's such a quiet retiring soul as well... What's a harpy?"

Paul drifted away from the group conversation to make a phone call.

"So remember, when I text you next, the helicopter is to arrive no less than ten minutes after. That's right, I want it hovering just above the Roof Terrace, showering petals... not too close mind. Don't want to blow their dinners away! The Star Artiste? Well, lower the rope ladder then... Okay, no problem, see you back at mine for a malt my ol'mate."

Mackenzie Davis reclined in the rear seat of her limousine and let the brandy roll across her tongue. She was a little surprised at her decision to attend at all, as tonight's function was somewhat removed from her usual tastes. More inclined towards intimate soirées on yachts moored off privately owned islands, it was obvious, for Mackenzie, this event was not for socialising. Her global company, which in part supplied the lifestyle to which her family had always been accustomed, specialised in appropriating exclusive, international patents on all things pharmaceutical, most recently cornering the World Market in DNA. research and organ transplants. Therefore, a hospital function such as this would be deemed a necessary endurance ordinarily given to a lesser associate, but when she had been contacted by the Ellis woman, apparently an Old School contemporary, she had inadvertently consigned to Mackenzie a crucial key towards a more personal goal.

Helen Ellis was a complete fool who had stumbled onto something extraordinary. She clearly had no idea of the genetic implications presented in the found x-rays. All she apparently wanted was to be a Big Fish in her tiny pond. It was different for Mackenzie though. She and all the Family descendants were able to perceive the bigger picture through their distinctive narrow, icy-blue dead eyes. She and her kin were more evolved beings, and it was Mackenzie's duty to make sure this status quo continued for it was in her bloodline to covet dominion over all others.

As the car turned onto the drive of the Beaconshill Conference Centre, she pressed the driver intercom.

"Is everything in position?"

"Yes Madam."

They were on schedule. Undercover company agents were stationed in the restaurant area, and the conference centre grounds, backed up by high powered 4x4 vehicles and waiting to strike. X-rays were not enough. A living specimen was always preferable. From the sorry tale told by eager-to-impress Helen Ellis, this Bagner woman had no one who would miss her, and even if she did, people go missing every day, without any fear of consequence from the real powers that be. This made Mackenzie's personal appearance tonight even more curious, for her family always kept their distance. They excelled in observing from afar the lesser mortals they made use of, occasionally tweaking a secreted wire here and a taut snare there, but always from a secure and distant balcony. However, though her family were strongly united, they were also competitive to the point of deliberately crushing another sibling's advancement should it perturb them, as they did not care to play nicely. Blatantly without any affection for each other, they chose instead to hold each other close, as it is wise to do with enemies. With a strange gut feeling she could not qualify, Mackenzie felt compelled to directly manage her pet Project Salamander herself tonight. She took it very seriously, as this had the potential to elevate her as the Alpha within the Family dynamic. Uncharacteristically the stress of this had taken its toll on her, with uncomfortable and truncated sleep patterns in the last week, and unsettling dreams of claws and talons carrying her away against her will. Experiencing an involuntary shudder at the dream memory, she rapidly drained the remaining brandy from her glass.

Chapter Fourteen

"Super show Helen!" mouthed yet another guest, shouting to be heard above the hubbub of the fully packed room. What a perfect evening it was, warm and balmy, with a million stars overhead. There were disappointing comments already being aired, but Helen dismissed them. In truth, despite all Helen's best laid plans, it was so far quite pedestrian, with nothing too outrageous, but equally nothing really as extraordinary as she had crowed about. The band was halfway through their pre-dinner set, playing numbers which were comfortable enough for a dining audience, and bordering on bland, so as to avoid prompting indigestion. Helen had explained to Eddie at the sound check, the surprise appearance of Angeliquita was to be the main attraction, and that they were to hold back from fully expressing their musical skills until she said so.

"Now remember Edward, Eduardo, your first cue will be just after dessert arrives, when every table will be alight with sparkler-lit Bunuelos fritters. This will be the time to change tempo." Helen slunk closer to Eddie, causing him to pull back his neck like a repulsed chicken." And don't forget your second cue when we have a sweeping spotlight over the audience, resting on the Star herself." Helen smiled her best coquettish smile, though Eddie's face gave away how easily he was resisting her charms. "You are to walk over to collect her from her seat. Now remember, she will feign reluctance. She might even pretend to run, but just keep a firm grip and get her over to front of stage to do what she does best."

The last remark was for the personal amusement of Helen. She couldn't wait for Angela to scream, *it was what Baggie did best*. However, Helen was to a certain degree, peeved the embarrassment would be over all too soon.

Well at least there will be the film of the night, she gloated to herself.

She had arranged for a Special Edition DVD to be available for sale, with all profits to go to the Hospital Fund of course. From the Finance Department table, Helen looked about her to check the room. No, Bagner hadn't arrived yet, but James Lockhart had assured her the taxi was on its way, with Angela on board. James had been especially vigilant to ensure Miss Bagner's place at table, and had personally booked a car himself. Everything was in place. Everyone who was anyone had arrived and were already chinking glasses over an diverse array of Chef Trevor's interpretation of Tapas. Flirtations oozed, promises and business cards were exchanged, sometimes both with the same incentive, that being a promise to be taken away from the ordinary. It was in a sense a masquerade of sorts. There was only one thing missing for Helen, or rather, one person: Angela. Then, just as she gazed across the wondrous sight of her creation, the double doors to the dining room opened, and in stepped Angela herself.

To describe Angela Bagner as making a dramatic entrance would be an understatement. She was radiant, glittering with poise and emitting an intangible inner energy which beamed rainbow-like as she moved. With her neon white hair coiled loosely into a chignon and pinned with a curl of night-scented jasmine and honeysuckle, she scanned the room, and spotting her hosts, she smiled with warmth that could melt ice cream.

Sweeping through the crowded room as if she were floating slightly above the floor, heads were turned, and whispers spread, as this stunningly confident woman, with diamante-sparkling dress and night-blue feathered cape, brushed past the gasping guests. It was as if the Red Sea had parted. But she wasn't at all aloof, she was attentive to everyone, greeting every eager face with candour and a refined "Hello," As she paused for a chair to be moved out of her way, she spotted Paul Hollingsworth seated with his company and made an immediate detour in their direction. Tina had popped out to the Ladies Powder Room, but Janice Brinkley had remained and was sitting wide-eyed and open mouthed as Angela approached, the fragrance of jasmine and honeysuckle trailing in her wake.

"Hello everyone, are you enjoying yourselves?" She looked around the table, offering a hand towards Janice, who shook it with a fluttering heart. "My name is Angie, and you are?" After exchanging introductions, an invitation to join their group was enthusiastically made.

"Thank you so much, but I must decline. I'm with some people over there." She waved towards her colleagues, all of whom were discussing whether or not it really was Little Miss Mouse Bagner. "But, I hope to see you all on the dance floor later, especially you Janice, and Elaine of course." And without a trace of shyness, she placed Elaine's hand upon Janice's, to which the two women beamed at each other with sheer glee. As the radiant Angela turned to leave, she added in honeyed tones, "and Paul, we must talk later, everything you've had planned. Great ideas, but you must understand I will be adding some caveats of my own."

The astonished Paul dropped his guard and began to stutter a garbling "yes", as this luminous Goddess in front of him, gently stroked his cheek and continued on through the crowded room. Shortly after, Paul left to find a quiet corner in the Cocktail bar, so he could make some unexpected urgent calls. *Had Elaine and Bill said too much?* If they had, no matter, his plan was turning out to be better than he had hoped, though admittedly, he hadn't a clue as to how, but for some reason he trusted it absolutely would. After all, he'd been dreaming of tonight's success.

Breezing through to where her open-mouthed colleagues were seated, Angela embraced each one as an old friend, leaving them stunned and, causing James Lockhart to nearly stumble over as he quickly jumped from his chair to greet her. Angela was not only dazzling, she was a phenomenon. Immediately conversation bubbled over every wine glass supped, spilling over onto the surrounding tables. Both men and women smiled invitingly and offered chairs in the hope this woman would grace them with her company. Everyone was captivated, and craving a morsel of her attention, clamoured like they were star struck. All except Helen, and not wishing to expose her true feelings towards this the goddess in their midst, Helen shifted away the chair in a welcoming gesture.

"So sorry I kept you waiting," Angela soothed to her party with a warmly open smile.

"Not at all Miss Bagner," James stammered nervously. "I think I speak for everyone here when I say... it wouldn't be the same without you!"

"Oh please James, call me Angie."

Everyone at the Finance Department table nodded, wide eyed and clearly pleased they were now the envy of the night, elevated by the distinguished company they were keeping. Their previously dull table had suddenly come alive, was bright and full of laughter. Sandra and Jeanette found themselves giggling like schoolgirls, flushed with the excitement of Miss Bagner's transformation, and basking in the unspoken idea that if she had, why couldn't they? In an instant, there could not have been a more carefree band of people in the room, and spreading across the dining guests was a happy virus manifest since Angela had entered. Helen was incandescent with indignation.

How dare she? She's acting as if it's her night!

This was quite true. Angela had blossomed in self confidence, and decided to treat tonight exactly as that: her night. It was not the outcome Helen had expected or desired, leaving her somewhat un-nerved by this apparition appearing in the stead of her nemesis. Who was she, and what had she done with Bagner? Gathering all the guile she could muster, Helen patted the seat next to her again to settle the late guest into her planned position. Angela was happy to respond, and as she sat down, Helen leant over to plant the obligatory double kiss of greeting onto Angela's cheeks. But out of earshot of the other table companions, whispered darkly into Angela's ear,

"I have made it my mission to destroy you."

Then with a superficial smile, Helen turned to hold court, as if nothing had happened, only to find everyone at the table, in fact everyone in the restaurant appeared to be ignoring her. Angela was now the centre of all attention, either directly or indirectly, for she had brought life to what had previously been a reasonably pleasant dinner-dance, and had charmed it into something of lustre. This night would be one they would each remember for the rest of their lives, and in times to come during its recollection, they would say there were moments as if time had actually stood still. Helen watched as Angela crooned to her admirers in delicious conversation. Each adoring devotee appeared relaxed and elated awaiting the next captivating crumb, their ardent gaze hanging on Angela's every word and smile.

This of course had a most adverse effect on Helen, aware she was suddenly redundant and forgotten. Laughter and smiles and adoration, those things were meant for her, but Angela Bagner had stolen them from her. This spinster adversary, who sat beside her, had somehow altered beyond her original self, having undergone some kind of internal revolution. This was ruining her plans, for bemusing as it was, Angela had become popular.

Wait until later Bagner! Helen seethed in her mind, and just as she did, Angela sweetly whispered in return.

"And with so many things you could do," Angela looked sadly into Helen's eyes and shook her head as if in sympathy. "You will only destroy yourself. Did you not know the best revenge is to be happy?"

Before Helen fully understood, Angela had nodded to a discreet corner of the rooftop, where two lovers were lost in the intense embrace of a passionate kiss. Then Helen's world came crashing in on her, for she recognised the couple, it was her husband Nick and his Personal Assistant, a young woman, twelve years Helen's junior.

Oh God, it was just all too clichéd!

All those trips abroad and film shoots away flashed before her eyes and she suddenly knew that all she had thought real, was false.

"You can change anything if you want to dear Helen." Angela rested her hand on Helen's, but this merely outraged her further. Tearing her hand away she squawked,

"Get off me, you, you... nothing!"

Strutting from the table, she headed through the crowded room to confront her wayward husband, knocking over glasses and pushing aside diners in her way. Striding through the tables, her mobile dropped soundlessly onto the carpeted floor. Always the gentleman, James bent to retrieve the phone and called after her. Whether or not she heard him, the steamroller that was Helen drove on. James paused and considered the object for a moment. Somehow it had landed on 'Diary', displaying momentarily a curious 'note to self' from Helen. It read: 'NB – Completed Charity invoices and receipts in Personal file.

Charity Invoices and receipts, what have you been up to Mrs. Ellis? Well, well, this might prove interesting reading, thought James, and tucked the mobile neatly into the inside pocket of his dinner jacket.

Angela sighed. She found no pleasure in the suffering of Helen Ellis, but she knew she was merely a witness to what Helen had created all by herself, and there was more to come.

Little was seen of Helen for some time, but to further compound her distress, she knew that no one had noticed her absence. Seeking refuge in the quaintly titled Ladies Powder Room, Helen sat with mascara trickling down her otherwise perfectly made up and botoxed face. Occasionally a woman or two would enter, gossiping about the evening,

"Not sure about the decor."

"It does seem to clash doesn't it?"

"How are you finding the food?"

"I feel a bit squiffy already."

But most of all, despite troublesome stomachs, the highlight of the night was the mesmerising vision that was Angela.

"Well, at least Helen got that right. Helen told me she booked the Special Guest Artiste especially for tonight you know. Did you see her come in? Wow!" one woman babbled while applying crimson to her lips.

"Oh I know, such style! I'd love to wear something like that, mind you, you'd have to have mountains of confidence to carry that off," replied the other, powdering her nose, "suppose it's because she's a professional. I hear Los Diablos have already signed a recording deal with her. They sound pretty good themselves... ooh I just love Cuban music!"

"Come on, let's get back, I don't want to miss her singing. You know my friend from yoga is here tonight with her daughter Lucy? Well, Lucy recognised her as the recluse who lives below her. Apparently she has the most amazing voice! You remember, Lucy is the one studying music as her degree."

The two chattering women exited, leaving Helen alone to groan. *So Bagner had fooled them all, a singer? How on earth did I not know of this?* The Woman who Helen had seen terrified in the Azure Height cafe all those weeks before, was nothing like the shining beauty who sat outside. Helen's entire scheme pivoted on the given assumption that Miss Bagner was dowdy irritant who needed to be taken down a peg or two. Still, all was not lost. Helen comforted herself by remembering the mutated humps on Baggie's back. In preparation for a big reveal, she had invited a certain team of hospital doctors, keen to carry out further tests on Angela. And then there was Mackenzie Davis. Now that was a stroke of genius, for amazingly she had accepted the invitation. Not only would Helen use Angela's affliction to facilitate even more public ridicule, but it was giving the devious Mrs. Ellis a lift up onto a higher rung on her desired social ladder. *Mackenzie had come!* Mackenzie Davis was one of the most significant 'It' girls at her old school. Back then, Helen had longed to be just like her, or even just to tread in her shadow, but that was not to be, for much to Helen's personal and secret shame, she was a Scholarship girl.

Fortified by the comforting, though admittedly illogical thought that she would still in some way get the better of her colleague, Helen brushed herself down and tidied her face in the mirror.

How could I have missed it? Nick's probably done this before, but to do this on my big night! I've always been far more discreet. Explains why there was never a tan mark around his wedding ring, must have removed it to appear single – What a bastard!

After this inner debate, she reassured herself that at least she could make use of the television film. Helen decided to contact their main offices the very next day. It was about time she did, as that was another thing Nick had been keeping her in the dark about.

Turning to leave the muffled security of the Ladies, she groaned again, only this time she gripped her stomach. Restoring her posture, she noticed a strange bending of the walls about her, and how the previously pastel coloured walls were now vivid and throbbing in solarised patterns. In addition she felt weirdly as if she were in slow-motion. Ignoring this warning, Helen pushed through the door to the restaurant. Everything was Angela's fault tonight.

While Helen was waylaid, nursing her narcissistic pride, Angela had surveyed the evening's guests. *What a wonderful night!* All these people she was yet to bring into her life... if she wanted to.

All of us are flawed, but we are perfect in our imperfection.

She thought of the wide expanse of their possibilities, some of whom she had visited intimately in her recent dream travels. There was Paul Hollingsworth for example, your traditional rough diamond, a little bit roguish admittedly, but with not a bad bone in his body. Angela decided she liked him. She liked his loyalty and his willingness to take chances. Then there was Eddie from Los Diablos. *What a wonderfully funny man!* It made her smile to think of him. He had struggled all his life to look after his family, but never gave up on his hope, Angela felt he deserved his dream to come true. Yes, such a wonderful night, with countless possibilities under a million stars, and she might never have met any of them, were it not for the misguided Helen. Angela felt a rush of empathy for the poor woman. As well as being a most unpleasant person, it was quite clear she was not a happy one. A Being who nurtured the illusion of happiness, but failed to grasp what was really important in life. Helen would have been appalled to know this, but Angela had begun to feel almost fond of her.

From where Helen had disappeared to, Angela could now see the previously entangled couple of Nick and his young mistress in an equally passionate altercation. When Helen had reached them both, she had grabbed the nearest pitcher of sangria, and thrown it over the pair of them. It seemed Nick was less concerned over the humiliation of his girlfriend than that of the soaked film equipment at their feet, blaming her immediately for not keeping it secure. It was ruined, however his chances for a big break in television were further magnified by the young woman's fury, who then threw scorn, or rather his equipment, over the balcony.

From her distant position, Angela sighed at how often human beings chose to waste their lives with trivial pursuits and empty ambitions.

Such a squandering of time and life, and with so many things they could do, she murmured under her breath, but her trail of thought was cut abruptly short. Something had arrested her quiet meditation, or rather, someone. Someone was observing her. Slowly looking over her shoulder and across the crowded tables, her eyes met those of a pale skinned figure in a silver grey dress, coldly staring at Angela. The seated woman was probing her with the gaze of dissection, and her narrowed, ice-blue eyes seemed to be trying to penetrate the depth of her target. Angela knew who this was; calculating amorality in the flesh, Mackenzie Davis, the shadowy figure who had steadfastly stalked her dream life. Ordinarily, the average person might not notice the deviant psyche that was amongst them. They would see her as attractive, compelling, flattering and so eager to know you. Indeed, it had amused her to overhear that apparently 'butter would not melt in her mouth'.

The irony was not lost on Mackenzie, as she felt absolutely nothing for anyone. She had been bred that way. In the dynamics of her clan, the motivating drive between herself and her siblings was to outwit and dominate the other. If you can behave in emotionless terms with your own blood, then it left a person like Mackenzie with no compunction when concerning others. If truth be known, Mackenzie's only saving grace and hint of humanity was her passion for opera, and young sopranos in particular. She admired the exacting skill of control that was required, and deeply respected the enduring aspiration towards perfection. Unlike her other stark domains, there was a strange license that the fine voice of an opera singer gave her; she could almost feel, albeit by proxy. Mackenzie Davis was in her limited public life, a great Patron of the Arts, and had personally guided the careers of those who caught her interest. To those around that circle, Mackenzie's philanthropy was renowned, a pillar, and blameless because of her evident altruism. However if anyone lingered longer in her company, a few survivors would tell another tale, one of sub-zero wickedness, and a lack of any concern or empathy for any normal emotion. Mackenzie was outwardly human in form, but inwardly she was a Being that held no qualms for manipulation or cruelty. She would entertain herself through the torment of others, by seeing 'feeling' people as insects under a magnifying glass in the sun, and she could spend an inordinate amount of time planning such recreations, examining how her specimens might struggle whilst their wings were slowly ripped away.

Angela knew this creature, for she herself was no longer the meekly subservient person she used to be. The days of beige, sufferance and isolation were long gone, and the Woman she had become was wise and in rhythm with the World. Yes, she did indeed know Mackenzie. She reminded Angela of cats killing for pleasure, and who played torturous games before they finally put an end to their victim's misery. This was nothing new, for there had been millions of this species throughout History, often holding positions of power; politicians, executives, even primary school Head Teachers. And here was such a creature, vacationing perhaps amongst these ordinary souls for some kind of humorous dalliance, like a hunter visiting a zoo might go window shopping, but instead her shark-dead eyes were focussed only on Angela. If this was to have happened about four or five weeks before, Angela would either have been paralysed to the spot, or might have run to the nearest exit sign, but not now. Angela was prepared for this meeting in ways that Mackenzie had no knowledge, which was strange, as Mackenzie made it her business to know everything about everyone who might stray into the scope of her radar. She knew all about the pathetic scurrying of Helen, she knew about all the subterfuge and scuttling of some silly man called Hollingsworth and, she knew about the enigma of Angela's wings.

What Mackenzie did not know however, was the realm of possibilities into which Angela was able to traverse, and how she could enter other people's dreams. Nor did she know of the Angela who could slow time and open up dimensions, transforming sometimes into an archaic goddess called Lilith. No, Mackenzie knew nothing of that. Mackenzie Davis, not her true name of course, for each of her clan had chosen a name to best suit their wanderings through the lesser worlds, as a smoke screen misdirection of where they had come from, and as a sleight of hand to what exploits they were really manoeuvring towards. More importantly, Mackenzie was not aware she was known by both Angela and Lilith for her true self, not just her assumed name, as many people had reason to change their identity, but known for the dreadful and abhorrent experiments she and her company carried out on all forms of life. Most especially, on animals and humans, under the lie it was for the advancement of science, but in truth, it was just because she could. Night time travels as Angela's winged self had made these atrocities known.

This time, the experiment specimen was to be Angela, a perfect jewel in the crown of Project Salamander, named after the creature whose DNA instructed missing limbs to grow again. What a prize for a bored Mackenzie that would be. She imagined an army she might grow, an army who could be repaired and sent to war, again and again and again. Her arid mouth watered at the thought. *Such fun!* True enough, Mackenzie didn't feel, but she did enjoy.

Mackenzie smiled a lizard's smile, having gained Angela's attention, she beckoned her nearer patting the seat beside her, but Angela merely held her gaze, looking back at her blankly, sustaining an impenetrable expression of inscrutability. Just for a flickering moment, Mackenzie twisted her brow in puzzlement. This was intriguing and would make this particular chase more satisfying, for she had epicurean tastes for sport.

"Miss Bagner, Angie... Angie!"

James completed an announcement, and was just leaving the stage, but she had slipped into a deep meditation and been unaware of the Grand Prizes being called. Apparently she had won something too, as James thrust a gold envelope towards her.

"Angie, Mrs. Ellis appears to be missing. I've made some announcements, you know, the prize raffle and so on. It is our night as a department, I wonder, would you say something too?"

"Of course James, not a problem at all."

With that, Angela rose from her seat and sailed like a galleon through the restaurant tables, with the balletic grace of someone who owned the space about her, The diamante on her gown coruscated as she moved, sending shafts of rainbow light over the diners' heads, and the swaying feathered cape, as it streamed down her back, seemed to have a life of its own, moving in syncopation to it's bearer. Suddenly, with a choreographed timing of musical theatre, the kitchen swing doors opened and a fanfare of waiters and waitresses shimmied in, bearing sparkler-lit Bunuelos; light, fluffy fritters, filled with a crème patisserie and dusted with sugar and nutmeg. The jittery apprentice Commis-Chef was in charge of these delicacies. Although there should have been only a hint of cinnamon, his shredded nerves after an evening of loud volume and deeply personal insults from Chef Trevor, resulted in him picking nutmeg by mistake, and then accidentally dropping the spice pot and its entire contents into the sugar dusting. Not wishing to be at the mercy of Chef Trevor's rage, the tremulous lad had hoped this would go un-noticed. Unfortunately, this was to be the last cherry on top of what was to be a night to be remembered, or possibly forgotten by some.

The young bespeckled registrar took a bite of a Benuelo, coughed and turned to his red nosed mentor to continue their observations on the evening's menu.

"So, I'm wondering. Do you think these foods could have a cumulative effect?"

The sage, red nosed doctor nodded his reply and they continued their discussion on the fact that certain foods, available in any supermarket or larder, have potentially hallucinogenic properties.

"But of course, the humble chilli pepper for example is in the same botanical family as potatoes, tobacco, and Deadly Nightshade, all of which can cause one to hallucinate if their fruit is ingested. Then there are the amazing hallucinogenic effects of particular kinds of fish. For instance, the Sarpa Salpa, variety of sea bream, served this evening is thought to be harmless and of course delicious, but if one makes the mistake of including the entire fish, say, using the bones for fish stock destined for a rice dish, a Chef might be in danger of serving his or her guests a very memorable meal. This can induce hallucinations similar to LSD."

His protege nodded attentively and added in what he hoped were impressive tones, "I've come across cases where ingestion of large quantities of fragrant nutmeg can, if eaten in excessive amounts, cause aberrations both visual and aural."

The doctors put down their forks, simultaneously stifled burps and concluded that, it would be ill-fated indeed to find all these ingredients in one set menu.

"Let's hope there wasn't any fish stock in that paella, dear boy or we'll all be in for a bumpy night."

From the brightly lit stage, Eddie suddenly spotted the scintilla procession spreading throughout the room and recognised his cue to up the tempo.

"Okay Boys," he waved to the rest of the band, who at this point had almost fallen asleep during their Easy Listening set, "This is it! Time to bring out the Big Guns!"

At this, the three cornet players trumpeted the change of rhythmic gear in unison, a klaxon sound boasting an entrance to take notice of, causing every head to look up. Eddie tried not to look nervous, for he couldn't see the spotlight yet. The directions he had been given by the Ellis woman were a little flaky, but he'd put that down to her being a theatrical type, and not wanting to appear out of his depth, had gone along with it without question.

Where was Ellis anyway? No matter. Always give 100% Eddie my Boy!

But his anxieties swiftly melted away as James Lockhart, genuinely in awe of the resplendent Woman he now clearly adored, stood up and began to clap enthusiastically, nodding to other diners to follow his example, which they duly did. They had been waiting in excited anticipation for this all evening. Their response was loud and passionate, and everyone was on their feet. It was all Paul Hollingsworth could do to wave 'Go on!' to the troupe of dancers waiting patiently on the outside perimeter of the rooftop.

Angela, gliding effortlessly towards Eddie, smiled to all she passed, shimmering with a presence the likes of neither Lossingham, nor possibly the World had seen been before. Behind her, a cavalcade folly of Brazilian Carnival girls, were sashaying their tropical tail feathers. By this time everyone was whooping and cheering at the dazzling spectacular before them. Such colour and music, it felt as if they were being transported to a different time and place. Of course, the cocktail of potential mind-altering chemicals in the meal they had eaten may have been playing a part in their experience. Whatever the case, everybody seemed to be having a deliriously enjoyable time, and when the object of their desire nonchalantly arrived onto the stage, playfully tickling Eddie under his chin, the place was in uproar. Angela whispered into Eddie's ear, he nodded back to the band to lower the volume just a little so she could speak. They duly pulsed an infectious groove of sound. Shimmying up to the retro microphone, Angela beamed a contagious smile and in a dulcet voice she purred,

"Hello you beautiful people. Thank you all so much for coming here tonight, to Las Estellas des Verano, The Summer Stars Summer Ball!" Everyone cheered.

"My name, for tonight," she giggled and turned to Eddie who was grinning back, "my name is Angeliquita, and this," she grabbed Eddie's hand and pulled him forward, "This is our marvellous main man... Eddie!" Again everyone cheered. Eddie grinned back, waved, and then comically placed devil horns on his head, pulled his demon tail out from his back trouser pocket, and clapped as the rest of the band followed suit. Then, one by one, Angela introduced each devil by name, and each introduction caused a matching applause. Eddie supposed she knew every player because of the demos he had forwarded via Helen Ellis, but Helen had no sooner received them than promptly binned them. Had he known this, it would have seemed mysterious indeed.

"And we are..." she flamboyantly flourished her arm in the air. "And we are, Angeliquita and Los Diablos! Let's heat you up some more."

At that, Angela and Eddie and the Band were one, launching into a Samba style version of 'Fever.' It was as if they had played together for years, and yet they had such freshness and energy, such wit and zip. It was as if they had brought with them the very Cuban sun itself, sending glints of warm light onto everyone and everything about them. When Angela sang, sizzling took on a whole new meaning; as hair on the back of necks rose, it sent electricity down spines, dilated pupils and in some more mature diners, tingles were favourably felt in some long abandoned places. The glittering dancing girls undulated in perfect rhythm with the congas and claves, their tail feathers bouncing provocatively to and fro. Whilst the bass and flute twisted in and out of the melody,

Eddie at last gave full expression to his beloved music, picking and strumming on his treasured Epiphone guitar. Eddie was in his bliss and could almost smell a waft of cigar on a mango scented breeze.

"... But what a lovely way to burn... What a lovely way to burn..."

For just a brief moment, and only just, there was a stunned silence, a roar of ecstatic rapture, followed by a sudden rush of guests filling the dance floor. Some grabbed their phones, either to film or photograph, some grabbed the gratuity castanets so as to make some noise, and some just grabbed each other, for reluctant partners were not allowed. All sensed they were in the presence of something special and they wanted to be as big a part of it as they could. From one song to another, Angela and the band delivered infectious joy. No one dancing could defy the urge to smile, because Angela was a force of Nature, a gushing spring, and the Devils and Audience were her thirsty attendees. She had intoxicated them.

This left most of the tables empty of people, except for a few stragglers here and there slightly worse for wear, after too many mixed drinks. These poor souls were slumped on folded arms but happily smiling through it. But there were those who seemed to have had a more acute reaction to the unusual qualities of the dinner itself. These agitated dinner guests appeared bug-eyed, and twisted the corners of tablecloths in their hands whilst they sat nervously looking about them. Some even hid themselves under tables. What it was they thought they saw was difficult to be sure of, but the next day the Management team found deliberate scratch marks, made most probably by sharp cutlery, on the topside and underside surfaces of more than one table.

Tina had managed to push her tiny frame toward the front. She had to make sure that her eyes were not deceiving her. Was this really the lovely woman who lived opposite her?

That lady was so quiet and reserved, it didn't quite match the girl up there now. But there she was.

It only goes to show, you never can tell. People can be anything!

Tina, now inflated with enormous pride, began nudging people alongside her.

"I know her!"

"One of my family's friends you know!"

"Such a refined lady!"

By this method of friendly nudging, Tina arrived directly front of stage. It felt like days gone by when she had sneaked in through an exit to watch bands at the Electric. The lead singer was in her element, her arms wide, thrilling in the joy she was exuding. Her voice had supreme verve and flexibility, so much so, the revellers felt as if they were lifting off the ground. If they had only looked down they would have been surprised to have found this was exactly what was happening, but at the end of each song, their feet would rest again, so no one seemed to notice. How much time passed was hard to say, but at last, Angela softly growled into the microphone,

"Sadly my Beautiful Friends, this is to be our final song of the night." There were plaintive cries of 'No!' from across the dance floor. "But I don't believe all good things must come to an end, I believe that... 'Everything is Still to Come!'" Turning to Eddie she half whispered, "In the Key of A, Cuban rhythm, and follow me!"

Eddie nodded. He had already decided he would follow this woman anywhere. The song was a rumba ballad which focussed on the rim rhythms of the timbales, the staccato cascara patterns and the accent strokes of the mambo bell. It was highly percussive, and onto this, Angela had allowed for the melody to be driven by the vibraphone, to call and respond to the keyboards. It was an impressive composition, especially considering she had written this during the few days leading up to tonight, but Angela had not just blossomed, she was fully in bloom.

"Todo tiene su razón... todo tiene su rima... todo tiene su temporada... todo tiene su tiempo... Everything has its reason... everything has its rhyme... everything has its season... everything has its Time..." she sang, to the echoing throng.

The whole audience were gyrating closely together, clapping hands, waving arms and shimmying shoulders. Janice and Elaine were bouncing next to Tina, trying to clap castanets together, but their efforts were inaudible. Not to be outdone, Tina had another idea. Jenny had given her something before she left, insisting she take it to the Ball, "You're going to need it Mum," she had said knowingly, and just to humour her, Tina had taken it. Diving her hand into the evening bag she was carrying, she pulled out a small object which she placed on her pursed lips. It was the bird whistle.

"Peenk! Peenk! Peenk!"

The alarm call pierced through the noise of the crowd and Angela froze. The band thinking this a musical break, froze with her, not realising the alarm that was ringing in the singer's ears, was sending a shockwave of heat searing through her feet. She looked about her as if searching in the crowd for a particular face, and indeed, she was. But to every member of the audience her gaze was personal. The piano and bass kept the melody and beat pulsing, while the rest of the Diablos never let their eyes stray from their Queen, waiting for the next thrust of sound. Angela looked about the room, clapping twice over and over at intervals as if to punctuate, and each time she did, piñata after piñata exploded in perfect time, scattering down onto the laughing faces, but instead of sweets and streamers, cascades of firefly-sparks hovered and caught in their hair. Some tried to hold them in their cupped hands, some tried to catch them on their tongues like snowflakes, but as each one touched, the time they stood in began to slow. Soon it was a blizzard of illuminated pollen, shrouding the partygoers from what Angela was really looking for. Her feet were tingling and she could smell something which rotted in her midst. Just beyond the crowd, on a table in half shadow, a seated figure lit a cigarette, and drawing deeply on the smoke, Angela could see the whitened teeth belonging to Mackenzie Davis. Mackenzie was pointing towards Angela on the stage, sending a languid order to three darkly suited figures to surround the area. Their hands were already slipping inside jacket pockets. Their instructions were to capture 'Dead or Alive', the latter preferably, and as soon as this spectacle ended.

Los Diablos had no idea of the diabolical scenario being played out beyond the crowd. They just presumed their Star had orchestrated the most amazing stage effects they had ever seen. *Better than a smoke machine* approved Eddie.

Then suddenly, something happened which would eclipse even this. Forcefully loosening her feathered cape, Angela pulled it from her muscular shoulders, and two huge, monumental wings sprang from her back, vaulting her high above and over the awestruck heads below her. The wings were not only alive in themselves, but alive with her. The slightest flicker passing across her staring face sent ripples and vibrations through the rich brown plumage.

A strange lighting effect seemed to be beaming onto the stage, as if a film of someone else was being projected onto Angela's levitating form. It was the Creature Lilith, and she was emanating shards of light of every colour contained in the amorphous sphere in which the she travelled. Everything around her however was still, caught in the last infinitesimal moment in which the Creature Lilith had leapt from. The Creature Lilith was bursting with strength and adrenaline, ready for the fight with the creature who called itself Mackenzie.

The Creature Lilith halted for a moment, her talisman floating about her neck, and turning her heart face from one side to the other, she inspected her target. Strangely, the target appeared to be unaffected by whatever had held others in a state of aspic, it appeared also to be amused with the diversion, and continued to inhale on its cigarette. In a millisecond blink, the Creature Lilith, darted to where her prey sat and launched her talons into the body of the Thing-Mackenzie. Tearing an opening in the air, the Creature Lilith took Mackenzie through.

Chapter Fifteen

It was a velvet night, with sweet smelling currents of air caressing the two airborne figures. The full moon turned behind the World they had flown from. All the myriad stars and galaxies had once again come to welcome travellers, willing the pair to witness their glory. The Creature Lilith flew in perfect sympathy with the element about her, knowing she and the surrounding expanse were of each other. Appearing like gold from a super nova, the Creature Lilith was equally rare, but as integral to the Grandest Story there was, Life.

In the grip of her talons was the creature Mackenzie, who unlike many of the pilot's previous passengers, was not struggling. Instead, the human cargo had decided for the time being, if there was any real time in this place, to employ the path of least resistance. This was mainly due to the razor sharp talons all but imbedded into her liver. This calm and composed strategy, served in other ways as Mackenzie wanted to watch and absorb this entire place and observe the mutant carrying her.

What pleasurable distractions it would make.

And what Mackenzie wanted, Mackenzie got. The first well practised tactic was to fawn and praise, to lower the guard of her victim, who would begin to believe Mackenzie as trustworthy, and therefore sensitive to hidden insecurities. Then the fools would tell all, disclosing sometimes the most intimate worries, and frailties, not realising Mackenzie was on a fact finding reconnoitre, searching only for information or services she could use. If any were found, Mackenzie would tolerate her targets repellent decrepitudes for as long as necessary. Once confidences were extracted, Mackenzie would use the retrieved foibles against the gullible innocents, only dropping the facade when there were no witnesses.

Even if the puny dupe were then to remove themself from the nightmare they all too late had awoken to, Mackenzie would be established as the most reasonable and caring of persons, incapable of behaving in such furtively calculating ways. At best, the result would be accusations of paranoia and the wrecked life of an unsuspecting ingénue, at worse, a darker pleasure would be wrought and people would disappear. Mackenzie didn't like waste though, as she would make sure these simpletons would be helpful in research trials abroad. Mackenzie even directed some trials personally.

And so she began.

"It must be so difficult for you to be alone, unless... are there any more of your kind?"

The Creature Lilith flew on, without reaction or answer. After an indeterminate time, Mackenzie tried again.

"Do they hurt you? Angela isn't it? Do they hurt you, your wings I mean?"

As the Creature Lilith was not of Mackenzie's world, and no longer manifesting as the Being Angela, again she gave no response.

"But so beautiful, such a shame that so few people would appreciate them."

Only silence came.

"You are clearly very powerful. Such muscles and strength. I would love to be able to fly as you do, but I am just a... weak mortal."

The Creature Lilith was well aware of Mackenzie's attempts to disarm her, but being Ages old, had dealt with this kind before. The Mackenzie's murky arrogance was becoming tedious, so the winged aviator decided to cut short the ritual. She plummeted downwards, dragging the Mackenzie behind her at speed.

"Come Janus, We are here."

The conveyer's voice was arcane deep, the sound of a mountain range which had become sand on a turning shore, ebbed and flowed in its throat. Mackenzie was delighted, as the sensation of surprise was one which had always eluded her, for Mackenzie was surprised by nothing.

So this is what it's like!

"Indeed," replied the Creature Lilith to Mackenzie's hidden thought, and landing in a darkened enclosure, held the passenger in one claw. Their resting place was surrounded by a perimeter of squirming and contorting blackness. Mackenzie was enthralled. If only she hadn't left her camera phone behind.

I wonder if the Sat Nav app might work here? Perplexing her considerably was the fact she was not yet attractive to the Creature Lilith herself, for all her efforts to disarm by charm had no apparent effect. It was extraordinary, for this was the very first time Mackenzie felt no control, and the need for control to Mackenzie, was as necessary as emotion is to most other humans. Control served as Mackenzie's equivalent expression of love or other such primitive feelings, but without their unfathomable and inconvenient lack of logic. Without control, Mackenzie's true appearance would reveal itself. The mask began to slip.

"Are you to leave me here in some kind of lesson of retribution?" Mackenzie sneered, "Who is it you are in service to? I will not be trifling with any idiotic notion of God!" She drew out the last word with spittle spray. There was not a thing, nor being which would be able to create Mackenzie's unique mind, at least, that's what Mackenzie thought.

"We Are All." came the short reply.

"What does that mean?" Mackenzie felt the loss of control again.

"It means, We Are All."

The Creature Lilith was too long in the talon to continue explaining the obvious to the disintegrating Mackenzie. It was time to perform the Law of the Old Ways, and she knew she would have to claw deeper into the dark to release the eons to power it. Such a farcical performance, soon the true face of Mackenzie would be made known by its own denial of 'We Are All'. Perhaps the Creature Lilith would show it more than What Lay Below. Using a taloned finger, she again bent over and cut deeply into the tissue of air and once more the Chasm opened up its earthy jaws.

"Oh you do disappoint me. A formulaic archangel comes to carry me to purgatory. Hell and damnation, blah, blah, blah."

Ignoring the snide jeering, The Creature Lilith outstretched the captive away from her. The more anger the Mackenzie voiced, the more it stank of rank sweat and excrement. It really was quite unpleasant, even to a Being of Ages Old. Thrusting the Mackenzie and its squalling protestations down into the pit, again the Creature Lilith waited. Time was of no consequence here, Time did not exist, or rather; Time did not restrict itself to a linear pattern, for Time had more of Vitruvian Man about it. In Vitruvian Time, Beings co-exist with other Beings in other times, rather like an onion has different layers, except the layers occupy the same space. Oh, she had enjoyed the conversations with the Gentleman who put the idea of Vitruvian Time to paper – *Leonardo wasn't it?* Now there was someone who made good use of his Time, although many thought him out of his Time. He was very interested in flight she recalled, and had made some rather attractive studies of her wing structure too. It was but a small vanity exchanged for the enhancement of his journey in that life.

Perhaps we will call on him again, but not until this task is completed.

Feeling slight vibrations from the ankles of the Mackenzie, she decided to leave it there a while longer. She needed to consider if this ritual alone would be enough. This one was a tricky one and would need to be treated with some delicacy. For here it was understood, the Law of We Are All meant every being is an expression of We Are All, therefore every Being is in constant flux until they gain the understanding of We Are All. There was nothing punitive in the process, the choices Beings made on their way would determine their outcome. For all Beings it was merely the journey to an understanding of the fundamental Law: We Are All. However, a glimpse of possible outcomes would be permissible, a 'sneak preview' might in turn offer an epiphany. After all, Beings must make their journey to understanding alone. The next Plane of Understanding would serve as a little guidance, or a push in a wiser direction. Satisfied with this as the wisest choice, the Creature Lilith nodded in agreement with the stars about her. Her commune with them had led her to the obvious conclusion. It would indeed require the next Plane of Understanding, for Mackenzie to progress. Rarely delivered but once conjured it would have inevitable outcomes.

Very well.

When the bedraggled Mackenzie was finally pulled from the pit, it was yelling in outrage as the Creature Lilith shook the dirt from its dangling legs like a small dinner bell.

"Is that the best you have? Do you really think that thing down there would shock me into your submission? Why, I've created worse in my laboratory!"

"Not at all, I just thought you might like to visit a relative." Her captor replied blankly. There was stunned silence,

"What?"

"To some What Lay Below are all the poisons of human nature, greed, anger and stupidity. Things we all share. We Are All." The Creature Lilith shrugged her shoulders, as to her it was self-evident.

"Do you know who I am? I think you will find I am nothing like the rest of the Human Race!" the Mackenzie raged in disgust.

"No, that is true, you are something more. You are the festering sore of generations of inbred ego." She glibly remarked. What Lay Below was put there a long time ago. One of your ancestors We believe. How was your meeting? Did you exchange addresses?" The Creature Lilith rarely laughed, but allowed herself a small titter on this occasion.

"Who Do You Think You Are indeed!"

"So what now? Am I reformed? Are you take me back so I might do penance to Humankind? I tell you now, they are not worthy of me! I do not think you realise who you are dealing with, or what I am capable of!" The gnashing teeth of the Mackenzie were exposed and saliva drooled uncontrollably from its voluminous mouth.

"Here we go," sighed the Goddess to herself. "Here comes the true face. It's going to start with the threats and so on. Why do some of them take so long to get it? Exasperating! Very well, the next Plane of Understanding it is to be then."

Slowly, the Creature Lilith repeated again, but this time as if talking to a very stubborn and stupid child.

"We... Are... All."

They shot vertically up through endless sky, through a sea of stars, which drifted in like luminous phytoplankton of every imaginable shape and luminescent colour. The Creature Lilith saw the Mackenzie had no reverence for the miracle about it, only a desire to consume everything for itself. Nothing moved it, and for that she felt pity for the Mackenzie.

What a two-dimensional world it must live in.

She was very much aware of the evil the Mackenzie was capable of wreaking. The depraved and grisly carnage the Mackenzie and her kind had systematically executed in the name of science or power was testament to this. It would always be a failed endeavour however, as the Mackenzie was nothing more than a torturer for sadistic pleasure. In a way, the Mackenzie was searching for some kind of feeling, for purpose, but the outcomes were absolute evil. Some well meaning Beings asserted there was no such thing as evil, and the Creature Lilith conceded this to be true in part. Evil couldn't exist in itself. In the Law of We Are All evil outcomes came from an imbalance of the choices all Beings make and, an intractable refusal to accept We Are All responsible for the choices we do make.

Such a childish idea to believe in a parental deity, when to put it simply: We are All. Anything else was superfluous. The Creature Lilith sighed again.

"Something bothering you?" sniped the Mackenzie who was trying to listen into her bearer's thoughts. They had been suspended for the longest of time or the briefest of moments.

"What is this place anyway?"

"It would be difficult for you to understand."

"Try me."

"Well, this would perhaps be likened to the opposite side of what your scientists might call a Black Hole, a place where all things are pulled into."

"Hmm, it doesn't appear to be very black here, in fact, it's, it's..."

"Quite the opposite."

The Mackenzie's words trailed away, as in front of the floating couple, a change was coming about of an astonishing kind. The innumerable stars were pulsing, growing, and drawing together into one coalescent mass, of multiplying bubbles of light. The indigo darkness was shrinking away, subsiding until there was nothing but all-enveloping light, pure light, light that was almost palpable, and held substance. It was the place where the Being Angela had been brought to, so as to find understanding. In fact, all Beings came here for this, over and over again, here to the Plane of Understanding.

Sometimes though, understanding takes a longer journey for the Beings resistant to the Law, as simple as indeed it was.

"So? What is this place?" the Mackenzie taunted scornfully again. She was unimpressed by what she thought she saw. "Is this Heaven then? What I could have if I'm good?"

How prosaic and uninspired was this thing called the Mackenzie.

Calmly taking its head into the complete grasp of its claw, the Creature Lilith was now resigned she must perform one of the two ancient laws of Time Without Beginning, (an additional clause of the Law, We Are All). With her face nearly touching that of the being in her clasp, the Creature Lilith took a deep breath. It seemed she was inhaling the very starlight they were both immersed in. Then, without breaking her gaze on the reluctant traveller, she released a stream of light, directly breathing into the Mackenzie's gasping mouth, filling up the stupefied creature with visions it had never known before. Life continuing as it had, purposely dismembering the weak and the vulnerable, so as to remove any vestige of humanity from their existence. Then, to its death bed, where the Mackenzie lay without remorse or regret for her actions, for everything it had done had been a way for it to *pass the time*. The Creature Lilith withheld the breath and looked deeply into the Mackenzie's confounded eyes.

"You asked what this place was. This is where you can travel to understanding, for unlike a Black Hole where all things go to, this is where all things come from." The Creature Lilith resumed the beam of breath, then...

Bang.

A sudden bang of no sound, of light within light, with the power to scorch and bleach all memory of what may have been before. But the Mackenzie did not forget, as she felt herself plunge into a watery world of throbbing red. A thumping heartbeat resounded in her ears, but it was not hers, it came from outside the ruby sphere in which she wrestled. Then came a pulling and pushing sensation, which dragged her blinking into some kind of more ordinary light than of the overwhelming place from where she had just been held. Yet she was still struggling, and gasping for air she let out a wail. Thrashing arms and legs flailed this way and that, desperately trying to find something to seize and hold fast to. She was being lifted, and something warm was being wrapped about her body.

"यह एक लड़की है"

A brown skinned woman in a sari was looking down at her. Mackenzie knew what she was saying.

"It's a girl,"

Consoling the crying young woman on the hessian bed she whispered.

"I'm so sorry Amreeta, the Saddhu was certain this one would be a boy. Perhaps if we give more offerings at the temple, next time we will be blessed."

"But what of this one Maataaji? What do I do with this one?" For the distraught mother life here was hard enough, but now with another mouth to feed, and a girl as well.

"I shall take her to the Science House, where the doctors adopt them. They say, it's for the best." She patted her daughter's hand.

The Mackenzie started screaming. She knew the ghastly truth of where she had arrived, near to where one of her company's research centres was established and one that was exploring organ donation and genetic hybrids.

The Grandmother looked down at the mewling baby in her arms and smiled.

"Good lungs on this one eh?"

Chapter Sixteen

The Creature Lilith was taking a rest. With one eye open and the other closed, she lay dreaming a dream within a dream. The dream was of a tropical frog on a dewy tropical leaf. Small as a thumbnail and emerald green, it lay like the Dreamer herself, quiet and still. The sounds of the rain forest dripped and echoed, echoed and dripped, sending tiny vibrations through the frond on which it sat. It was just being.

The Creature Lilith often visited this particular point in the stream of the Law. It was a good place to rest and replenish. Such deep joy would come bubbling up through the map of her veins, carrying all the wondrous stories of how Beings travel to understanding. Whether bitter or sweet, each path had the same destination. Sometimes, even for a Being such as She, finding an oasis of calm in a dream of a tropical frog, on a dewy tropical leaf, was the wisest choice she could make on her journey through Vitruvian Time.

"We Are All."

The Creature Lilith murmured in her half sleep, and in reply, the small green frog chirruped a tiny croak. How long she had lain there was of no importance. her heart shaped face resting on one hooked arm, the rest of her reclining body lay as if in a hammock, only her cradle was a scoop of starlight. It was strange if one were to watch how the Creature Lilith and the Being known as Angela would flutter and shift in focus. Oscillating between their two appearances; one, a mature human female, the other, much the same, but with talons and claws and great owl wings.

The two Beings were occupying the same space, but both were from, and in, different dimensional layers simultaneously. Their individual particles were indivisible and yet: each was aware of their own singularity. The Creature

Lilith was becalmed in Time, for having performed the ritual of the Old Ways, so as to push the Mackenzie through the Plane of Understanding, quite frankly – she needed a lie down. The energy required for the task was enormous, but in this layered world, as the Being Angela referred to it, existing energy was forever expanding and contracting like the tides of an ocean, regenerating all which had gone before, and all which was to be. Every Being which entered and exited from this place shared the same attention from the Law, whether a Being was in decline, or a World was being born, each were carried on a wave, rippling outwards into infinity, like static from a radio. Listening to these waves was how prayer was answered.

The Creature Lilith loved to discuss this with the Great Men and Women of History who she would visit in dreams. Of course, she would not present herself always in the appearance she manifested now, she would be careful to dress appropriately so as not to cause alarm, and she would only visit those who sent invitational vibrations through the stream of the Law. It would seem rude to appear without a request, 'cold calling' Beings was not the way the Creature Lilith did things. She was like other archetypes of her age, ones who had moved to such an understanding of the Law that they could traverse in Time and Space. Not only that, she was able to listen and hear the movements made by a Being approaching, even from billions of light years away, for when there is understanding of 'We Are All', it is a relatively simple thing to do to feel the presence of All. Self explanatory really, but she did remember the lad from Württemberg had much to ask about this.

"Very untidy chap that Einstein, left an awful mess to clear up, fiddling about with atoms and uranium and such."

Ah, yes! She was deeply moved as to how all Beings travel, in all their different ways towards the Law. Some go by religion, now that certainly could be a confusing and darkly comedic path, waylaying Beings for many an eon or two, after which time there was no guarantee a Being would be any nearer to understanding. Some had the notion understanding We Are All was determined by gender, or even by species! Then there were some power-hungry charlatans who would use the *idea* of the Law to harness for their own personal gain, taking advantage of the fear other Beings carried concerning death.

Dressing up Business as Redemption – hah!

Some Beings take their chances, and just get on with things, with no real desire to understand, but now and again will wonder why their life was such and why their lot always seemed to happen to them. Some would sense the Law and would try to harness it for their own personal gain. Now these Beings were very entertaining, and had raised a wry smile on the Creature Lilith's face many a time through their comic escapades, running around for ridiculously long periods of time. Her most favourite variety, with whom she engaged with most, were those who sought understanding through Science. Fascinating creatures, so determined to synthesize everything and anything into a formula or concrete definition, when all the time the answer they were seeking was right in front of them, all around them and inside them. It was simply 'We Are All'. It embraced all, and was all, forever changing, forever still. Nonetheless, the Creature Lilith thoroughly relished administering a gentle influence here and there. A little persuasion might steer their behaviour in more predictable ways, without imposing her own view. It left Beings the option of free will. That was the theory at least but in practise it was a different matter entirely, and generally very repetitive. It was infuriating how slow they were to learn. But in her own personal journey to deeper understanding, the Creature Lilith knew non-judgement was necessary to deepen her own patience and compassion.

How very irksome it is though, to witness time and again, Beings missing the bloody point. How many wars? How many starving? How many fools thinking they should be King?

One time she had spent a delightful afternoon in an alabaster palace, situated in the Southern Hemisphere of the Being Angela's world. Some idiot ruler having amassed an obscene amount of wealth and power had called a Holy man to converse with him. Really what he wanted was assurance that he was bound for what he thought of as eternal glory, due entirely, or so he thought, to all his impressive material achievements and wealth. Surely he would be reborn in a state of true understanding? The Creature Lilith remembered hardly being able to contain her mirth when just at that moment, a long line of ants came trooping across the cool marble floors, passing between the King and the guru. After a pause in the conversation, the Holy Man gestured to the insects and blithely said,

"Emperors all."

He then promptly got up and left. Though she had journeyed since, the length and breadth of Time, the Creature Lilith knew very little had changed for most Beings which travelled. They were slow to evolve.

Such funny things, and yet We do love them so.

Her closed eyelid flickered. The small tropical frog on the dewy tropical leaf had jumped, just one jump forward, across his green leaf kingdom. Soon he would leap beyond its edges, and the Creature Lilith would wake.

For now she stirred in her one-eyed sleep. The other eye, was watching for ripples, keeping vigil over the pool of light where her resting head hovered on a pillow of night. When she had pushed the Mackenzie through, the beautiful darkness had returned to act as shelter to her depleted form. If viewed from the world below, her position would appear to be a night full of stars. Here though, looking down, the pool of light at her side was an opening of possibility, an outcome reserved for the Mackenzie alone, and tailored for her alone by the Mackenzie's own choices. Direct intervention such as this was a rare event for the Creature Lilith, but there was only so much that she would tolerate, and though she knew she would face outcomes herself from this action, she considered it a small price to pay for this necessary transgression.

For the meantime she lay with one eye open to the stars about her, each one a window onto another possibility. Her free hand still held tight onto the cord of light attached to the Mackenzie in her new state. A wailing, impoverished female child, born as a beggar, onto a mountain of landfill, where her new family scraped a paltry existence from the rubbish of the wealthy. It was dirty work, but apparently in this world, Beings such as these had to do it.

She glanced back into the flickering form of the Being Angela, and through the exchanging quantum of light, She and She communed on truths, such as how photons of light might carry thought, and with thoughts, prayers were heard. Photons bounced off the two sisters' faces like a sprinkling of refreshing rain. Hundreds of trillions of particles whose paths were interrupted by their smiles found their direction forever changed. It was the most the Creature Lilith could give the Being Angela, and she knew much of this knowledge would be mislaid in the mortal's return to her world. Nevertheless, the Being Angela would be forever elevated in her understanding now, and perhaps by this, might in turn influence the journeys of others in her world. The Creature Lilith hoped so, and hope was a powerful force that Beings from all directions had yet to fully comprehend.

Suddenly, there was a tug on the cord of light and the Creature Lilith resumed her watch. Something was happening down in the Mackenzie's new state. She widened her wakeful eye to focus more attentively.

The Old Woman trudged up through the stinking heap. It was early morning, and already a foul smelling miasma was rising with the heat, but the Old Woman had lived so long with this rancid vapour in her chest, she no longer gave it any attention. Generations of her family had once lived in fresh smelling air, farming in the valley below the mountains outside of this sprawling city. It had been a meagre living, that was true, but at least back then she could hear the wind in the trees when she surrendered to sleep after a hard day's labour. Her family seemed more content then and would attend the temple with their treasured bowls of rice and sprigs of hand-picked flowers, gathered from the valley base of the mountains overlooking their lives. All changed when her husband died and their children's hungry bellies were empty. So she had come here to the detritus and dirt, in the hope of something better. Something better! That's what the others had told her.

"Come and collect glass, and plastic, and cloth. If you're clever you can get a shop on the rubbish mountain itself. Ganesha, the remover of obstacles will help you!"

Then they coaxed her some more by adding tales of real treasure sometimes found and a story would be told, of a son of a friend's friend finding a gold watch, or collecting enough discarded rupees to buy a small scooter. This story ended with the young man going on to taxi for an eminent businessman, who then benevolently took all their family into his grounds to live and work. The Old Woman sighed as she reached the peak of the putrid mountain. Her mother used to tell her stories too, in which everything would become right, but lost gold watches and winning a broken glass lottery was not a story she wanted to tell her grandchildren.

She looked down into the cotton papoose tightly bound against her. Such a lovely little girl, if she had her way she would not be walking to the Science House to give her away, but she knew she must. It would be better for the child than to remain here. Already she could see the scrabbling bent figures of the ghetto children, climbing the levels with sacks in their grimy hands, foraging for whatever they might find of value. Some were fighting over broken computer parts, while scavenger birds circled overhead. At the far off gateway another full-to-bursting rubbish truck was pulling in with more filthy treasure to salvage.

"Well my Little One, soon you will be clean. No more make do or hunger for you!"

The child started screaming as her Grandmother spoke. Never had the Old Woman known such a child for crying. The neighbours next to their tarpaulin hovel had usually been very accepting of noise, you had to be, it was live and let live in a place like theirs. But even they were driven to distraction by the howling of this latest baby.

"You must be feeding her too much!" they joked.

If only that were true, then she would not be standing on this hilltop of decaying debris, trying to memorise the features of her granddaughter's face before she gave her away to a stranger. This gift was a baby of just seven days old, and the Old Woman knew she would never see her again. None of the children who went to the doctors at the Science House were ever seen again. The Old Woman imagined the life the little girl was soon to have, with clean sheets and hot food, bath time and books. Yes, books! She would have an education. She would be able to read, and one day might come back to tear down this mountain, so that trees might be planted for the wind to play in. All these hopes were whispered into the ears of the crying infant. Most especially, she hoped somehow her love would be remembered. Such a love, that was strong enough to give her Little One away. For a moment the baby stopped crying and opened her puffy red eyes to look up at the Old Woman, observing her dark eyes and the curious crescent birthmark on her wrinkled cheek. Her Grandmother's face, leathered by a life of relentless struggle, had never lost the hope she carried for her children. Hope was all she had. A tear fell from her eye onto the baby's face and it began to cry again.

"Well I hope you don't make that noise when they give you your first bath time my Little One," she chuckled.

The refuse truck set her down on the dusty roadside.

"You'll have to make your way from here yourself Maataaji," The driver called before leaving. "Here, take this for the journey!" and he threw down a soft drink can. It had a smiling face of a young woman in a glamorous sari on its side. Beautiful teeth and hair shone with cleanliness. The Old Woman regarded the face and smiled back. Perhaps this was a sign of her Little One's future success. Tucking the can into the cloth of the papoose, she started to walk the long track to the Science House.

The Being Angela was watching now, through the open eye of her winged companion. Mesmerising at first, Angela witnessed, as if through a spy glass, the domed world spread deep below, with every happening and Being on its surface was visible to her, every building, leaf and tree in the constant moment of the world they watched. If a closer view was needed, the Creature Lilith simply squeezed gently on the cord of light in her hand for the scene in question to jump into focus for closer inspection. The Creature Lillith quite enjoyed this process, remarking to the Being Angela on her apparent significant influence upon 20th century cinema. Not that she wanted to brag, though she did admit vanity might be a flaw in her psyche, but no Being is completely perfect. As the Creature Lilith was later to remark,

"All Beings are a work in progress, and a Being's work is never done. There is always room for improvement."

Down in the convex world, they watched the Old Woman trudge on, carrying her precious cargo. Walking for nearly two days, she was clearly exhausted. Milk had been begged along the way from a passing farmer, herding goats. Another man helped with a ride in his straw filled cart and she had slept in its warmth for an hour before he set her down. The Old Woman felt a little sad to leave the creaking carriage. The smell of the straw and the rocking wheels had given her the sweetest sleep she'd had in years. A sleep not had since she had left for the city. So now she walked on, determined at least one of her family would be saved from remorseless toil. That night, curling her body around the baby in an abandoned goatherd's hut, she thanked the Gods for watching over them, and sent up a prayer for her Granddaughter to stop crying.

Yes it is difficult not to interfere, the Owl Woman replied to her companion's thoughtful questions. *But lessons are best learned through experience don't you think? Here, We are just presenting our friend with possible outcomes. The Being will in time come to 'We Are All', but the Being must decide how long its journey will be by the choices it makes. We cannot force it to make a choice against its will. No one can. Anything forced on a Being against its will is not a choice.*

The Being Angela drew nearer to see, intrigued by how exactly `the Creature Lilith controlled the cord she was holding.

Would you like to try? Here, take it for a moment.

Suddenly the Being Angela felt the cord of light pulsing in her hand, pouring through her fingertips and up her arms, until it filled her entire being with a tingling sensation bubbling in every molecule. It was somewhat akin to lying in the shallow surf on a shoreline as frothy waves rushed over her. She gasped in her thoughts.

I know this! The garden and the Blackbird – Mr. Messenger!

Her tutor smiled.

Ah yes, the Being Gabriel is a fine ambassador, but please pay attention, in order for the continuum of the energy flow to be maintained, you must allow the Law to flow back from you.

How on earth do I do that?

The Being Angela was perplexed.

May We remind you Dear One, you are not in Kansas now?

The Creature Lilith chuckled, she thought herself terribly amusing but had in fact a dreadful sense of humour. She was forever quoting 20th century-isms, for she considered it an interesting era, albeit a little kitsch.

Perhaps this might help, We have visited these Beings in your world to offer singing lessons from time to time, and We know how you enjoy singing!

In an instant, the Being Angela was transported into the body of a dark haired woman, dressed in fur and skins and standing in a circle of seated people in similar dress. A soapstone trough filled with a blubber-fat fire burned in the centre of the wood lined room. Its light, and that of the soapstone lamps hanging from the eaves, lit the faces of some twenty hide robed people. Flickering shadows danced across their weathered faces, almond eyes glistened in the lamp light, and a smell of earth and moss pervaded everywhere.

Each person in the circle listened intently to each other, swaying and moving as one, while a man softly tapped a rhythm on a circular skinned drum. The tribe's outstretched, open hands waved to and fro, capturing the drum beat as it was released into the air. Then, when the beat fused with her heartbeat, the Being Angela found herself singing, inhaling high notes through her nose, and then dropping quickly into low notes as she exhaled through her mouth. As the drummer listened to her increasing breath, his beat kept pace with her guttural notes. Playing amid the two tonal sounds by the muscular changes she made with her lips, Angela created a circle of sound until, there in the centre, she sensed a third sound. It was an unmistakable constant drone between the two: the buzzing sound of silence. When the circular song was completed, the hide skin woman sat down and an old, old man stood up to speak. Around the sod house, a wind curled and sang over its roof.

"The Spirits of the Great Raven are with us all tonight. Thank you Anernurk."

Oh. I understand now.

As quickly as the understanding fell into her mind, the Being Angela immediately returned to the pool where the Creature Lilith was resting. With the cord of light pulsing through her, she sent a thought of what she wanted to see, down into the umbilical. The convex turned, and there on a dusty track walked the Old Woman, only now her steps were slower than before, as one foot dragged after the other. The celestial pair watched as the Old Woman approached a large wire fenced compound, guarded at its entrance by a uniformed young man. Beyond this stood a large white and windowless building. The only visible door was set to one side of an L-shaped annex projecting from the right.

"Namaste," The Old Woman bowed to the sentry with her hands palm to palm.

"Namaste Maataaji. What are you wanting here?"

The young man was proud of his officialdom, and adjusted the calico jacket of his uniform. The name on his badge was written in English and said 'Rishi', but the Old Woman had never learned to read. However she could understand pictures, and the small logo of the World held in a cupped hand told her she was in the right place. A long while before, some foreign doctors had come to the rubbish mountain, to offer help they said. They had seen so much desperation in that place, that as well as offering some medicine and clothes, they said they could give the children a fresh start.

They had a 'Science House' outside of the city and from there the children might be freed from all these sorrows of poverty.

Many of the first children to go thought it a great adventure, promising their families to send back whatever good fortune they could. There were so many tears, but it was the only way out that the downtrodden parents could see, so they tied small keepsakes to the children's wrists and ankles. Some even managed to make necklaces from beads they had found and placed these around thin necks, making their children promise not to forget them. The doctors seemed so kind, and listened so attentively to them through the interpreters that they won the destitute diggers' trust and the children – mostly girls, were taken away. Each doctor wore a badge of the World in a cupped hand.

Rishi looked the frail Old Woman up and down. She reminded him of his own Grandmother who he missed so badly. He had been recruited to this lonely place from a village hundreds of miles from here and it felt too long a stay for a country boy like him, but it had been a chance of a lifetime for his family ensuring regular money sent home.

The Company was keen to only employ workers who had no connection with the area, which was curious as there was migration from all across the country. Even here the World was shrinking. Working in shifts, his counterpart would relieve him after ten hours in the security hut. To Rishi his hut was a palace, with a little stove and a rickety bed. He even had a radio on which he could listen to the wider world. In moments of tedium the pop songs of Bollywood would sometime possess him. Then he would dance around the shack using his walkie-talkie as a mock microphone, making believe he was a cinema star. On one occasion he had left the walkie-talkie on and inadvertently entertained his co-workers on the speaker system throughout the complex. His colleagues, being bored also, decided this was too good an opportunity to miss in ribbing him with hoax calls over the two-way radio.

One of the gang thought himself an excellent mimic, and in the sweetest old lady voice, teased Rishi to distraction.

"Rishi-Jaan, Rishi-Jann, my Darling. What do you think you're doing? Dancing round like a monkey buggar!"

"Rishi-putra, my Son. Are you well? Is your throat sore? 'Cause you might think that you're Mukesh, but you sound like a coughing crow!"

"Rishi, Rishi, my Mishti, my Sweet. Are you washing properly? Cause I can smell you from here in the village and you're stinking like buffalo dung!"

The sound of four grown men, buckled in fits of eye watering laughter would follow over the speaker, and Rishi would blush and shuffle and frown. This baiting continued until, remembering his Grandmother's obsession with regularity, Rishi shared his homemade lassi with the jokers, adding the ingredient of his beloved Grandmother's special triphala churna.

The potent laxative meant he was left alone after this. His Grandmother would have approved. She always had a mischievous twinkle in her eye.

Only occasionally the telephone would ring and a deadened flat voice would give him directions. His employers were a strange people, rarely seen by either himself or his colleagues. They had disappeared for the last six months, he had heard rumours there had been something called 'bad press' which had shamed them, and had brought uninvited visits from more people abroad. Rishi understood shame, dishonour was considered a sin in his upbringing. When you are poor, your wealth is your reputation. Whatever they had done, they had left quickly and the building was largely locked up, and serviced only by a skeleton crew necessary for security and maintenance. Rishi had arrived as they were leaving, so he had only a brief memory of their departing vehicles speeding away in the dust. The last one out of the compound shouted some final commands at Rishi's Supervisor from the back seat of a limousine. For reasons unknown, the man was angry. He was baring his teeth like the wild dogs back home. The image that stayed with Rishi for a long time, was a moment when the doctor's sunglasses fell, revealing a pair of the coldest, narrow dead eyes imaginable. Rishi had seen eyes like those in a European magazine left in a train station waiting room. It was The National Geographic, and the eyes were of a Great White Shark. Sometimes, even now, when Rishi was really homesick and scared, he dreamt of the Shark Man in the last car leaving.

"Come into the shade Maataaji, I will bring you something to drink."

In the relative cool of the hut, the Old Woman sat sipping fruit juice from a plastic cup.

Plastic, everything is made from plastic these days.

Even the chair Rishi offered her was plastic, making the heat stick to her resting arms.

"Who have you got in there Maataaji?" he asked cheerfully, pointing to the bundle she still carried.

"My Granddaughter, we came to see the doctors," and she gently patted the grizzling baby on the bottom to comfort her.

"What is wrong with her?" Rishi had arrived long after any children had been at the compound.

"Nothing, there is nothing wrong with her." The Old Woman looked down at her small charge and smiled. "She is perfect. When will the doctors return?"

"I don't know, they haven't been here for a long time. I could ask my Supervisor when he arrives tonight. Where are you staying?"

"The Taj Mahal Palace," the Old Woman replied dryly. It took a moment for young Rishi to realize she was making a joke.

He could see from her clothes and worn fingers she was tired to the bone of being poor.

"Maataaji, would you do me the honour of sharing some supper with me? I hardly see anyone here on this job, and you and your Granddaughter look like you could both do with a rest. When my shift is over, I go up to the white building and sleep in one of the cots stored in the hall. There's plenty there. We're still clearing them from the dormitories. You could rest for the night, and I will try to find you a doctor for the child. What is her name?"

"She is only nine days old, I haven't given her name to her yet."

He was a kind young man, and reminded the Old Woman of her husband when she had first met him, practical and eager to please. She accepted the invitation. When the sun was lower in the sky and the next guard relieved his shift, they ambled across the compound to the annex and an evening meal of lentil dhal and chapattis. While Rishi prepared this offering, the Old Woman looked at where she was to sleep. They were in a long sterile room, with double doors at either end. Tables and chairs were stacked together, as if just delivered or waiting to go somewhere else. Rishi had taken down a table and two chairs. He was delighted to have company at last and he wanted to impress the old woman as though she were a visitor from home. In a way she was. He fussed and clucked and pampered her as best he could.

The Old Woman found this highly amusing and stifled several chuckles to preserve his dignity. Men were not supposed to serve women, especially ones of her caste, but she was tired, and it seemed to make him happy, so she played along as honorary grandmother. The little family sat and ate and chatted about their villages, how much they missed them and what was wrong with the World now, while the baby continued to cry. On finishing their meal, Rishi went to find another cot from the stack while she peeled lychees from a plastic bowl.

No doctors, oh well.

Sleep was beginning to weigh heavy on her eyes. Having decided to let her life now be guided by the Gods, she had found no answers to help the child now. The baby seemed to have quietened, for she was as exhausted as her carer. No amount of screaming and wailing had made her conscious mind known to her bearer. Nodding with fatigue, the Old Woman dropped a lychee and watched it roll away across the tiled floor, stopping next to some bulging refuse sacks labelled with parcel tags. Not wishing to waste good food, she went to retrieve it, and as she did, could not help herself from sneaking a look inside the bags. It was force of habit.

Sometimes you might find treasure!

Her wrinkled hand froze. What she held had made her old heart clench with anguish. A bangle made from glass beads and strung on a plait of remnants of sari cloth. It was a keepsake from one of the children who had gone before, made by a loving, but painfully poor parent thinking they were doing the best they could. It wasn't just one keepsake, the whole bag was full of them. Tearing open the other sacks it was the same, keepsakes and leftover belongings of children on a great adventure. It sent a chill through her tired bones, and if the Old Woman had been able to read, she would have seen the labels spelled, 'Incinerate'.

"Good news Maataaji, my Supervisor says they will be here next week. The doctors, they're coming back!"

But the hallway was empty. The Old Woman and the baby had gone.

It was nearly dark, and the stars were twinkling above them. Far away was the faint glow of the city, something new since the Old Woman had been a girl. So many things had changed. Finding a dry ditch by a Banyan tree she lay down out of the wind, wrapping her threadbare sari around the baby in her arms. This was the only answer she had left. It was an old tradition in which a girl child was left to the Gods when there were too many mouths to feed. It was the custom for the child to be abandoned alone, but the Old Woman was too tired and could not bring herself to leave the girl child now. It was something no mother she had known ever wanted to do, but in this world, girls were not seen as valuable. Value was given to a gold watch, or a piece of plastic, or a boy. Yes, everything had changed, and yet the Old Woman knew of the important things which never changed. She held her Granddaughter closer. This tiny heart was ten days old now, old enough for naming. Taking the lucky soda can from the papoose, she poured a little over the baby's head, and whispered into her right ear,

"Namaste, I bow to the Divine in you and I give you the name Bela, and the name Ananta. They are yours, and all I have to give you, with my love, my Dear One, for Time without end."

Under the rising full moon, the Old Woman rested her head with the World as her pillow, for she was so very tired and yearned for the shroud of sleep. The stars looked down from their portholes of light, watching the Old Woman and the baby in the ditch as they died. Above their heads, the wind played through the leaves and both dying Beings clung to the other as they journeyed on.

Chapter Seventeen

The bead of dew slipped off the leaf as the tiny tropical frog leapt from its emerald throne and into the dark oblivion beyond. The Creature Lilith opened her one sleeping eye and was awake.

Now We pull.

She instructed in thought to the Being Angela, and they began. The surge of the vibrating currents was immense, and the apprentice was amazed to feel the heavy tug from the world below. It was similar to pulling wet clothes from the depth of a pool, weighted and resistant, but the more they pulled, the lighter it became. In the umbilical cord of light which linked them to Beings below, colours curled in and out and through its length, reorganizing the ascending bubbles rising from the two deceased bodies in the far away ditch. The cord's depth appeared to be bottomless, and heaving the pulsing atoms through the pool of light, the Being Angela could see how the particles were reforming into a human shape, and into the Being Mackenzie. But as the other molecules were pulled through the porthole, they burst outwards, dispersing their scintilla-like phosphorescence onto the starry sea. The Being Angela felt a connecting thrill as they spread, for rushing to meet them, came wave upon wave of other particles. As they mingled, the newly dispersed particles were carried away. What was left in their talons and hands was the emerging body of the Mackenzie.

"What have you done to me?" she screamed, her wild eyes were bloodshot and weeping, and she twisted and turned like bait on a hook. The Creature Lilith was unperturbed, knowing the deed was done and the outcome successful. Using her flight feathers, she gently stroked the distraught Mackenzie into calm, and patiently waited to speak.

"You've put something into me!" the Mackenzie sobbed, choking out its words. "What are these things under my skin? I can see them wriggling. Are they parasites? Tell me!"

Sure enough, just below the surface of her reconstituting tissue, rivulets of colour were weaving into threads, stopping at junctions of limbs as if to converse and exchange directions, then they would suddenly turn and disappear under, only to re-surface again at another site on the Mackenzie body. They had purpose.

"Are they nanomites? They're doing something, I can feel it!"

The Mackenzie was out of control and it terrified her. The Being Angela could see that although the writhing form before her was mostly the same, something, as yet indefinable, had changed within it.

"Nanomites? No, these particles are of a far deeper refinement than crude microscopic robots. You are merely experiencing Dual Molecular Dispersal Transference at what you might term, a sub-atomic level, or which other Beings in your world call..." at this The Creature Lilith stretched backwards and yawned, before uttering, "Death."

The Mackenzie was silent, and returned her captor's gaze with confusion.

"To be as precise as We can, during the process of Dual Molecular Dispersal Transference or DMDT as We call it, vibrational residue occurs, whereby one Being will overflow and leave a partial impart into another Being. Dispersal is after all, something all Beings will experience in their journey to understanding We Are All."

The Mackenzie gasped as the full ramifications were beginning to dawn in her.

"You mean this is only something like an echo in my body?" she stuttered.

'Not an echo – more of a merging if you will. A Being experiencing DMDT will then carry the temporal DNA of the transferring other.'

A look of utter repulsion surfaced on the Mackenzie's face. She had thought herself impervious and separate to others, that she was of a Higher species and set apart. While lesser mortals had yearned to find some kind of belonging, the Mackenzie had arrogantly strutted through her earthly life revelling in her singularity, she had proudly considered herself to be the only one of any importance. This had maintained for her an unquestionable and steel-like sense of Self, and had bestowed on her from birth the belief she had an unequivocal right to dismiss all others as lowly and of no importance. Now running through her veins was the irrefutable truth that she was not alone, making her sense of glorious, singular coherence dissolve. What remained was a tangible vibration of the Old Woman who had been her Grandmother in the world just gone, a beggar and a benign one at that – a kindly grandmother. Battling to reform back to her familiar self, she was wracked with contempt and self loathing; to the Mackenzie this had been a desecration of the grossest kind.

"You mean to say, you have infected me with that pathetic old hag?" she protested. "What was that place, a phantom? Have I been drugged? Am I now dead, or is this my imagining?"

The Owl Woman's reply was erudite, but her tone had something of the monotonous drawl of an air stewardess about it.

'Not at all, the world you left is real enough, it is but a possible outcome, created directly from your own choices."

"I didn't choose to go there! Why would I choose to go to a stinking piss hole like that? Do you think I am insane?"

The Being Angela expected a retort from her tutor for this particular remark, but instead she calmly repeated.

"It is but a possible outcome, created directly from your own choices. Your denial cannot become Truth."

The Mackenzie was clawing at her skin now. The coloured threads of light were forming a fabric beneath the surface and integrating into the muscle and bone and blood.

"But I can feel her in me," she retched with revulsion, "I can feel this overwhelming love for me! She has impregnated me! I am violated! Now I am..."

Then catching her words in mid sermon, the Mackenzie's eyes widened realising the bitter implications.

"and now I am compelled to do the same! I am fractured. I am a flawed and weak creation, because I now have feelings, like every other grovelling gutter waste! I am imperfect!"

She fell into a heap of despair, copious tears of loss for her departed, impenetrable self and, if truth be known, tears of grief for the Old Woman known as Maataaji who had cared for her. This was the worst thing of all, and for the Mackenzie it was an absolute disaster. These repugnant emotions she was now party to filled her with dread and raised questions as to her survival. The Mackenzie knew that in the world from which she had been kidnapped, there were those who could sense differences and vulnerabilities in their playthings; familial ones who would delight in finding new and unique ways to pass their time at the expense of others. She knew this for she had been one of them herself. Lifting a heavy head she entreated.

"So what now? What do I do now? Is there a cure?"

The Creature Lilith found this to be enormously funny and only just stemmed her laughter. It was vital not to judge when guiding Beings to a deeper understanding of We Are All. However, it was archly comical, for despite having ventured into different dimensional strata, the Mackenzie was still completely unaware of the cold-faced irony in the drama she played an active part in.

"Outcomes change as Beings change their choices," was the blank reply. "We Are All."

Clutching the Mackenzie firmly in her grip, the Creature Lilith brought it close to her saucer-large eyes and inspected its completed form by turning it this way and that to check for any changes. The particles had finally settled and returned the shape of the former Being in all but one physical detail; a tiny, barely noticeable crescent-shaped blemish on the Mackenzie's cheek. Satisfied that everything was as it should be, the taloned hand relaxed to become a cradle. The reluctant passenger was stupefied, and quickly fell into torpor, repeating a mantra over and over again under its breath.

"We Are All... We Are All... We Are All..."

Rising up and spreading her enormous owl wings, the Creature Lilith was indeed a magisterial figure, commanding an authority of Ages Old, but for a brief moment there appeared an expression on her heart-shaped face which alluded to a weary sadness carried there. A sudden rush of sympathy welled up into the Being Angela, for despite the fierce nobility of the goddess before her, there was a manifest tender affection towards the little monster she carried in her palm, and this hint of humanity overwhelmed her witness.

Such a lonely way to travel, you do so much and yet are rarely known for what you do.

The Owl Woman began to laugh.

Oh Dear One! We are far from lonely as We journey deeper into We Are All. Can you not feel it? We Are All is here, now, around us and in us, permeating through all the Layered Worlds?

The words poured from her with a resonance of multiple sounds, as if all the bells in all the worlds were ringing at once. Then, suddenly the indigo sky in which they both floated peeled back a layer, unveiling a throng of Beings cascading and migrating in and out of each other. Awestruck, the Being Angela found herself brushing them away from her face like gossamer spider's silk. The most extraordinary thing was every single Being was aware of the other, and each was a part of a larger formation of waves pushing forwards and onwards. Waves circling became millions and billions, until they all became part of a starlight murmuration: a current of Beings of one mind. Seeing that the spectacle had made her companion tremble, the Creature Lilith wrapped her wings around the Being Angela so as to reassure her, and when she outspread them again, the startling vision had gone from their sight. The Creature Lilith had no desire to traumatize her young charge, for despite her ferocious nature, she was nevertheless maternal, and this was effectively a child she was guiding.

Now Dear One, We must leave, places to go, Beings to meet and so forth. You must gather your strength. Be watchful. Be mindful. Prepare your face for the faces you are to meet.

The Being Angela looked anxious.

How long before we meet again? I mean, will we meet again?

She was indeed a child. The Matriarch paused for a moment and then patiently replied,

A Being We once met with said, "...being with you, and not being with you, is the only way I have to measure Time." As to outcomes of meeting, well, that will depend upon the choices you make, and We trust you will make wise choices to that end.

They talked at length. The Being Angela listened attentively, reading her pilot's parting thoughts. She was to return to her world and plan her choices to come, whilst the Creature Lilith was to travel on with the Mackenzie to an undisclosed destination.

Away into the indigo night, the thought forms of the Creature Lilith and the Being Angela began to separate. Their farewell gestures melted like the reversing film of waking dreamers. This was the way Beings would often learn in the Layered Worlds, sometimes slowly remembering fragments as if waking from a dream. However, the Being Angela remembered it all, or rather, as much as any mortal mind was able to without breaking their sanity.

They have such tender frames and sensibilities.

For now Angela was going back to her world, with her memory mostly intact: unlike the Mackenzie.

Chapter Eighteen

"Viva!"

A gargantuan piñata exploded, 'BANG!' just above their heads, sending down snowstorms of confetti and streamers, all emblazoned with the logo, 'Viva!' The baited breath of the audience rang out at last with triumphant applause. They had been held captive, waiting for this High Priestess of Song to give her next command, and here it was, 'Viva!'

Long afterwards, recollections of the night were many and varied, but the most commonly voiced accounts suggested a feeling of everything and everyone being held together in a moment of Time. It would stay with them as one of the most memorable events of their lives, though curiously many details were altogether absent. Certainly in the days that followed, it seemed there may have been some problem with the food. The doctors present had come to the aid of some of the night's guests, and due to the many disorientated party goers ending up in A & E with gastric complaints, a call to the local Environmental Health officer was made. Thankfully for Chef Trevor, nothing was found within the dinner remains to be either contaminated or illegal. After robust reprimands had been made, to the effect that a sound knowledge of foreign ingredients would be better advised for any future culinary experiments, the matter was closed to the great relief of both the Conference centre management and the Hospital Charity who had, in effect, commissioned it. However, the nervous apprentice Commis chef did take note of the experience and one night, a Eureka moment struck him as to how he could use this knowledge to his own advantage. In time, his adventurous concoctions were discovered as festival favourite 'legal highs' and, even appeared at the top of a Sunday supplement's list of best seller alternative cookery books, entitled 'Freak Out Foods and Tempting Trips'.

But that was for another time away from this summer night.

"Viva! Viva! Viva!"

The whole crowd were chanting and Paul Hollingsworth could not have been happier. Angeliquita was magnificent. How she had achieved this he had no idea. The Woman was incredible. Perhaps it was a hydraulic boom giving her the illusion of flight in the Grand Finale. No matter, he didn't care, for already the internet was flooded with mobile phone uploads of this moment.

"Viva! Viva! Viva!"

Whatever had happened to the camera crew was of no consequence either now. A late arriving local news team were on the spot to report the last exclamations of a uniquely entertaining night. Jackie Brent had an exclusive and was delivering a gushing commentary on the show.

"As we look across at the adoring audience, we can see the discovery of our own, home grown Stars, 'Los Diablos', with a glittering performance from 'Angeliquita', the shimmering songstress who has won every heart here – truly the People's choice!"

Paul clapped his hands and let out a cheer. This was so much better than he had hoped for. Top advertising companies could not have done more than this.

He decided from that moment on to continue listening to his gut feeling. It had always served him well in the early days and somewhere along the line, he'd forgotten how to use it. That was about the same time his business began to show tiny fractures and profits started to fall. *Never again though.* He had put too much into it and too many people now relied on the business for their living. Besides that, he couldn't have built it without them. The night of the Summer Stars Ball became a turning point for Paul Hollingsworth, and not just because of the upturn in the Viva! Product fortunes. Paul had felt something shift in what he supposed was 'trusting his instinct', though Angela would give another interpretation. Even so, as Paul looked around him, he felt a renewed connection within his life. His life had until tonight, seemed like a forgotten coat in a cloakroom. All this had changed by following an idea from the Rendezvous Café. Things were fitting into place, and he knew he was in the right place and at the right time. Looking over at a strange noise to his left, he realised the Ellis woman however, was clearly out of step, having had no inkling someone else would commandeer the show. The distraught and dishevelled Helen appeared to be slumped on Angela's chair at the Finance table, babbling to herself whilst scratching what looked like tallies on the table top with a cheese knife. The roving spotlight finally found its destination, allowing perfect footage of an apparently demented Helen, unflattering as it was, to appear on the internet the next day.

Not a single person in the audience wanted Angeliquita to go, she was their sweetheart siren who belonged to them all now, and a desperate fervour began to mount. Rapidly the situation was becoming more than little tense, as the crowd closed in towards the stage, hopeful of seizing just a moment longer in her presence. People began clamouring to be at the front, and some tumbled over, nearly crushing poor Tina and several others around her. Becoming increasingly desperate in the noise and crush she frantically blew on the bird whistle in the hope of attracting attention from above.

"Peenk!"

Angela could see the danger, and pulled Tina up onto the stage to safety. As she did, she watched Mackenzie's dark suited associates, alerted by the sudden appearance of a television crew, disappear like cockroaches, along balconies and through exits. Their commandant was gone, leaving their assignment defunct. The only evidence of Mackenzie Davis having been there was a still lit cigarette smouldering in an ashtray, and a pair of handmade silk shoes tumbled beneath an empty chair. As only a few had noticed her there, only a few noticed her gone, and then only briefly. People disappear all the time. Thankfully, this time it was Mackenzie Davis and not Angela Bagner. For although Angela's winged persona had retreated to a degree, she was under no illusion, the flight into the other Layered Worlds had not been a dream. She did not mistake the imminent peril to be over: this was but a lull in the tide. Sensing possibilities spreading out across distant fields of Time, she perceived there was potentially more to come. Vigilance would be key to predetermine her own possible outcomes. Despite all her experiences there would be no time for rest just now. Angela could feel the Creature Lilith in her being, fluctuating in her consciousness. The movements within her were incredible and she knew this was because she and Lilith were ultimately the same expression of the Law and that the two female entities could never be parted, regardless of Time and Space.

With barely time to feel relief at her escape from Mackenzie's plans, Angela knew it was time to go. The fitter members of the adoring and somewhat intoxicated crowd were starting to climb onto the stage, but how to make her exit safely? It had to be without raising suspicions of her acrobatics being more than extravagant stage effects. As Angela quickly gauged her options the loud buzzing of rotor blades came roaring down and a moment later the helicopter, showering the uplifted faces of the audience with scented petals, hovered closer to the rooftop. A typhoon of streamers, hairpieces and feathers blew away from the dancers underneath. Paul Hollingworth smiled widely, showing the glint of a gold tooth. His old flying buddy had come up trumps with the perfect solution.

Holy-moly, you pulled a blinder there Paul me ole' mucker!

"Viva! Viva! Viva!"

An unfurling banner, screaming the Viva! slogan dropped from the helicopter. Beyond the banner Angela glimpsed that it was weighted down by an emergency rope ladder that backed it, and she seized her opportunity. Holding Eddie's face with both hands, she kissed him firmly on the mouth and said,

"We'll see each other soon, okay?"

Then grabbing the lower rung, she stepped on, blowing kisses and chanting 'Viva!' with the cheering crowd below. Just above her, a smiling figure was yelling down to her with an outstretched arm.

"Come on, everything will be right now!"

Safely transported away from the rooftop, Angela thanked her angels of sorts, two very nice young pilots, one called Gavin, the other, Rory.

"You have striking blue eyes," Angela mouthed loudly over the engine noise.

Thinking she was passing a flirtation, the young man blushed and laughed off any connection, insisting he had inherited his eye colour from his father, along with his mop of fox red hair.

"How long have you known Mr. Hollingsworth then?" he asked her on the journey to Paul's estate.

"Oh, hard to say, feels like a long time and yet no time at all."

Arriving within the hour at his mock regency mansion, Angela was offered a royal welcome by Paul's housekeeper, who urged her to wait for his return. Not wishing to explain her feathery appendages, Angela declined, insisting she must rest in her own bed, and would contact him personally at a more convenient time. A chauffeured car carried her home to gather her thoughts.

She was now the captain of her life, and she knew her choices alone would reap the outcomes she desired, though not always necessarily in the way she might picture them. There was much to be done as, quite literally – Time was of the essence. Practical plans must be made to ensure happier circumstances for the people she had come to open her life to. In so many ways she wanted to put her house in order. It was obvious there would have to be necessary changes, and ones which would demand a change of address to begin with if she were to make full use of her Time. However, these changes would also require some careful strategies and a degree of guile. The Mackenzie woman had left a lasting impression on Angela. There was no doubt in her mind others like this person existed out in the World, beyond Angela's former hermitage life. Angela also knew she had not seen the last of the Mackenzie, for she could feel her when, closing her eyes and pausing her thoughts. Tremulous threads tingled in her skin letting her know the tread of the Mackenzie on the Earth.

Angela had choices of course; one was to continue as she had before, with her head down and as little correspondence with others as possible, forgetting these extraordinary events and trying to put them behind her, perhaps rebuilding herself in another inconspicuously beige town somewhere. But like it or not, she had emotionally invested in people: Jenny for example, who had unknowingly helped Angela heal her own grief from a scalded childhood, her neighbours Monsieur Pierre and Miss Bee, who had taken her in as their own, and all the other kind faces she had awoken to in the last weeks.

Smiling to herself Angela listed the many she had warmed to, Tina, Eddie and the boys, James Lockhart, Paul Hollingsworth and his friends. So many lives she felt love for. Good fortune had always been around her, but she had been unable to perceive it. Most of all, she had come to have a loving relationship with herself, and now she would never risk losing this. This left her with the wisest choice she felt best to take. She would settle her affairs in Lossingham, leaving small gateways open so that she might physically visit or connect on occasion, but there would be no more beige wherever she was.

For some months, Number 33 was silent, and though many visitors would come and go, trying their luck by knocking on her door, no one saw or heard from Angela. Jenny in particular was most upset, and would keep a watchful eye on all the traffic in the street in case Miss Bagner came back. The little girl missed her friend.

One morning the letterbox clattered, waking Janice and Elaine from their sleep. Janice stumbled happily downstairs, to find a hand delivered envelope on the hall mat. Yawning as she made coffee and croissants and still half asleep, only when returning to snuggle up to Elaine in the warmth of the quilt, she finally opened it. Out onto the bed covers fell a short note, with plane tickets and hotel reservations paper clipped to the back.

"Hello Young Lovers," Janice read aloud. Elaine laughed at this, spilling crumbs across the bed. "Hello Young Lovers! I have no use for this holiday as I have other travelling plans. Please accept these tickets for your wonderful selves. I hope you always share music wherever you go. Angie."

"Angie, who's Angie?" puzzled Elaine.

"You know, she's the Goddess who brought us together!" Janice giggled. "Shall we go?"

"Funnily enough, it's in just the area I'd like to go house hunting. All those lavender fields and sunshine. I was thinking you might help me."

Much later, in the months and years to come, whilst they held hands in the evening sun on the veranda of the Côte d' Azure home, they often wondered how their friend Angie seemed to know exactly that here was the place they ought to be – growing young together.

Angela had her name to live up to with more than just this pair of lovers. It had been good to meet Eddie and the other Boys in the band. They were a great bunch, and Angela had warmed to them all, but to Eddie most especially. She felt he was a hard working man who deserved to have some of his hopeful ambitions realised, and in a desire to help make his dream come true, had approached Paul Hollingsworth.

Setting out her terms with the understanding she would only allow her name 'brand' to be eponymous with 'Viva!' if she and Los Diablos were fully sponsored in a tour and recording contract. It didn't even pass Paul's mind to simply find another Diva. He knew there was something uniquely magical in Angie as he liked to call her and as she liked to be called. She stipulated her connection with 'Viva!' would be conditional on the product's Fair Trade sources and, for a limited period of time, although renegotiation of any future involvement would still be a possibility. Paul was suitably impressed by her legally acute mind, identifying loopholes and advantages qualified lawyers would miss.

"I've taken a shine to you Angie," he said one day, looking her in the eye, "You're straight with me and I appreciate that. I wonder if you'd like to accompany me to a spot of horse racing? Dress up, drop of champers, you know – dead posh. There are a couple of business associates I'd like you to meet. See if you could give me your opinion on them?"

Angela declined saying that she had some other more pressing commitments involving travel, though she added she intended to continue looking in "from time to time". He never did quite understand why this had caused her to laugh so heartily. Los Diablos were delighted that she had contacted them with her dovetailed business plan. Regardless of her mature years, Angela had fitted into the music of the band like a hand in a glove. Paul recognised there was a bigger opportunity here than just coffee. When at last he approached Los Diablos with an initial management contract, their first assignment involved them being filmed on location in Cuba, assuring them this would be their biggest of breaks.

After the Summer Stars Ball, there was so much widespread publicity, Paul realised he couldn't just restrict Los Diablos to only an advertising campaign. He was going to move into the Music Business, possibly even Film Production. The possibilities seemed endless, as each new idea fed the next. So, to ease into this new world of possibility, Angela acted as Paul's adviser for a long time and they became firm friends.

"You've got an eye of a hawk!" Paul Hollingsworth would often be quoted as saying in the years that followed. "Brains and Beauty! Angela my Dear, you have them both and I've got at least one out of the two. But which one?"

"Careful Paul," Angela teased, "hawks have got rather nasty claws, as beautiful as they no doubt are."

In fact, years later, 'Brains and Beauty' was to be the title of his auto-biography, as to how he had discovered Los Diablos, the world renowned Latin 40s fusion band. He soon realised Angela was not a Woman to be trifled with, and not wishing to threaten his friendship with someone who he had grown to deeply respect, he honoured his promise not to reveal her whereabouts or circumstance to anyone. Anonymity would, in the turn of things, become very important to Angela.

Neither did he forget their meeting when she told him the next concert was to be the last one. Los Diablos were established and he was now a highly successful Music Entrepreneur. It was true Angela was a natural star performer, but the bright lights of fame bore no attraction to her. He had tried to persuade her otherwise, but she had repeated again she didn't desire fame.

"Fame, hah! Really Paul, you ought to know by now I don't need confirmation of my worth from anyone," then she added in a lower tone, "When you don't crave validation, you become a most fearless and fearsome individual."

"But why would you want to be feared?" he had asked. He still bore an endearing streak of naivety.

"Well, the outcomes I am pursuing will make necessary the wearing of armour at times." She answered enigmatically. "It's a matter of knowing your enemy."

No matter how much he pressed her, she would never divulge who her enemy might be, or come to that, who on earth could possibly see her as an enemy. He decided to put it down to Angela being an arty type with eccentric idiosyncrasies. Paul had to admit there were times when she was definitely fearsome, especially when defending people she cared for. Some over-zealous promoter for example, thinking that he could, and would, take more than was contractually agreed, might make the foolish mistake of assuming Angela would be a walkover just on the merits of her being female and of a certain age. That promoter would live to rue his patronising ways, if he dared to cross Angela. Flashing a look of defiance, her voice lowered to the sound of a growling mountain, the gentleman in question would visibly shrink in stature and self esteem, and suddenly relinquish any claim. At all other times however, her now many friends and associates only witnessed Angela to be the epitome of grace and courtesy, with kind, enquiring and reassuring words to all around her wherever she travelled. This was certainly true for the time she spent in their company, though there were episodes when she was absent and her whereabouts, a mystery.

When Tina and Martin opened the letter from the solicitor, they first thought they were being taken to court, but as they read, fell back onto their sofa in astonishment. The letter outlined an instruction from their client Miss. A. Bagner to create a trust fund for all the Collins children, with the condition that as an entire family, they annually attend a musical event chosen by their benefactor, the aforementioned Miss. A. Bagner. The first of these events was to be the International D'Art Lyrique: air tickets and hotel reservations to follow.

"International dart lie-rike? How do you pronounce this Martin?"

"Dunno, but we're going!"

Pierre and Miss Bee sat together under the shade of wide spreading fig trees, outside the Jardins cafe. Miss Bee was dozing, having eaten and drank her fill, the remains of her sugary sweet rum cup only serving wandering ants. Monsieur Pierre smiled and patted Angela's hand. She had just brought another two beers to their table to while away the mellow afternoon. They were listening to some young musicians playing on a low stage in front of a large mural of peasant revolutionary workers. Angela smiled back, Pierre was the closest to a living father she could hope for in this life, for even though he would never be the same as her own, she felt blessed that Pierre allowed her to treat him as such. She felt sure her late Father would have wanted this to be. He never wanted her to be lonely. An invitation to an opportune film shoot had been happily accepted, and now here she was in the bosom of her chosen family. It felt idyllic. Just beyond the wrought iron railings, a little tricycle taxi peddled by along the dusty, palm lined street. A car horn sounded and a polished blue Cadillac pulled up. It was Eddie and his family.

"Hey there! Angie! How are you guys?"

"We're fine. We just had lunch and we're having a bit of a siesta," she answered, nodding in the direction of the sleeping Miss Bee.

"Okay, we're probably doing the same back at the hotel. Need to get some rest before the gig tonight. The kids are all tired out from our trip to Coppelia's ice cream parlour."

This was a bit of an understatement, as his Boys in the back seat were battling each other over a comic book, with drooling ice cream down both their t-shirts. Eddie's partner Sal was sporting a Jackie O style headscarf and sunglasses combo, having successfully zoned out from the Boys' commotion. She possibly had something stronger than ice cream in her system.

"Good idea. I think you both need it," Angela added with some sympathy. "See you later for the sound check!"

"Don't be late now!" Then away he went, puffing on his cigar down a sun drenched Havana street.

Angela turned to Pierre.

"Are you happy Pierre? Are you enjoying this holiday?"

"Awwh, Mizzabahg-nah, youse a hulliday evreeday!" He squeezed her hand. "We'll go bak home soon, but youse allwayze in here." He patted his chest and grinned again, proudly displaying his gold tooth. "You still wears it tho, don't youse?"

"Of course Pierre, I will for always." She held her hand over the talisman hidden by her dress, and although she knew she had no need of it, the powerful thoughts and prayer Pierre had imbued it with, made it something she would treasure forever. Then she kissed the old man gently on his ebony cheek and they both returned to quietly enjoying music in the Cuban sun, both Father and Daughter, feet tapping in perfect rhythm.

Chapter Nineteen

The last person Helen Ellis expected to arrive at her door was Angela Bagner, but there she was, bold as brass as they say, with a glowing complexion and carrying a bunch of flowers no less. It appeared to Helen that her nemesis must have done well for herself. She even looked taller.

"Nice shoes," she found herself blurting out. "Are they Jimmy's?"

Her visitor looked down at her floating feet. She smiled, knowing now how people see what they want to see. It's easier for them that way.

"These old things?" came the throw away answer. "I've had these forever."

The flowers were beautiful. This was surely a confusing way to gloat over her misfortunes. It wasn't the way Helen would have responded, but then, Helen would not have bothered to call at all. She was still smarting from the aftermath of her failed misdemeanours. No matter how much she had tried to wriggle out of her responsibility, all roads had led back to her.

All those carefully diverted telephone messages and medical files concerning Angela, steered directly to Helen as their destination, and the later hospital enquiry found Mrs. Ellis as having compromised the integrity of the hospital's reputation through the fraudulent misappropriation of funds. It was obvious to the doctors now: they had been hoodwinked and were the unwilling victims of a dreadfully crass publicity stunt to promote some cringe worthy television documentary by a superficial television company. *Growing wings! What fools we would look if this was ever made public!* The suspicions raised during James Lockhart's audit had been fully confirmed by the mobile phone records of Helen Ellis' fraudulent enterprises, in the guise of charity.

The rewards of her cheating were very short lived, as Helen really did not have the intellect for highbrow crime, and a local building society is not the place to stash your loot. With the understanding she return all monies received, and that she sign a disclaimer to the effect that she would not reveal any details of the events leading up to and during the Charity Summer Ball, the best resolution for all involved was for her to leave her employment under a cloud. After the secreted funds were returned, the whole matter was hushed up, despite lingering hints and attempted exposés in the Press.

Nick had abandoned her at the first hint of scandal. To his credit he admitted himself as the adulterer, so the decree nisi was more likely to be in Helen's favour as long as Nick didn't contest it by petitioning for custody of the children. He did not. The inevitable divorce ended swiftly with a parting of their ways and distribution of assets, although there was a brief altercation over the ownership of their extensive collection of vinyl records, circa 1977 to 1983. Before the settlement was finalised Helen downsized considerably into rented accommodation, fending for herself and her two children Ruby and Elliot. Her aspirations for her offspring to attend only private schools were now dashed on the gravel drive of her life, or rather now, on the narrow paving stones of her front garden. Ruby and Elliot however flourished with the change in their schooling and began to blossom in confidence as now they didn't feel the pressure to out-perform their peers. They began to enjoy being children at last.

Of course, even in her woeful sorrow and fleeting shame for being caught with her hands in the biscuit tin, Helen began to alter events in her mind as to what had actually happened and why. She was clearly having some kind of breakdown, brought on by her husband's philandering. It wasn't her fault at all. It was she who was the innocent victim. Poor Helen.

So some months later, it came as a complete shock to answer the doorbell, only to find her rival, Angela Bagner standing on her doorstop, smiling broadly and pushing a huge bunch of lilies into Helen's hands.

"My favourites! How did you know?"

"Hello Helen. May I come in?"

Quite taken aback with the surprise visit, and with the forthright voice with which the woman spoke, Helen let her in. They sat in the back kitchen for some time before either spoke, Angela continued to smile sweetly. This was not the woman who Helen had known and gleefully patronized. This woman was confident, had poise, and on the face of it had a reason to be. It was most unnerving. While Helen looked anxiously about her, she couldn't understand why Angela appeared to be shimmering. There was a translucency about her, but she decided it must be the sunlight. This was odd, for though she had lived in this house for only few months she had never noticed light like it. She scoured her brain for something to break the silence.

"Tea?"

Angela nodded cheerfully.

"Love some!"

Retreating to the kitchen counter, Helen busily filled the kettle, rattling cups and spoons in an attempt to fill the silence. There was no gallery to play to here, and her obvious embarrassment due to recent intrigues was acute, due to the fact she knew they were known by her visitor. She rummaged through a wall cabinet for no apparent reason, hiding her confusion and reddened cheeks. Automatically she reached for a tin and removed its lid.

"I'm afraid I don't seem to have anything to offer you. Someone's had them all," she began, then realizing the subtext of what she had said, she turned to look at Angela. The humour was not lost on either of the two women and they both burst out laughing, continuing until tears rolled down their faces. Then Helen's tears fell heavier and she began to sob.

"Look, why are you here? If you've come to see if I'm sorry, well, I'm sorry. Okay? If I could change what I did, I would, but I can't. I was an idiot."

Her visitor quietly looked back at Helen with an understanding expression. She had no desire to make Helen feel uncomfortable and she patted Helen on the hand.

"Yes, you have been an idiot."

Helen looked aghast and a little indignant as well. She wasn't used to hearing things as they were, especially from a person she had maligned purely out of her own insecurity.

"But now you have a fresh start, for nothing remains as it was. You can begin again. You will move forward. It really is never too late to start making the right choices for your life."

Taking an envelope from her bag, she placed it on the kitchen table in front of the sobbing Helen.

"What's this? You're not taking me to court are you?"

"It's for you and your children. Open it after I've gone," then she stood up and made her way up the hall, closing the front door quietly behind her. On opening the envelope, Helen found details of a holiday in a small seaside town. It had a pier, a sandy beach and little tea rooms to relax in. The note read:

"Spend some time with your children, and watch the waves roll in. I promise you, it will be time well spent."

"How dare she come here and tell me."

She nearly screwed up the booking form in resentment, but something prevented her, a niggling thought in the back of her mind of – *what if we did?* Pinning it to the cork board, she decided she would talk to the children when they came home.

"Bloody woman, how bloody dare she?" Muttering up the stairs Helen was initially outraged by Angela's kindness.

How would she know how to bring up kids? Still if it's for free, more fool her. What did I come up here for again?

Curiously, on her way back a bewildered Helen found a small soapstone Buddha resting on her bedroom mantelpiece.

Funny! I must have misplaced it in the move.

It was a far cry from their latest trip to Thailand, but when Helen mentioned the seaside holiday to the kids, they jumped at the suggestion. They had previously been so used to tutors and after school clubs acting as their substitute parents, they thought the novelty of being with their Mother alone was nothing short of an exciting adventure. They were to stay in a Bed and Breakfast as well. Ruby and Elliot had read about those places but had never dreamt they would go, and Helen although reluctant to admit it, was amazed at how it became the number one subject discussed at breakfast and supper and last thing at night. The prospect of a simple seaside holiday outshone all the expensive summer camps they usually had been packed off to. It was a shame Dad Nick wasn't to join them, but this was nothing unusual. Communication with him had been normally by Skype or mobile, since long before their parents parted.

What a glorious thing it was, to do nothing but play ball, fly kites, picnic, and read. The Landlady of the B&B was delightfully kind, allowing children to be children, to make noise and have pillow fights, and even let them walk her mongrel dog Mabel, down to the beach for ice cream and paddling in the sun-shimmering waves. This idyll might have been taken from a children's book, full of easy laughter and wholesome pursuits. Never had they enjoyed each other's company as much. One evening, as they nestled together, wrapped under a sandy blanket by a beach bonfire, they were bathed in the rich colours of the sunset, and they watched the waves come gently rolling into the shore.

"Thanks for this Mum. I'll never forget it," said one.

"Me neither. Can we come back here?" said the other.

Helen didn't reply, she just held them both closer as the waves rolled in.

"You know, if you watch long enough, they look like they're standing still," said one. "The waves I mean."

"The sea is playing its music," said the other. "Listen, can you hear it? It's like a lullaby."

So they sat there for hours, watching and listening to the waves as the golden sun went down.

Despite the homespun holiday Helen and her two children shared together, like many other Beings, Helen Ellis was slow to learn. Her freshly found commitment to turning over a new leaf was short lived, and she quickly forgot the simple wonders they had discovered. Then, an offer came with an unexpected phone call, from the television company which had played its part in her downfall. The offer had arisen because of her internet notoriety, earned from the unfortunately popular film of her public displays on that fateful charity ball night. A producer saw the comic potential and Helen was invited to appear in a series of reality game shows involving further public humiliation, and enduring the ghastly experience of sucking up to whom she deemed to be the lower classes. Despite this initially distasteful proposition, Helen soon rose to the challenge and became a regular contributor to celebrity magazine front cover stories. In this faux fame way she attained what she thought of as a semblance of happiness at last, and all future vacations were secured by promotional contracts.

Thankfully, her children never forgot the bliss of their seaside heaven, and would emulate its nostalgic charm in years to come with their own families, by returning again and again to the little seaside town which had given both brother and sister a sense of something real.

Ruby returned to school and blossomed in Physics, most especially when her class explored waves using spectrometers. There had been a curious moment when under a tunable stroboscope, the passing waves in a wave generator became one, as a single wave captured in time. Ruby was enthralled. It was just like the waves she had seen on their seaside holiday, and like the Japanese wave print at her Father's new house. She grew to become a physicist, specializing particularly in the study of wave motion in all its forms. Her brother Elliot took to music, classical mainly, but later went on to use music for therapy in mental health care, by harnessing repeating sequences of music to stimulate or calm certain areas of the brain. Most importantly, every year, as their families expanded and spread their wings across the country, their annual meet would always bring them back together again like homing pigeons: back to their beach. All that was, except one. Nevertheless, Granny Helen would sometimes make the effort to call them there from the Channel Islands, when she remembered.

Chapter Twenty

Down in the fabric of the layered worlds, a sun scorched patchwork of possibility rippled in its unique timeline. This was just one of many alternative outcomes in the infinite multiverse dreamscape Angela had come to know. Like a finely delicate mille feuille pastry, each different timeline revealed a different outcome of choice, and in one the Creature Lilith had placed a burden to rest.

In the relative shade of a ramshackle wooden veranda, a rusting shop sign hung motionless above where the Old Woman squatted, just out of the blazing heat. Round and round, in circular movements, she turned the grinding stone, while buzzing flies circled about her head. The grain she had in the mortar was small, but at least there was some. There seemed to be less and less every day since her husband had died, leaving her with only one unmarried son and too many daughters to support. She sang a song under her breath which she had been taught by her own Mother.

"Sixteen men,
There are here,
Seventeen women,
Twenty children there are,
And dogs and cats,
There are the village ploughmen,
A spoonful of rice,
A spoonful of lentils,
A spoonful of flour,
Just a pinch of salt."

It was a little heirloom of where her family had come from. Within its words and rhythm contained every generation fed with miserly rations. It was a song of their survival, and a song she had given to her own daughters to treasure, for she had nothing else she could give them. With two saris, both white, one to wear and one to wash, she was considered prosperous. The saris she wore before, in colours of turmeric yellow and cinnamon red, were but a threadbare memory, for as a widow she was obliged to wear only white. Other women squatted nearby in clusters on dusty rugs, each engrossed in their daily task. Some ground the grain and some moulded the dung cakes. Some boiled the water over the dung cake fires, and each with a song they sang alone or together. The sentiment of each labour song was rooted in their common experience and one they all shared, of abject poverty. From hand to mouth, and cradle to grave, this was their lot, and yet despite this, the Old Woman smiled as she sang and proudly turned her grinding wheel, flicking the flies away from her aged face as she did so. She was no longer the Daughter-in-Law serving her late Mother-in-Law. She was now the Rani, or Queen of her family. Now she was Maataaji, albeit a widow too.

Once she had been the beautiful Jyosana, meaning 'Moonlight' and named so due to the crescent birthmark on her cheek, but when she had entered her husband's family, she had become nameless, taking the beatings that all girls and women would, because it was their duty to obey without question. Obedience, what a word to live by! Her caste had been designed by the Gods for this role in life, and they meekly accepted this in the hope that at some time in their future, and after so many lifetimes, the dice might fall differently in their favour. The condition of course being that they followed the rules of obedience in this life. Maataaji was not so sure anymore, for she had seen changes approaching the borders of her village. Tales of the City and the riches to be made there were luring the young men away with promises of the

West. Her unmarried son was yet to find a suitable wife to bring in a dowry, and he was already talking of moving on to where his fortune could be found.

"Maataaji! Maataaji! Come quickly!"

The Old Woman looked up and shielded her eyes with her gnarled hand to see. Even though it was early morning, the Sun was already fierce and its glare made silhouettes of the children running towards her through the muddy dust of the wild mustard fields. It was hard to distinguish them from the chattering monkeys who played alongside, and as they ran nearer, more gangly children joined them, stopping barefoot games to be part of the commotion. Little happened of any excitement in the village. Everyday was much like the last, and every person was just grateful for another day. From across the fields, the swarm of skinny, shrieking children came, making the cotton pickers stop briefly to watch, while wandering cows meandered past, unaware of the ruckus as the children neared.

"Maataaji!"

The lead spokesman of this group was one of her cousin's grandsons. Her cousin had been blessed with so many boys, it was a needling pain for the Old Woman.

So why is he searching for me? She had enough work of her own to do.

"What is it Sachin? Have you lost your Mother? Or has she replaced you with a monkey?" the Old Woman quipped, much to the delight of Sachin's laughing friends, who each then began an impersonation of the scruffy urchin as his simian self. It took a while before the small runner could be heard above the whooping.

"Maataaji! You must come with me. I've found her!"

Sachin was nearly beside himself with excitement, already pulling at the Old Woman's hand. Even though she was only a lower caste woman, she lavished what treats she could upon them. The treats were her stories, and Sachin and all the village children would consume them with relish, for there was little else for them to eat.

"Who Sachin?" The Maataaji swiped his hand away, "Come on Boy! I have work to do! You can see I am busy. Who have you found?" It was hard to feign impatience with any of the children here, as every single one was a treasure to her, but she had her role to play.

"Your Varali!"

At the announced name, the Maataaji was struck silent and sat up, and Sachin, not knowing she was in a state of shock continued to babble on, eager to impress his beloved Storyteller.

"You know Maataaji, the story of the Lady who came from Moonlight. Don't you remember telling us?"

All the children squealed in agreement, perplexed the Old Woman was not overwhelmed with the same level of enthusiasm as they. Instead she just stared blankly ahead. A quiet passed over their faces. They were hoping she might leap up and dance with astonishment from the news.

"I do hope Sachin," she firmly uttered, slowly gathering herself to stand, with aching joints cracking loudly. "I do hope this will not become disagreeable to my friend the cane. I would not want him to beat your backside for your silly jokes."

She waved her walking stick in front of her, commanding a path between the gang. Sachin was thrilled and grabbed the Old Woman's hand to gain authority over his peers, and to his great pleasure, the Old Woman shooed the other children away.

"Where are you taking me?" she asked, warmly squeezing his hand after the other children had reluctantly returned to their games.

"Up by the bend in the river." he beamed. "I was looking for Aam fruit, and I found her there."

By the time they got there it was late morning, and the heat intolerable. Though her step had been slow, the prospect of the grove of trees was a welcoming destination and the journey to the river's bend had been pleasant enough. Her small companion was determined to entertain her with his own story, as to how he discovered the character she had told him of: The Lady who came from the Moonlight.

"The best bit is when the Lady promised to come back on the second day of Magha, even though everyone was sad to see her leave. I know it's Magha. I heard the Elders in the Panchayat talking about it. Well, I did see the New Moon coming last night too. Here we are," he declared proudly as they reached the curve of water. "And there she is!"

He pointed across the stream to a rocky outcrop near a small spinney offering shade. It was the place which led to the mountain region towering over the village. The Old Woman strained her milky eyes, trying to focus on what it was she had been brought to. All she could see were large boulders, baking in the dazzling sunlight. Sachin was himself disappointed in her reaction, but not wishing to give up on their quest, he urged the Old Woman over the river's stepping stones.

"Don't worry Maataaji, I'll help you!" he tried to assure her, "If you fall in, I'll pull you out."

"And if I fall in, I'll pull you in and drown you!" she snapped. There was something not quite right in the air about them. It felt electrical, like before a storm. It made her nervous.

Sachin however, was wiry for his age and nutrition, and wasn't daunted by the Old Woman's grumbling as he tugged her up the other bank. He knew her bluster was all for show and that she had the kindest heart, much like everyone from the village, even so, she was somehow different from the rest. Some of the stories she told were from the past, from their ancestors, and everyone knew those, but Sachin's favourites were the ones the Old Woman made up herself. The ones in which real people appeared. His uncle had bought a wind-up radio, which had become a new centre of attention for the whole village, if the signal was right. He would make Sachin or one of his brothers hang from tree limbs to secure the crackling sound of the Big City music shows. Tales of western wealth and forbidden fruits would filter through the crackling airwaves, bringing unsettling and tempting souvenirs to their simple way of life. Some of the bigger boys in the village were already talking of leaving, but this held no interest for Sachin. He preferred sitting close to the Maataaji Storyteller who could make dreams come alive with her words.

Away from the river and under a Banyan tree, the Old Woman sat to rest and wiped her brow with the corner of her sari. The Boy offered her some water from his tin flask, which she sipped gratefully. It was quieter here, as the noises of people had slipped away with each footstep they had taken. Now all that could be heard were the whirring buzz of cicadas, and the wind rustling the leaves above them.

"So tell me, what is it you have found Sachin?" she asked at last.

"Not what, Maataaji, who."

He heaved her to her feet and led her beyond the tree's shade, to a mango tree growing alone just behind the rocks. A large reclining mound of what looked like ragged cloth lay in front of the onlookers. The two stood in the stillness for quite a time before they spoke, and only then, when they realized the mound was breathing. It was a person!

"See Maataaji! It's her. Look at her face!"

Treading with faltering steps, the Old Woman moved towards the mound, her legs trembling for fear of waking whatever it was under the cloth. Death and shrouds were commonplace in this life, but not a life from death. She had heard of such things, but they were stories she chose not to tell children, otherwise she would never have had a restful night. As she got nearer, she could see the outlined features of the person's nose and chin, and she knew immediately this was no one from this area, nor possibly from this land. The shape and form of their bones were far too different. She stretched out her shaking hand and lifted the muslin away from the sleeping figure. What she saw made the Old Woman let out a scream and fall to one knee, only just catching her fall with her trusty stick. The sleeping figure continued sleeping. Sachin sprang to help her up.

"Maataaji, are you all right?" Sachin begged her, "Is it not her? Is it not the Lady who came from the Moonlight?"

The Old Woman nodded and gulped. It was indeed the Lady who came from the Moonlight. There could be no denying this, for it was a sleeping woman who should not be there. A sleeping woman with an identical crescent moon birthmark as the aged Maataaji, only with one important difference. The woman was white.

It was late afternoon and still Sachin had not returned. She had sent the Boy to fetch men to help with the sleeping white woman and while he was gone, she kept a vigil beside the stranger. The Day chased its shadows across the dust and the cross-legged Old Woman. Before Sachin had left, he gave her a fresh mango he had picked from the tree above, as well as his tin flask of water. Then, promising to be as swift as his skinny legs would let him, he had run to find help. The white woman continued to sleep on. Gentle shaking by her protector could not waken her from sleep. Such a deep sleep the Old Woman knew would only come from travelling a very long way. Travelling perhaps across lifetimes. The sleeper was dreaming, for her eyelids flickered and she murmured something underneath her breath. Something indecipherable to the low caste woman at her side, for it was in another language. A lonely figure in the dry earth, the Old Woman wept and prayed.

"Oh Prajapati! Lord of All the Creatures! Is this she? Is this my Varali?"

Maataaji's watery eyes looked down upon the sleeping figure. White skin, and pale as the Moon. Such a sign of beauty! She knew many darker skinned women who would willingly bleach their skin to win a pale complexion such as this, thinking it would somehow make them more beautiful. But her Varali had not had pale skin. Her Varali had been as brown as an Areca nut and as small as a sweet mango. Small enough to be held all too briefly in the palms of Jyosana. Her beautiful Baby had not stayed with her long enough to be named, but if she had, Jyosana hoped she would be called Varali, for the child had inherited the crescent moon from her Mother's own cheek, and Varali meant 'Moon'. The Child had been born too early, in the time of Magha, bringing the New Moon to the valley, but her Mother-in-Law had taken Jyosana's Little Varali away, for there were too many girls in their family to feed that year. It was a question of Pride and Purse.

The Young Woman had used her imagination to survive this dreadful separation. She imagined the child Varali sleeping in a mango seed, and being planted in the ground under the New Moon, and watered by her Moon Mother's tears. She imagined the Mango Child growing overnight into a vast and luxuriant green tree, full of Aam fruit which fed all who loved it. Villagers met by it, children climbed in it and lovers made honeyed embraces under it. Her leaves decorated wedding parties and the homes of young newlyweds. Wood was reverently taken from her branches, offered to Holy Puja and Hawan prayers, and given in respect to sanctify funeral fires. Then, on the night when the Moon became full, a strange and beautiful Lady appeared underneath, with skin as pale as the Moon, singing a silvery song which filled all who heard full of joy. Everyone in Jyosana's imaginary world cried tears of happiness when they heard a song of Amrita fill the night air. They begged her to stay, but Varali gently explained she was to go onto another place where all Beings must go, and promising she would return on the night of another New Moon. In this way, Jyosana's imagination had given her Child a life lived with purpose, albeit for the phase of one moon.

After all these years, and countless times telling the story of the Lady who came from the Moonlight, Maataaji had almost forgotten how her story had first begun, until now. Now her Varali had been called from another place, from beyond this earth, bubbling up like a forgotten water spring in drought. This white woman was dressed beneath the shroud-like cloth like most white westerners, only her silk gown was long and silvery grey, and her feet were bare. It was as if she had been taken from her bed and carried away to this far off place in her sleep. The Maataaji knew a woman like this did not belong here, and yet, here she indeed was, belonging somehow to the Maataaji. Wiping the stranger's lips with a little water soaked on the corner of her sari, the Old Woman whispered a prayer for clarity, laying down the Aam fruit as an offering, in the hope the Gods might look kindly upon her. Without knowing who this pale creature was, a tear fell from the Old Woman's eye, splashing onto the white woman's cheek, but why she cried for this stranger was a mystery. The grief she was told long ago to disregard, had in truth only been buried in a shallow grave alongside her baby daughter. The covering was thin, and this sleeper had brought all the past to the surface, for now it was exposed, and the pain was still acute. She longed for another chance, and the woman on the ground was her possible redemption.

People tend to believe what they are presented with, so she chose to believe because she needed to. The Boy Sachin was right, this must be her Varali come back to her. The crescent birthmark on the woman's pale skin was identical to her own. It must be a sign, but she would only be certain when the sleeper woke. Then, just as instantly as the Old Woman had thought this, the flickering eyelids of the white woman opened. It took a while for her narrow, ice-blue eyes to focus and see the guardian looking down on her.

"Maataaji?" the stranger murmured, "is that you?"

The council leaders looked down on the Old Woman sternly. They had been discussing the situation for what seemed like hours, but it was only now in the early evening, that they had stepped from the meeting house to speak to her. The Panchayat Elders were not to be refused or challenged, certainly not by women, so Maataaji was prepared for a fight if it was needed. There was something indefinable which connected her to the strange white woman, for although neither spoke the other's tongue, this foreigner recognised Maataaji. This was odd indeed, for the Old Woman had never travelled beyond the village outskirts in her entire life, and yet, here this strange white woman was, holding Maataaji's hand ever since she had woken under the Mango tree. Briefly, and only briefly, the Old Woman had pulled her hand away from the blue-eyed woman, who had until that point, sat beside her passively eating the mango, while all the time staring vacantly ahead as if half blind. It was only when the Old Woman took away her hand that the stranger become distraught, wildly looking around her as if there might be a bird of prey above their heads. There were many such birds in the foothills of this mountainous region, but none which Maataaji knew would attack humans. The unseen assailants disappeared as soon as the Old Woman took her pale hand again, except from that moment on, the white woman began to scratch at her own skin, while mumbling something in her own language.

Much like a mother and child, the two had remained together waiting under the shade of the Mango tree for the men from the village to return, and while they waited, the Old Woman sang a loris lullaby to soothe her Varali, who had returned from Another Place.

'Moon Uncle who lives far away

Cooks delicious sweetmeat

Moon Uncle who lives far away

Cooks delicious sweetmeat

Eats it from a plate

Gives a small bit for the Baby in a bowl'

She crooned softly to the white woman who clung tightly to her wizened hand like a child afraid. This was Mackenzie, a woman of wickedness but now reborn without memory of who she was, or how or why she was here in this deserted part of the world. She was a sleepwalker, as she had not fully awoken to either her present geographical position, nor to the molecular changes which had transpired whilst travelling into the Layered World. All Mackenzie knew, or rather sensed, was somehow the person she clutched with her gripped hand, was her Maataaji and, her Maataaji was the safest place to be. Maataaji would protect her. At the heart of a creature like Mackenzie was a supreme survivalist. She remembered she had been in danger, and danger for Mackenzie was to be out of control. It had been the most frightening experience, for not only had Mackenzie lost control, she was doubtful that she had found it again. There was something under her skin, and scratching with her one free hand, blood began to trickle and congeal along the track lines of her nails, and soon, smelling the iron-sweet liquid, flies were crawling over the glistening wounds. Unaware of the stranger's terror, the Old Woman carried on singing gently to her, occasionally flicking away the feasting flies and sometimes chiding Mackenzie by firmly pressing her hand to prevent the scratching. Neither woman understood the other's language, yet somehow they understood each other on another level. One would protect the other.

When the men finally arrived, there was much shouting of orders and directions, with each man competing for dominance over the situation's control. Some of the village women and their children had joined the party as it neared the outskirts. A white woman, here! It was the most exciting event to happen in a long time, not since the white doctors had visited years before. They had come looking for young men to staff their building near to the city, but had left with none, moving on to the next village beyond theirs. The tales filtered back had left a taste of regret among the young men who had remained, and the arrival of the mysterious white woman had quickly rekindled talk of adventure. Many spoke of how they would not let another opportunity for fortune to slip through their hands. If this woman could offer anything similar, they loudly promised to make a different decision this time! It was this which had disturbed the five Panchayati Elders most of all. Boys and Men were considered most valuable in their world. Losing boys to the big city would be like losing a ruby to swine. Unthinkable! They had deliberated for hours and had finally decided the removal of the white woman, and all she represented, was imperative in order to keep the quiet equilibrium of their little empire. She had to go before temptation took root, and go as far away as possible.

"Take her to the mountain temple Maataaji," instructed the Head Panchayati firmly. "Take her there. It is clear you and she have karma together." He pointed to the birthmarks on both the women's cheeks. "They will know what to do."

The ground beneath their feet was hard and rocky on the mountain path to the temple. The Panchayati Elders had sent her on the longest journey of her life, for they had sensed the arrival of this white woman might be a herald to change they were not yet prepared for.

Sachin had offered his companionship, but she had declined for this was to be a pilgrimage like none she had ever heard of before. Sweetly, he had sought out various goods for her journey, filling his tin flask with fresh spring water, collecting fruit, and chapattis rolled in leaves, and wrapping these in a linen shawl. He even found some sandals for the white woman to wear and the Old Woman put them on the sleepwalker, as carefully as any loving mother would.

"Thank you Sachin," and bowing to the small boy, palms pressed together, honoured him. "I will never forget this."

"But Maataaji, you will be coming back, won't you?"

She affectionately patted his head.

"I think I can say we all come back Sachin."

The two women walked in virtual silence. On occasion the Old Woman would sing to help keep her mind from aching bones not truly in a fit state for such a journey. The white woman made little mumbling sounds, almost like a whimpering infant, when their two hands were parted on a narrowing of the pathway. Then she would grab onto the corner of the Widow's white sari so as to not lose contact with her aged protector. The air, so chilled and freshly scented with mountain herbs, was beginning to thin, making headway slower than Maataaji had hoped.

On a wide, rough path, in the evening light, the pair sat down on some patches of grass to rest. Rich colours of a purple and pink sunset tinted the white sari, until she appeared no longer as a widow in white, but Jyosana the beautiful young wife again. Jyosana, who had made love under sultry stars, when her body was lithe and gravity had not got the better of her. Jyosana the young mother, full of hope for her life, holding the hand of her lovely Varali who had returned to her.

The two pilgrims were bathed in golden light, making their skins almost the same hue. Jyosana squeezed her companion's hand and smiled. From this new level, the Old Woman could see all the way across the valley, down to where her village nestled next to the mountain range behind it. So small! She had not realized how small their lives were. Everything before was set in a rhythm, carved into rock as to how things were supposed to be done, turning everyday like grain in the grinding stone. It was how things were supposed to remain, but not now. From where she sat she could also see the distant silhouettes of the Big City on the far horizon, growing, spreading, and getting nearer. *All is change! In the blink of an eye!* Lowering her head, and contemplating the dirt at her feet, she sighed.

From ahead of them there came the sound of footsteps, and of more than one person too. Jyosana and Mackenzie sat upright and exchanged a look between each other, as three shaven headed bhikkhu, Buddhist monks in yellow and red robes emerged from a bend on the path, their beads and begging bowls bouncing against their stride. They were each of an indeterminate gender and age, though under the shade of a deep red parasol, paced the oldest of the three monks, judging from the deeply set lines etched into his smiling face.

"Namaste."

The three beamed and bowed to the two women. Jyosana bowed in return, while Mackenzie remained mute.

"Tell us Sister, of your journey," asked one, in a quiet and subdued voice. "We are all listening."

The words seemed to echo across the ridge of the mountain on which the five of them gathered. The air tingled and slowed into a suspended moment, and Mackenzie appeared to become more aware of her surroundings. All three monks looked intently at the Old Woman, and she felt compelled to tell her story, of the Lady Who Came from the Moonlight. Of her lost Varali, and of the white woman found under the Mango tree that she thought was her daughter returned to her, because she had not let her story die.

"And why do you believe this is she Sister?"

The three smiling monks gathered around Mackenzie to look more closely. They seemed to be reading her face like a detailed map, as tiny micro-expressions flitted across the woman's skin in infinitesimal muscular spasms, revealing the location and identity of the bearer in Vitruvian Time.

"She shares my moon mark here," she pointed to her cheek and that of her companion. "And I feel her inside me. She must be."

After some time, and as one, the three monks turned their attention away from Mackenzie and onto Jyosana. The oldest of the three visitors spoke directly to her.

"Yes Sister, you have met each other before, there is a strong karmic bond here indeed. But as to where and when your lives entwined, We do not feel We can tell you now. We can say she has travelled far, but not in miles, for she has come from Another Place, and perhaps Another Time."

The two other monks nodded happily in agreement. The old monk continued.

"We knew of your arrival for many moons. We shall take her to the temple to help her understand her journey to here. We have prepared a place for her to rest and wake."

The Old Woman tightened her hand on Mackenzie. To lose her Varali again was all too much for her aging heart. The monks smiled as one, and the oldest monk reassured her, laughing warmly as he did.

"You will of course come with us Sister, if you wish to. We have prepared a place for you to rest and sleep."

They beckoned and turned, walking away up the steep path towards the monastery in the clouds. Only one monk remained to patiently help the Old Woman to her feet and lead them to the temple. Younger than the other two, she could see from the contours of his face that he had more in common with her reborn Varali, for despite his weathered brown face, he looked like a white man who had lived here in the mountains for many, many years. Only when she found her focus, she recoiled, stumbling backwards a little.

Is this a god? The monk had eyes of a colour she had never seen before in her lifetime and she was transfixed.

"Are you ready Sister?"

The Old Woman nodded meekly. Taking his arm she continued gazing at his face, and into his turquoise eyes.

Chapter Twenty-One

The great, majestic Creature Lilith had chosen her form. It was a necessary procedure, for there was not a Being who was exempt from Choice and Outcome, no matter how much they might run or protest. Due to her own impatience, she had interfered in a Being's chosen path, and now she was paying the piper. She was reborn. There is an aperture of time during Molecular Dispersal Transference, (or MDT as it is known in the layered worlds), in which a Being is unaware as to what they have become, let alone what their outcome might be. Lilith was in such a state, between her fluctuating astral self and the new self. The thoughts of Lilith the goddess during this period did not quite fit the form she had squeezed into and as someone might come to from anesthesia, she was still filled with thoughts of what she deemed, a higher nature.

"It is an easy mistake to make, this thing called existence, perceiving it as random or a roll of the dice," Lilith pondered. "In all fairness, the outcomes of a Being will not always directly reflect their choices in their experience of Now. But it must be said, although a Being's outcome may seem haphazard, accidental even, deep in the bottomless flow of Vitruvian Time, We will find the current of choices which have surely led to..."

"What are We wittering about now Lilith?" a vibrating multitude of slightly irritated voices boomed through the Flow, like the relentless crashing of wave on shore. "As if We didn't already know."

The Creature Lilith sighed. At times she was aware her musings bordered on pomposity, and despite her transcendence into a higher state, she was still at times an opinionated creature, albeit a well intentioned one.

As a Being moving towards understanding 'We Are All', she accepted there was not even a single *plankt of time when she was truly alone (*0.00000000000000000000000000000 000000000000005391 second to be precise). But oh! What she would have gladly done for an occasional moment of solitude, or some comfort in the sweet territory of silence! It would be in those occasional moments of resistance, she would find herself 'turning down the volume' of connection between herself and other Beings in the Flow, purely because she wanted the sensation of being alone. The sensation was illusionary, for there was not a Being who ever truly was. This invariably would cause her to veer off course, and foolishly flirt with the delusion of being alone in her thoughts. The Creature Lilith's imminent outcome was due to her interference with corporeal lives, and the direct result of one such dalliance.

"It can be so very tiresome, knowing the bigger picture so to speak. Takes all the surprise out of things," she complained wearily. "Necessary We suppose, as We become nearer in understanding. It is the ego We carry which, again and again, halts our growth. Daring to assert that We are unique, that there has never been any Being like We before or since! True, We have an expression which is matchless, but fundamentally, We Are All. Hah! How we miss the Being Garbo, she knew how to carry Ego with integrity and panache. What was it she became again? We must look her up."

The Creature Lilith was evolving. At first glance, her vibrational self had indeed shown the appearance of a mythical goddess, but this was merely an affectation on her part. The owl wings, the talons, why, truth be known, she had a whimsical hankering for such a formidable persona, and through its adoption had hoped to assimilate these qualities of ferocious assertiveness into her core. This vanity had been her undoing, and there was now a need to re-establish some basic humility.

Gravity from this part of the layered World was beginning to anchor her new form, the vehicle of which was very different to a mighty goddess. Feeling the sand and ebbing tide glide rhythmically over her horizontal body, she sighed, and as she did, bubbles of foamy surf tickled her feathery mouth, and she let the rush of brine and gurgling detritus surge through her. The Creature Lilith knew this was as it should be, and that in the constant flow of Now, she knew also that no Being was just flotsam and jetsam. There was a purpose for all.

You are what you eat...or is it, you become what you project?

Answer came there none from the firmament, and Lilith knew We Are All heard her thoughts, but had chosen not to comment. Lilith was a much appreciated Being in their number of course, but the expression of her Being in this moment of Now was considered a little jejune, awkward, adolescent even and evidently a Being who was still making unwise choices because of her juvenile ego. For an angelical such as Lilith, originating from only a remote past this was not uncommon. All Beings had at some time been at the mercy of ego. Why, from that viewpoint of Time she was just beginning! Such a long time she had travelled, though for the Creature Lilith, her lifetime was but a blink of the Cosmic Eye.

When the universe was young, before the formation of stars and planets, she had looked about her in wonder, as just a tiny thought floating in the Great Mind. When protons and electrons combined to form neutral atoms, her conscious mind began to stir. And later, when photons began to travel freely through space, she had first begun her quest to understand. Lilith had conversed with the Old Ones, those who knew the Before of existence, and they hinted as to how All had come into being. There had been Another Place, in which Beings had longed for deeper understanding of their purpose. Through quadrillions of years and millions of yottaseconds and kalpas, they had ploughed, and sown, and reaped their choices and outcomes, until finally, the Beings became One-but-not-One. And in that transcendent silent sound, the simultaneous expression of We Are All exploded into the next state of Being, like a celestial piñata. In turn this became our universe as we know it now. Lilith could still feel the relic radiation tingle on her skin and lingering static made her feathers stand on end at times. This universe was merely the next stage towards understanding, and the Old Ones considered themselves quite a sprightly and youthful band. "Time is relative," they said.

It was true Lilith was ancient, but in comparison to the Old Ones she was very young indeed. For Beings at such a young age, even angelical ones, it was almost expected they make unwise choices, but to acknowledge each one could create unbalance in the Flow. Too much attention to 'me, me, me,' would be to the detriment of 'We'.

To explain some of the underpinning principles of residing in the Flow of Now, to Lilith, the Being Angela's new found love of earthbound Cuban music was a perfect analogy. As Eddie later explained to Angela,

"...well, Cuban grooves are a puzzle I'm still working on. When you break down Cuban music into its different components like, you're playing to your own time you know? But knowing that everyone else, (and I mean everyone), has their own groove they're playing to. There are so many time signatures it might be seen as impossible on paper."

"But how do you make sure it works?"

"Listen, takes dedication right? You kinda have to let go of the outside of yourself and free up the inside, then it feels like," Eddie paused for a moment to find the words, "then it feels like you're gliding through a summer sky, big and endless like, and everyone up there is in the groove with you, doing these amazing tricks, in and out, without bumping into each other, 'cause everyone seems to hear each others' thoughts. You feel this stillness that moves through you and everyone else. It doesn't matter that you're all different, in fact, it's the different timings that make it.

Takes a lot of practise, as long as you're aware like, and you keep hooked in to all the other players, then the groove will fuse." Apologetically he added, "Yeah, I know this sounds a bit hippy funny fags, but when I'm in it, I feel like I've found my place. In the groove I'm accepted and so is everyone else. We're all one like."

The collective voice of We Are All reverberated throughout the layered worlds.

"The Being Lilith must move towards understanding through her own choices and outcomes. The Being Lilith is a neophyte, a novice, and, like all novices, can learn in no other way."

The budding Lilith reluctantly agreed with their insight, which was indeed wise and astute, but nonetheless irksome. Most teenagers, like the impatient Lilith, resist sound advice, and oblige their parents to muster tolerance and serenity. And so it was with Lilith and We Are All. The parents must watch as offspring blunder ahead, with the gauche arrogance unique to their age, and which will in the end, trip them up, landing them in proverbial excrement.

We think this must be an example of 'Shit happens' We suppose. Lilith sighed, wriggling herself deeper into the sand. *Where We are in existence, is of our own making, and from our own choices made before.*

It wasn't as though she had made no effort to adjust her sometimes 'knee jerk' reactions to lesser evolved Beings. Lilith was still moving towards understanding the essence of We Are All, and through the unfolding countless millennia, she was becoming more fluent in its accents and nuances. Vitruvian Time is certainly not an undemanding language. In Vitruvian Time, Past, Present and Future tenses are discarded, and instead, the main structure of communication could be described as, 'One-and-not-One'. This meant if an initial thought from a Being was centred, regardless of language, all linguistic meaning would merge and communication would be faster than light. Some of these evolving Beings were known to converse in nothing but haikus, and considered them to be a greatly underestimated artform. Haikus were often mistaken by fledgling angelicals to be an easy poetic formula to perform. Unfortunately, the Being Lilith created veritable travesties of haiku, but then, this was but another common failing of Youth to write indulgent and dreadful poetry. A passion for rudimentary physics led to one of her more presentable earlier efforts,

Surge of the ocean

Like V equals lambda F

Push tides eternal

After a few eons, Haiku made way for the more fashionable Metaphor, allowing a thousand possible meanings to be housed within a single sentence. Unfortunately for The Creature Lilith, her Vitruvian language skills fell far below the Metaphor mark, landing smack in the middle of Platitudes. And Lilith's platitudes had all the cheesy qualities of a pound store poster of puppies in a bucket.

Generally though, it was agreed the wisest choice for an angelical was to ignore fashion and move towards the 'One-but-not-One', linguistic state in which the bonds linking Beings to We Are All would overlap and fuse into a perfect vibration, mistaken sometimes for 'silence'.

To illustrate, the burring sound of Silence is still found in far off, wild and forgotten places, where the intrusion of modern life has not yet penetrated. Silent places allow for a Being to hear their own true thought, and in turn gain a greater ability to sense those of others. The Being Angela had impressed Lilith greatly in her rapport with the vibration of Now. There was also something in her akin to the goddess herself which she recognised in the seemingly innocent earthbound creature. This perhaps had contributed to her taking the Being Angela 'under her wing' as a potential apprentice angelical. She was what, in 20th century Western parlance would be known as, a natural.

Angela's internal cry for redemption had sent ripples through the flow, and Lilith had heard her call. So many Beings utter empty prayers, learned by rote, like lucky charms, but it is the sincere and beseeched invocations that carry through the layered worlds, which are answered, for their cause is a true one. The goddess had duly responded, without considering the outcomes of her choices, and instead she had judged and acted. Choice such as this is fraught with accusations begetting accusation. What did come first, the chicken or the egg? Who cast the first stone?

Meanwhile, the slowness of some earthbound Beings to evolve was understandably frustrating to the nth degree for a creature such as Lilith. Impatient by nature and so intolerant that she even irritated herself, across Vitruvian Time progress was potentially a lengthy tedium indeed. Lilith knew she needed to evolve away from her predisposition to conceit and judgment, and towards exhibiting a little more forbearance when it came to judging how quickly a Being may or may not learn. She needed most of all to make choices from a position of authentic compassion. This was a tough road to travel and most definitely a less frequented one. The recent case of the Being Mackenzie was a case in point, resulting in Lilith's present form here in the sand and sea. Lilith had left her with the Old Woman who had walked the long track on another timeline, all to protect her young granddaughter. The Mackenzie had chosen the destination herself, for it is a well known fact in the layered worlds that a life of a Being will be pulled back to the same places and peoples, so as to re-enact unfinished business and, unlearned lessons. It was a little like returning to the scene of a crime.

The goddess could sense the time-path would lead to some elevated Beings known as the Sangha, high in a mountainous region. There the exhausted Mackenzie would heal from her trans-dimensional realignment, and the weary Jyosana could find rest in the Deep Sleep she yearned for.

The earthbound Ones who lived in the mountains were fascinating Beings, able to exhibit patience in ways Lilith could not comprehend, and if the Mackenzie was to awaken from her previous habits of behaviour, she would need to learn at least some of their gentle ways. It had taken her an extraordinary measurement of time to become the beast Mackenzie, and so it would take extraordinary actions to rebalance her. In the process Mackenzie might even realize how she and her hosts were both in fact alike. It was for that Lilith hoped, for had those same wise ones not taken the goddess into their care and seclusion all that time long gone?

The Creature Lilith knew the Mackenzie, as she too had once journeyed along a corrupt path. They had made no judgment, which was the key to opening her eyes, albeit partially. The Ones from the mountains shared a comparable ability to read micro-expressions on a face as the Mackenzie could, expressions which the ordinary Being might try to hide, a skillful trait of both Buddhist and psychopath. The enlightened Ones from the mountains, residing in the constant flow of Now, had chosen not to rise into the layered worlds, but instead saw their aspiration as guiding lesser evolved Beings towards understanding.

It could not be said that the Mackenzie had not evolved, but the succession of unwise choices she had made so far, in so many ways, and in so many lifetimes, had only steered her on a distorted course. It was out of step and out of rhythm with other Beings. The Earthbound Ones from the mountains would be able to guide her onto a wiser passage. On this new path the Mackenzie might understand that by helping others she met with on her journey, she would be helping herself also, as well as satisfying her hunger to hold dominion. On the face of it, the Being Mackenzie was indeed a creature of despicable means and actions, but the sum of a Being's outcomes is not discerned or judged by their surface choices. The conundrum was somewhat like a hall of mirrors, where a mirror reflecting another bends back and back into an impression of infinity.

...and what of the Being Mackenzie's 'victims'? What choices had led to their outcomes? As reprehensible as the Mackenzie was, she was but one thread in the Great Fabric woven on the Loom of Life...

"Be vigilant in your use of Metaphor young Lilith," came the voice of We Are All. "Be mindful of all things, especially those of the Now We reside in."

It was sound advice. We Are All was acting in the best interests of the Creature Lilith's journey to understanding, and understanding did not require platitudes or navel gazing. It required 'being' where and what you were, in any given moment of Now.

The Creature Lilith duly withdrew from philosophising, to return her internal gaze to the manifestation she was in at that very moment. She could sense an approach. The vibration of footsteps sent shivers across her reclining flesh. To listen in to the sounds about her required a conscious disengagement from We Are All, which in itself was a welcome relief.

Chapter Twenty-Two

Under a glorious blue sky of high summer, an elderly Elliot leisurely strolled across the familiar stretch of beach towards the lighthouse.

He watched as his three grandchildren and terrier dog, ran here and there along the shoreline, pausing on occasion to look into rock pools and squeal with delight over strange worlds hidden there. His family had been coming here for years, long before the children had arrived, and even long before he had met his wife.

Years ago his late mother had said one day, out of the blue, that she was taking both himself and his sister on a seaside holiday, and without doubt, it had been the best thing to happen to their previously lonely lives. At the time, his parents were estranged and paid little attention to the children, instead mostly palming them off to endless clubs and camps which enhanced their social prestige, rather than inspired their children.

That pivotal holiday had allowed both brother and sister to be kids, to play and explore and be themselves, and he and Ruby had blossomed in the wonders. As the years passed, the siblings grew in confidence and began to ask questions about life. In the process, they found some questions took time to answer, if there were answers at all. Questions like how a pebble became a pebble, and how it might once have been part of a mountain as high as the Himalayas, and, how one day the pebble might be sand. It was where Elliot had first kindled a love of music found in natural things, and where his sister Ruby had first begun her journey as a particle physicist, sitting with their mother, watching the waves roll in.

There was something about this place which reconnected a soul with the fundamentals of things, just through the simple pleasures of living. Time seemed to slow here, only to speed up again as the end of their stay drew near. In the relatively small window of time when they did stay however, they were as one. He and his sister Ruby had sworn an oath to each other to come back. So while their mother had retired to more salubrious surroundings, as they became adults and parents themselves, they were true to their promise.

Part of the pledge they had set in motion, was to never neglect their children because of misguided ego. As children, they had witnessed their parents fall fowl to the disease of ego and were determined not to do the same. As Elliot crunched through the sand he considered the way in which their mother had recently died, quite inconspicuously whilst on holiday alone. In fact her demise was only discovered when the new guests arrived and a maid came to clean the 'Do Not Disturb' room. It was all very sad. He and his sister loved their mother, despite her horrendous social climbing and snobbery. She really was just a silly woman who was obsessed with the superficial, and whose botoxed face needed very little embalming from the funeral parlour that had received her. Nevertheless, they both shed tears when they buried her, because they knew in her heart she loved them. Their father meanwhile was still very much alive somewhere, doing very well it seemed, successful on his own terms and on wife and family number three apparently. He had never really engaged with either Ruby or Elliot, having been absent one way or another throughout their childhood. Now looking at his grandchildren at play, Elliot wondered why so many people missed the precious gift of life for the sake of baubles.

How awful it would be not to be missed!

The little seaside town became a place for annual family get-togethers of the two evolving and expanding tribes. It wasn't perfect. It was much like most coastal towns, provincial, caught in a loop, and as vulnerable to the encroaching world as anywhere. On the tidemark, nomadic plastic cups and bags tangled in the thrown up seaweed. But to Elliot, Ruby and their families, it was the perfect antidote to an otherwise frenetic everyday life, crammed full with modern distractions. When they came here, it was to discard the clutter and nonsensical pressures of linear living. It was where each of them could laugh, listen to the seagull cries, watch the constant flow of the tide, and where, if they sat for a while in the morning or the evening light, they could hear their own heartbeat should they choose to listen. Elliot the Boy had even thought one time he could hear all the different rhythms from across the World come rushing to this shore. It was like an orchestra warming up, which entwined, seemed to link and become one: a global syncopation.

The composition which had launched the name Elliot Ellis, was a piece inspired by those early rhythms, composed by Elliot the Man, and performed by impoverished Indian street children, who made orchestral instruments from the rubbish found on the landfill where they lived. Unlike his parents' apparent need for fame and gain, he and his sister longed to make a difference in the short stay they had in the World, and if truth be known, both brother and sister knew they were who they were, because of their parents' counter views. If not for them, they may have never asked, *what other way is there to be?*

"Grandah! Grandah! Look what we found!" the children huddled over the seawater filled bucket and dropped in yet another treasure with a satisfying plop. "What's the name of this one Grandah?"

Grandah Elliot surveyed their find, and then began to speak methodically about the creature his young prospectors had pulled from the deep of a rock pool.

"Ah now," the grandfather slowly considered, "notice the reddish-brown colour, and its characteristic pie crust edge around the oval carapace shell. Can you see the black tips to the claws? This my Dears, is your Common Brown Crab," he added, tapping the side of the bucket. "This is Cancer Pagurus!"

"Well I'm going to call him Keith!" said one grandson defiantly.

"You got to name the last one," another grandson argued, "and Stewart's a stupid name for a starfish!"

"It might be a girl crab?" quietly suggested his granddaughter. "We could call her Peggy."

The two older boys paused for a moment before laughing out loud.

"With those claws? Of course it's a boy!"

They began snapping claw hands at each other in mock crab battle. The granddaughter looked forlorn, at which her kindly grandfather stepped in.

"Now Boys, you are gravely mistaken if you think the female of a species is the weaker, or less aggressive than the male. There are many, many examples in the animal kingdom which..."

But Elliot's grandsons had seen a new distraction, and were already running across the sands.

"Come on," said Grandah Elliot, taking hold of his granddaughter's hand. "Let's put this gal back where she belongs. By the way, where's Snifter?"

His granddaughter pointed to where a group of beach combers were gathering, and when the pair caught up with them, they saw that Snifter, their Grandfather's loyal but ever-curious terrier dog had his nose flat into the sand and was breathing in something unseen. A fisherman carrying an old bucket was looking over their shoulders and nodding approvingly.

"He's come to give me a hand, has he? Or a paw maybe?" The man asked, but when met with blank faces he added, "For my fish bait. He'll help me find 'em."

The children looked to their elderly guardian for explanation, and he gestured to where they were standing. Tiny piles of curled sand, like unravelled knots of wool, sat in piles and dotted the surface as far as the sea's edge. By each coiled cone were saucer-shaped indentations adjacent to the pile. The fisherman bent over where Snifter was enthusiastically snorting, his tail a wagging blur. The man took out a small trowel from his jacket and began to carefully dig down into the dip on the sand.

Down beneath their feet, the Creature Lilith twitched. In the transition to her new expression, she had now lost some of the greater memory of the Being she was before, and with each twitch of her segmented body, her higher consciousness strobed. This loss of consciousness was as it had to be. Anything other would be horrifying, if a Being was undeveloped in its understanding. Ordinarily it was necessary of course, for Beings to lose memory entirely when they returned to, a new, corporeal form. Of course for Lilith the purpose of this particular body was to return her to a deeper appreciation, to a sense of the humble, to remember how far she had come, and how far she had to go and: to remember there was no need to rush in the constant flow of Now.

There in the warmth of her mucous filled chamber, she yearned to perceive the sun. Sensing its warmth filtering down through her crystalline universe, she wriggled again, drawing down salt water through her feathery gilled mouth. Water, some say, may carry memory, of where it has been, and what or who has travelled in it.

Why was it Beings such as Angela could be defined in their basic makeup to be nothing more than buckets of water and a bag of minerals? They were something other than a mere collection of chemicals, something more than just H2O. Had they not made their choice of being so they might experience tears?

The Creature Lilith knew that primate Beings could cry, that canine Beings will also cry tears when distressed and some elephant Beings as well. Each tear carries the ingredient of its cause. Oils, antibodies, enzymes, and natural painkillers, released when stressed, are all suspended in salt water. Yet time and again Beings make choices, returning them to a place of tears, both happy and sad. She knew her arithmetic. On average a hundred and twenty litres of tears in a lifetime she thought, though The Creature Lilith was unsure as to how scientists might measure this.

In her quest to develop a more deferential modesty, the Creature Lilith had emerged, or rather submerged into the physical world, as a blind invertebrate who basically ate the microbial debris and shit of the sea. After each gulping salty spasm, she would indecorously evacuate a skein of muddied sand from her back end, her purpose simply to eat and shit all through the brief existence of life. Like all other Beings, she had a vital part to play. She was to re-work and re-oxygenate the sand, as well as serve as a food source for other animals. This was her necessary lot, for possibly four or five years, during which time she would be obliged to consume crap, occasionally breed more of her kind and avoid if she could, becoming a tasty morsel for fish or fowl. The humour was not lost on her. You are what you eat indeed. If ever there was a way to remind a Being as to how haughty she might have become, this was it.

To some What Lay Below contains all the poisons of human nature. Things we all share. Well, We got that right.

And now above her, the sand sky was falling in. The ceiling of her subterranean cell was descending about her, and giants were stalking her world. Suddenly, she was being pulled up.

"It's horrible!" the boys leered at the squirming creature. "It hasn't got any eyes. Can we take it to school?"

"What is it Grandah?" asked the granddaughter meekly.

"This is Arenicola marina or better known as the lugworm, or sometimes the blow lug." Elliot began to speak with animation. "Very interesting creature this, children. Very important for cleaning up the beach."

"She's fat and disgusting!" The two boys pulled faces at their sister.

"FAT? OUTRAGEOUS!" Lilith squirmed in the fisherman's gloved hand.

"Well in fact, the lugworm is both male and female," the old man raced to his granddaughter's defence, "which means it is a hermaphrodite."

"Yuck! Kill it!" The boys were jumping on the spot.

"There is something quite amazing about this animal," Elliot continued, ignoring his grandsons' delight in destruction. "Lugworms also have a clever way to avoid being eaten. The part of them which is usually exposed to predators, that would be the tail, can be re-grown if part of it is bitten off, similar to some lizards. I know there are geneticists who are studying animals like this to see if they can find ways for humans to re-grow limbs."

"Let's cut off its tail and see what happens!" the boys exclaimed with demonic glee as the thought of Frankenstein type experiments piqued their interest again.

"Oh no," interrupted the fisherman," this one is fat and juicy, just right for catching a bass."

"FAT? AGAIN?" Lilith twisted indignantly in his grasp.

The fisherman closed his fingers around Lilith's wriggling form. Elliot's granddaughter meanwhile was clearly upset and looked to her grandfather with glistening eyes.

"Well I think she's beautiful. Why can't we just leave her be?" She protested to her brothers, each completely unaware of the majestic being in their presence. "And I shall call her, Lily."

A brief look was exchanged between the two men, and Lily the Lugworm was placed back into the muddy sediment to resume her so far, surprisingly eventful life.

Chapter Twenty-Three

She looked at her watch again, regarding the second hand tick forward in time. *How funny, the spaces in between each tick hid so much from this linear world.* It read half past seven. This was an hour's difference to the clock on the building opposite her. Her half closed eyes wandered in their gaze, while the periphery of her vision was blurred and out of focus.

"Time," she murmured, "such a curious thing. The onward flow of the constant Now."

The woman on the ledge was coming to, up from the depths of a dreamy reverie, and not yet fully in her body. Below her, scurrying life looked a little like ants.

Theoretically, I am potential energy. If I fell now I would create velocity. And should my body hit the ground, I would release heat. How clever life is. I had better not fall.

Her bystander thoughts floated lazily around her like passing clouds, observing the woman on the window ledge and this scene in Aix-en-Provence. This was the place she had whispered to in the window of the travel agents, and that she remembered now. Sleepily stretching out her arms, and with closed eyes, she let a soft trilling warble ascend from her throat. A cloud of birds swept up from the square below as shadows moved quickly across the cobbled ground, and the Sun began to shine its light fully on the day. Warm dry heat slummed on dusty pavements, and people below were setting up market stalls to sell fresh fruit and vegetables under striped canopies. The Diva's song had attracted attention from the ground, and someone looked up, shading their eyes to see what or who was on the window ledge high above. Suddenly coming to her waking senses, she hurried to hide, and tumbling backwards through the open window, fell into the cool, bijou bedroom behind her.

On the iron frame bed laid a carefully packed rucksack, with a holdall, passport, purse and a laminated list of global time zones. Flicking open the passport, her portrait stared back at her sternly.

'Angela Valerie Gealach.'

The new trans-temporal abilities that she was still in the process of refining meant Angela, or Angie, had no real need for a passport anymore, as clearly she could travel a different road, by different means. However, from now on, when visiting old haunts and new destinations, appropriate dress would be necessary in this corporeal world so as to retain an appearance of a Being who was part of things. She would always have to have a story to back her comings and goings. This fabrication would be nothing new to her, falsehood was something she was already well practised in. Had she not lived as 'Angela Bagner' convincingly for years, even enduring an intimate relationship under another similar pseudonym, that of Valerie Bagner? These entirely conjured characters had served to conceal much of her original self. Perhaps it had been a necessary evil, if she needed to remain out of the spotlight for a while.

Just supposing, before she had left home at seventeen, she had decided the Monster who had damaged her as a child, must be removed from the planet. Her continuing nightmares may have inspired her cause and finally driven her into action. It would have been a fairly simple plan to execute, for example, perhaps after arranging a meeting through a dubious personal advert, she might have lured the Monster to secluded farmland during perhaps, a national celebration, such as a Royal Wedding. In order to undertake such an enterprise, as much undisturbed time as possible would have been required, and so in that hypothetical scenario, Angela, or Angie, might take advantage of the fact that the general public did seem to enjoy a good wedding and their collective attention would be elsewhere. One could imagine the Object of Base Corruption puffing on his pipe unguarded, oblivious to what was meticulously planned for him.

"So innocent, just the way I like my girls. My Girls."

Once sullied, his victims were left like empty shells, there would always be another and another. In light of this, an observer might well agree that whatever happened would be his just desserts. In a way he was simply being returned the favour. But it is so easy to judge. There may have been a situation where he might have become the prey. If so it would be entirely his own downfall, surely? Just supposing say, the Monster had been enticed by false promises, to a lonely, disused farm outbuilding, where a tantalising ingénue, paraded provocatively. If she had been nearly naked save for a paper overall and rubber boots, what then?

If slowly, she had coyly moved nearer towards his drooling jowls, with a strangely marked talisman hanging by a leather cord about her young neck and against her young breasts, what might that lead to? He would have been very wrong in thinking she might invite yet more delightful degeneracy. Curiously she might have carefully placed her discarded clothes away from the scene in a plastic bag, simulating an almost ceremonial ritual to further engorge her audience of one. She might even at an earlier time, have removed her body hair, and with it all markers of pubescent maturity, so as to allay any suspicions from the Monster about her juvenile suitability. Of course, if so, this same near nudity beneath the paper suit, would serve as the perfect method allowing her to walk away, from anything, seemingly unblemished. In this hypothetical senario, more than unblemished, 'squeaky clean' would be easy to achieve. By making use of the agricultural power washers, designed for sterilising areas for livestock, it would simply be a question of a quick wash down.

An observer might guess that removing any body hair would also lessen any forensic evidence left behind, and confound investigators looking for the person or persons responsible.

The Monster however, would not suspect that the Innocent had already drugged him with medication obtained to subdue an ailing parent. The Monster would be equally unaware, that the sedative dosage administered would be just enough to keep him incapacitated, but not so much that he lost consciousness throughout his 'learning experience'.

He needs to make the cerebral connection.

There may even have been a slight altercation, in which the Monster had fought against his small assailant, during which, her young hand may have been cut, but of course, if this had been an actual event, the cautionary application of a gag and plastic fence ties would have been sufficient to curb any further struggle. Then slowly, but nonetheless savagely, the Virago might have carved and cut and slashed the Monster apart with a chiselled flint taken from the field outside. She might even have carefully delivered a commentary to her victim as if they were part of a corporate training film. In such a circumstance it might have been necessary in the latter part of the task to make use of the claws of perhaps a Bengal Tiger or the talons of a Bird of Prey. Such items were very rare of course but people can have the strangest of collections. Perhaps items like these would be obtained from a collection of antique artefacts inherited from a father. If this had been the case, her homespun skills in dressmaking might have been put to good use, customising perhaps some robust leather gloves to accommodate the talons. Musing on the scenario, it would have been a whimsy of fine detail, but if it had happened, it would be a token of affection in that; she would have wanted her Father with her, albeit in the treasured charms from his Motherland. She might have even imagined him being a little proud of how she had taken command of the situation.

He would have wanted to be there.

Then just supposing much later, after the removal of all the offending internal soft tissue had been satisfactorily completed, the architect of this hypothetical scenario was to leave only the flayed skin and carcass behind, as perhaps a poetic postscript to the Monster's many victims. This would of course have meant that when the Monster's remains were finally found, the little forensic evidence which survived to tell any kind of tale would be flimsy indeed. After wild foxes had used the offal to feed their young cubs, the bones and flesh might then suggest a tale of terrible animalistic carnage. Investigators might easily come to the conclusion the victim had been dispatched with the cold cruelty of a creature bereft of emotion, rather than calculated rage. Pathologists would be left dumbfounded by the lacerations on the cadaver performed not with knife but with claw. Urban myths might grow as to the killer being an escaped panther which had roamed the moorland for some years before.

Truth be known, truth is in the eye of the beholder. The investigating police might have already known of the Monster's proclivities and had little sympathy or inclination to pursue legitimate answers or justice on his behalf, and ultimately the likely identity of the perpetrator was never established. Supposing then, by an extraordinary stroke of coincidence, a local farmer, worrying about his sheep, shot an escaped black panther on nearby moorland. On inspection, blood matching that of the murdered man might be found under its claws. By finding this supposed predator, perhaps stolen months before from a local coastal zoo, detectives might be relieved to put two and two together, happily pushing the answer five into a closed file. Whoever might have stolen the beast would need an accomplice or, a remarkable way with animals. The same detectives in this conjured tale might never have found the Monster's pipe, though the remains of his tobacco stained fingers told them he was definitely a smoker.

Often a person with predatory psychopathic tendencies might keep mementos of a kill to remind them of the power they wielded. However, it was unlikely the panther had kept the pipe as a trophy. It was noted the panther had the remains of a state-of-the-art pacemaker, found semi-digested in its stomach. But of course, all of this could be just murderous fantasy. Perhaps just a dark flight of fancy from the troubled mind of a violated child, longing for vengeance. Anything is possible.

During this time, the seventeen year old Angela Gealach was as they might say, long gone. She left home, adopting her middle name of Valerie and took Bagner as her surname; a name derived from an old story passed down from her Great Grandmother to her father, and then to his daughter Angela. Bagner was the Child Angie's attempt of pronouncing the word 'Bhaggna', meaning 'escape' or 'flight', and the tale it arose from was of a strange and beautiful woman who had flown from a different world in answer to the prayers of her beloved, earthbound Mother. Angela's father had arrived from India in the charge of a young Scottish woman, who had offered opportunity and education. Jeannie Gealach was an idealist determined to make changes in favour of social justice, and rather than send money to a distant, sponsored child, she had decided to take more direct action. As part of a company of musicians and artists travelling to more impoverished areas of the World, encouraging peace through education and culture, they had found themselves in the urban wastelands of Western disregard. Jeannie Gealach's little band were working with children from a rubbish mountain on a city's outskirts when she had befriended the boy Sachin. A strange little boy, he was underfed like the many others, but had an odd way of asking questions which seemed quite other-worldly,

"How do I know you hear the same sounds as me?"

"What is the colour of love?"

"Is the Universe real?"

And,

"When does Time end?"

The musicians and artists (Jeannie being one of the latter), were making instruments from the waste and junk with the children. Oil cans became drums, biscuit tins changed into stringed guitars and old tubing lived again as whirling winds. After a time, Jeannie recognized the boy Sachin had a sensitive gift for music, and decided to approach his parents with an offer for their son to live and learn in her country. They were overjoyed. He however, was reluctant to go, but his mother and father were eager for him to escape, so they praised the Gods for such good fortune and sent him tearfully away.

He grew up in a colder clime, surrounded by love and music and art, but so as to keep the memory of his previous life alive, he would recall again and again the stories his old Maataaji had told him. His marriage to Little Angie's mother had been an unwise one, but imbedded in his personal code, was a sense of obligation, duty and obedience, besides this, he could not leave his children alone with his wife, especially his shy and fragile daughter. Little Angie made her beloved Father tell his tales over and over. An especial favourite was the story of the Lady who came from the Moonlight, perhaps because she so longed to have a loving Mother of her own. For her, 'Bagner' became equated with 'hope'.

The persona of Valerie was to be one of 'quiet mouse', and perfectly suited to being overlooked. This was an easy transition, for despite being a child of incredible imagination, she had learned early on the skill of keeping quiet when necessary. Disappearing into obscurity as an adult became easy enough too, whether in the anonymity of a couple or as a woman alone.

There came a point when Angela announced to the Night a refusal of any more dreams of shame and guilt, and sure enough they stopped, or rather, she could no longer remember them. Neither could she remember what had happened, or what she had done. Just as she began to master her new personality, Love marched into her life at long last, and she found herself quite unprepared for its blunt impact. The character Valerie had spun out of control and despite her apparent amnesia regarding the despatched Monster, she continued to be haunted each night with dreams of Hell, and each day with feelings of self loathing. The carefully chosen charade was too difficult to balance alongside real emotion, yet it was vital she remained an unknown. During every passing day she became more unsettled by the yearning to tell all: to be herself. The only thing clear was that she loved someone out of her reach, and so in fear of exposure, Valerie in turn had disappeared and became Angela in Lossingham.

It had been the perfect ruse, a shy spinster with no family to speak of, impeccable in her work and a blank face in public. Her commonplace was her camouflage. The sort of person no one would notice and no one would miss. These masks had served their purpose. Often though, her seemingly empty expression would become a canvas onto which it was all too easy for unrequited paramours or shallow minded bullies to project their own needs and desires. Gradually as she immersed herself into the character Angela Bagner, more of her true self struggled to be released like a bird in a cage.

'Angela Valerie Gealach.'

Passport photos never really show the true person, and certainly not now. Now she was Angie, a woman with a mission known only to her. She would adopt the mono-stage name of, 'Angeliquita,' deliberately fostering an air of outrageous mystique allowing her to travel the World with perhaps some carefully chosen companions, loyal and secretive about her whereabouts or private inclinations.

Now, the best way to hide is in plain sight, and so she reverted back to the name on her birth certificate. She would be Angela Gealach, her Father's adopted name, changed on leaving his motherland. Angela Gealach had plans for travel, but not in the linear corporeal world alone. During her timeless conversations with the Creature Lillith, they had discussed what it was 'to Be', and what it was to be: 'a Being'. The Goddess had even spoken favourably on the Being Shakespeare, adding immodestly about some influence she'd had on his writing when he suffered from 'block'.

"First of all, We must ask our self, What are We here for?" The Creature Lillith had been so patient, gently guiding Angela when it must have been like infant's building blocks to her. "It is very simple. The reason We are here, is to celebrate and prove the limitless power of We Are All. And that is why," she added with a wry chuckle, "that is why Beings make so many, shall We say, unwise choices. For if We didn't, and We were always wise in everything, what would We learn? We Are All moving and changing in the flow of Vitruvian Time. Therefore, how else would We move closer to understanding We Are All?" Lilith smiled a wide serrated smile and added. "We know it is hard to conceive, but even We still make unwise choices and We accept We have to face the outcomes these create."

At this point the Creature Lilith did sound somewhat reminiscent of an early 20th century earthly, stereo-typical school marm, circa 1950, which would have appalled her as she looked dreadful in tweed.

"But what exactly is this, this, We Are All?" Angela felt foolish as she asked, because she could already feel the answer rising up into her conscious mind, like bubbles from an upturned vessel in the bottom of a well. "I... I think I know. Is it that we are all part of a collective mind, and that we are all expressions of this collective mind?"

Her tutor smiled reassuringly.

"Hold on tight to that thought Dear One. You are so very close. When you return to your world much of what you sense here will submerge, and as our mergence will have for you a perceived distance, your memory will be lost to a degree."

The Owl Woman's companion looked dismayed. So as to alleviate any possible anxieties, she quickly added,

"We have visited several excellent Cetacean Beings in your world who We know would be more than happy to educate you in Vitruvian Time Travel, when they're not getting intoxicated on puffer fish of course. Yes, We found them to be greatly progressed towards understanding. Unfortunately their names are unpronounceable for Beings such as your kind. They have a marvellous method of alternating their two brain hemispheres, one is always in what you might call an REM state, while the other remains in the conscious state. They change these around of course, to maintain equilibrium of the two. We thoroughly recommend you visit with these dolphins, so as to further develop your existing abilities. Then it will be a virtual hop, skip and a jump before We will be meeting again in next to no time." Her last remark she thought terribly amusing but it was lost upon the artless Angela. The unworldly woman was too busy trying to lodge all she was being told into her memory banks. How to practise living in the flow of Now, the need to visit puffer fish loving dolphins for trans-dimensional time travel lessons and, to guide those she knew were making unwise choices. It all suddenly sounded quite ridiculous, mainly because she also found it so acceptable.

"Heavens! I only need to don a cape and I'll be a super hero!"

"Well, We don't often wear a cloak We grant you, but We are nonetheless... quite fabulous."

The Creature Lillith chortled with a grin. Time had not improved her comedic skills in the least, but she was working towards it. At best she was achieving camp.

When Angela did finally return back to the moment she had left, back to piñatas and henchmen and silly, silly escapades in ego, her mind was made up. Regardless of how much she had become fond of pottering in her Lossingham life (jam-making was such a satisfactory hobby), now she had been introduced to the layered worlds, the setting point of her wild plum conserve paled when compared with trans dimensional time travel. It was a close second admittedly, but second nevertheless.

A plan of action was forming. Number One, she would engage in moving towards this idea of, We Are All. This might require honing her skills in the Flux of Now. She had noticed on the window ledge how her physical body had not quite synchronised with her Vitruvian body and had appeared to fluctuate, giving the appearance of two images which had not quite successfully superimposed. Perhaps a visit to the cetaceans endorsed by the Creature Lilith might prove fruitful in adjusting this. Number Two, she would help others come to understanding as well. After all was said and done, the tenuous relationship she had briefly experienced with Mr. Messenger had been no less pivotal in her present evolution. Angie began hoping she might do the same for someone else. And Number Three, (and most importantly), she intended to keep watch over choices made by other Beings. The games some Beings played could be wide, diverse and tragically, often depraved. Taking on the role of a cosmic 'guidance counsellor' would hold them in check and nudge them hopefully, in the wiser direction. She would rebalance the worlds of the two domains from the menace of damaged souls, and there was one in particular she had in mind to begin with.

'They had started something like that in the Finance Department hadn't they? Mentoring? It takes one to know one as they say.'

Angela was determined to play amongst them to bring a balance as much as she was able. A stratagem of conscious subterfuge was to be her life now, and in order to do that, she considered the cover story of a globetrotting entertainer to be the most viable. During her experience of travelling with the Creature Lilith, some residual goddess DNA had merged with her own. The result was an extra sensory receiver of sorts, whereby she could locate like-minded Beings nearing understanding of We Are All. Whether engaged in wise choices or not, the pulse of the flow in her veins would enable her to trace their co-ordinates should she choose to focus upon them. For example, she could sense the Mackenzie was safe in the World and, for the time being, the World was safe from the Mackenzie. The reforming one had travelled with the Sangha, who the Creature Lilith had described to her as 'community of the excellent ones'. Strictly speaking their name referred to those who had achieved certain levels of understanding. Angela knew their newfound companion had spent a short time in the Mountains before they parted company. It was difficult to pinpoint an exact location, but it was definitely in this world and time.

"They are fascinating Beings you know. As they have moved towards deeper understanding of We Are All, they have developed a similar ability to read micro expressions as to what your world would term as a signature profile trait of a 'psychopath'."

The Owl Woman looked at the Being Angela as if it were self explanatory.

"They not only discern truth, they can also perceive to what degree a Being is fused in Vitruvian Time. That is why they can understand how and where a Being has manifested from and, where they are likely to manifest to. Everything has a positive side you know."

She arched her eyebrow and nodded to Angela with a knowing smile, adding,

"No Being is all bad. You should understand this."

It would be easy to make a judgement as to the hypocrisy of Angela's enterprise. Yes, it was extremely possible Angela had indeed been a cold and calculating murderer earlier in her previously sorry life, but who now was better experienced for the job of protecting a newly changed Mackenzie? Fresh from the Layered Worlds, some sympathy had to be found for Mackenzie now that she was capable of empathy towards her fellow Beings. And who was better equipped to shield Mackenzie, should she meet her dangerously powerful global family, bent on rising to the top of any heap made by Mankind or Monster? It could be no one other than Angela. During the unfathomable passage of time spent in the company of metaphysical Beings such as Lilith, Angela had begun to look more deeply into her own beginnings and consider why she had experienced all that she had. In particular she considered her childhood. Had it really been as black and white as it might appear? Was it fair that she had previously relinquished herself of any responsibility? Wasn't that what victims were allowed to do? Who was to blame, the chicken or the egg?

Inaccurate. When does anything begin or end?

Briefly she had sensed, in her night time flights, and during her practise of slowing time, lingering moments left from long before any memories of her present life, moments in which she heard an echo from a past self, a self who was angry, ungrateful and deprecating of Life all around them, a person who thought only of their own interests, to the point where...

Was it possible I chose my Mother because I needed to see my own reflection?

It was not exactly an epiphany, as it was still much too clouded, like a tarnished mirror, but it was enough to allow Angela to begin appreciating what the Creature Lilith meant by moving 'towards understanding'.

If you wish to understand the outcome you reside in Now, the goddess had slowly delivered, *reflect on what choices you have made, and if you wish to sense what your outcomes will be, reflect upon what choices you are making.*

As for Mackenzie, alone, it was to be a sure journey to disaster, but with the help of a fledgling guardian, such as Angie, there might be some hope of transforming the darkness of both women, for no one knew what it was like to be totally different in a crowd more than Angela or Angie. An owl in daylight will notice things that others cannot: micro expressions of truth.

Yes, it would be perfectly understandable to judge, but it has to be admitted there was without doubt, serious mitigating circumstances to be taken into consideration. The deceased Monster had previously left Angela emptied of any self worth, existing on the outside, looking and functioning as everybody else, but at her core, there was something so out of place, out of time and always in flux. People around her would have been repelled and even attack if she had not played her acting role. Unexpected episodes of dancing on tables were at odds with the 'shy and retiring' profile she had previously employed, but a new artistic temperament could be the perfect explanation. Then if at some point in the future, in the timeline she presently resided in, someone should join all the dots, and venture to bring about any kind of historical legal justice, Angela could easily cite a background so troubled, it was nothing short of a miracle she had not strayed off the path of righteousness any further.

Perhaps the small matter of hypothetical torture and murder could be seen in this light as nothing more than a 'blip'. It would be a difficult case, as there were obviously manifest symptoms of Angela's mental ill-health. The partnership with Los Diablos would be the perfect vehicle to establish her as an icon of charitable virtue, and protect her from any future attacks. Here in Aix she could de-stress from all the recent changes and get her mind clear, so as to be one step ahead of any inquisitive interest.

Such a long journey, but when seen from a different perspective, it had taken her no time at all. There was indeed, 'no time like the present'. On the first night in Aix it was so warm, she had fully opened the top floor window to see a huge smiling moon shining down on her. A full moon, a time for ripening, and a time for fulfilment. When she slept, it was such a deep sleep she might have been at the bottom of the ocean, and she had thought perhaps that her wings had fallen from her back, like antlers out of season. Inspecting her back now in the small armoire mirror, to the centre of her spine were the remains of what they had been. Two bee sting bumps, side by side, and she smiled at how beautiful scars could be when they were healed. As she had reached to touch the little blemishes, she felt the outline and softness of her wings and realised they were still there and attached. The Creature Lilith had explained to her as best she could, as to how her wings had become.

"When you met with the Being Gabriel, some residual DNA from both he and the broken bird Being, transferred over into you."

With her eyes closed and her wide spread palm, she sank into the moment she stood in. The plumes were reverberating at the speed of dancing photons making them invisible to the human eye, but those beautiful downy feathers were still with her, and they spoke to her. Hovering there, about seven centimetres above the bedroom rug, she lovingly stroked her back for what might have been a lifetime, in an eon without age. She remembered it all, everything she had experienced in this world, and as for anything she had known in any other, she accepted them as possible outcomes, for anything was possible in the layered worlds of We Are All. It was only a question of making changes to the type of choices she had previously made when she had been, Angela-the-Owl-in-Daylight, Angela-the-Beige and, Angela-the-Virago.

"There are many kinds of Angels."

There had always been a choice, and now at last she felt comfortable in her own skin, with or without visible wings. Angie patted them affectionately. They had brought her to here, to where she had some different understanding of how to be. Journeying into the layered world had shown her this, how even though everything is always moving on the tidal pull of change, it is nevertheless unchanging. To say it was simply past, present and future would be an inadequate description, but it was an easier explanation for an average Being in motion to comprehend.

True Time was the moment in which everyone stood, in the onward flow of the constant 'Now'. Behind the black and white facade of so-called good always overcoming apparent bad, she knew each Being was in a flow, a current of an endless sea, a sea of possibilities moving to a greater understanding.

The conclusion Angela had come to, was that Beings were at their most powerful when they resided in the 'Now', for it was here their future was created, and now she had tasted power, she intended to have more. But what was it that Lilith had told her? To beware the word should. She had said,

"Religion for example, can attract Beings you might call bureaucrats, those who love setting out regulations, and subsections, and rules, and shoulds and should-nots. Sad really, because in truth, there are no definitive rules in We Are All, other than We Are All responsible for our choices and the outcomes they create. Knowing this will help us deepen our understanding, as everything We think, say or do will ripple out into other Beings' lives. As we move towards understanding, We are striving to employ caution and spontaneity at the same time, an impressive skill to wield," adding as an after-thought, "a little like walking a tightrope over a ravine whilst brandishing a long sword. We learned this from a Being called Genghis – Tamujen to his few friends. Very entertaining fellow. Awful bad breath."

The morning was passing quickly, and Angie sensed there was urgency for her to leave, for there was a twinge of anticipation in her feet and wings which told her something was awaiting her. Would she need a disguise? Would her secret remain invisible?

"Ah," she whispered to her reflection, "people will see what they wish to see. They fill in the gaps, so they think they understand. We already have the potential to perform all the necessary criteria of elevation, but We cannot ordinarily recognise this. We suppose it's a bit like how bees see our blue sky as purple, only because they can perceive spectral light waves We cannot see and colours We have never seen. It requires effort to evolve. We just have to look in a different way."

Angela dressed quickly and decided to breakfast in one of the cafés she had seen in the street below her hotel. Carefully putting on the rucksack, tucking the passport and purse into the holdall, she slipped on some espadrilles and then made her way downstairs. Running down two steps at a time, the holdall swinging on the whitewashed walls, her hand playing xylophone on the wrought iron railings, she skipped, with her beloved talisman hiding under her dress. Waiving at the concierge, she stepped into the sunlight. So warm! She stood for a moment with her eyes closed, soaking up the heat into her skin. There was an echo in the sounds around her, and she headed towards the main source of the hustle and bustle. Not too far from where she walked came the distinctive rise and fall of a carousel's calliope. Here was the street she had known of from her recent dreams. Dappled sunlight played through the deep green of the lime trees lining the pavements, on which dozens of tables, laid out with crisp linen, stood under the shade of brightly coloured awnings in the morning's golden glow. They looked welcoming and were lively with people, but one cafe in particular drew her attention, partly because of its name, L'Oiseau Du Nuit. The Night Bird. It seemed to beckon her from its black and gold framed window, with soft notes of Latino-jazz and a delicious aroma of freshly brewed coffee wafting through the open door.

Angela sat down at table near to the door and ordered coffee, cognac and a croissant from the aproned waiter. Already there were plenty of other customers enjoying the air near to her table. Many of them were overseas visitors, in town for the music festival Aix was world famous for. Fedoras and foreign newspapers rustled in the lavender-scented breeze, and conversation from all walks of life were exchanged with passion, over coffee and Gitanes. While she waited in the half shade, she felt the warm sun on her skin and relaxed into the gentle noise of life around her. Her heart was full, alone but not lonely, at peace and certainly contented. Shading her eyes, she watched a vapour trail trace across the blue sky. Where were they going, those people up there? In another century, aeroplanes might have been seen as visions or nightmares. It was all a matter of perspective.

"If God had meant us to fly," she joked to herself, "She would have given us wings!"

The waiter arrived to interrupt her mind's wandering as he returned with her order. Leaning back in the cane chair, she took it in turns to take sips of coffee and cognac in the sun. Glorious! In the reflection of the Cafe window, she gazed at who she was. White hair, golden skin and a strong face. Yes she was happy being the age she was too, but more importantly, she was happy as to the person she had become. She was kind, imaginative, courageous, yes definitely courageous, but most of all she was open to possibilities.

Inside the cafe window, Angela was being watched by a woman standing just behind her reflection. A little younger than Angie, with almond shaped eyes and a tussle of brown-black hair sprawling over her shoulders from a loosely held chignon, the woman was looking intently at her through the window. Stepping out from behind the glass, the smiling stranger walked from the café interior straight towards the seated Angie. Angie felt her wings tingle.

"Puis – je vous connais de quelque part?"

"I'm so sorry, my French is very rusty," Angie smiled, offering the woman the empty seat next to her. There was a strange familiarity about her which Angela could not quite place.

"Do I know you from somewhere? What is your name?" The woman translated, in an accent rich with sunshine.

"Angie, though I'm open to suggestions for a new name. And yours?"

"Ange, like an angel," the woman laughed flirtatiously. "I am Catherine. You seem familiar to me. Are you a singer in the festival? Or have we met in my dreams?"

Angela blushed. Never had she met with such a forthright and audacious an invitation as this. Admittedly it was a somewhat overworked line of flirtation, worthy of a well ripened Camembert. But it has to be said, that as Angela had arrived at this point in her life from a place where certain subjects had been completely out of bounds and unspoken, in particular a preference for gender, she was thoroughly enjoying this refreshing turn of events. This beautiful woman called Catherine was brazenly flirting with her and Angela loved it. Their conversation danced from one subject to another, melting sweetly like ice cream in the warm sunshine, punctuated only with laughter and smiles. The waiter came and went with lunch and pastries until the end of his shift, under the orders of Catherine, the owner of L'Oiseau Du Nuit. Catherine was a French-Canadian who lived happily alone, above the cafe. She did not suffer from loneliness as she had many friends, always busy with supper parties and such. Catherine explained she had visited one year, to take part in the Aix International Music festival. She had arrived as a tribal throat singer, but became smitten by the torch song. After the festival was over she found she just couldn't go. The warm climate was too inviting, and so she had made her nest.

"It was as if," Catherine said, looking straight into Angie's eyes, "it was as if I was waiting for something or... someone."

Then, in a somewhat premature gesture of intimacy, the alluring Catherine dropped the shoulder of her loosely tied top, to reveal a beautiful pair of raven's wings tattooed on the sun-kissed skin of her back.

"I am a secret angel," she cooed, "do you like?"

Angie spluttered in astonishment, dropping her coffee cup and smashing it on the ground.

"I'll get you another," Catherine giggled. "I didn't realise I would have such an effect on you, but I'm so pleased I have!"

While she was gone, Angie looked about her. This was certainly a turn of events, yet somehow not entirely unexpected. Her vision of this place washed over her and she smiled. Here, she had just decided, was possibly her new home, for she felt as though she might belong. The cafe was nearing the end of its busy lunchtime and was slipping into a dream-like sleepy afternoon. There were still many customers enjoying the air, including one linen-suited man in particular, who appeared to be watching her from under a white panama and behind dark sunglasses. Curious as to his interest, Angie returned his stare and the man gently waved at her. He slowly folded his English newspaper and stood up, making his way through the tables and chairs towards Angela, now Angie. When he arrived at her table, he tipped his hat in a gentlemanly manner.

"Good to see you again Miss Bagner, or is it Miss Gealach today?" He sat down beside her, placing the newspaper carefully in her gaze. Taking off his sunglasses for a moment, the distinctive turquoise eyes gave away his true identity. It was Gabriel Messenger, the man who made dead birds fly. Angie was understandably speechless, and he patted her hand to reassure her. Stuttering slightly, Angie ventured to speak.

"I read your book," she quietly said, no longer shocked at his presence."Good ideas, but dreadful platitudes."

"Sorry about that, We are still trying to get to grips with Metaphor. We think We will leave Haiku for the Time being."

The two angelicals paused before laughing together. It was a relief to realise they could relax their guard, if only for a short spate of earthbound time.

"We were keen you made the correct timing for this moment, so We took the liberty to give you an early morning call after your, erm, travels." He looked directly into her eyes and she realised it was he who had been knocking that morning, bringing her to from another journey into the layered worlds.

"I, We, We didn't hear you." She stammered, attempting to employ the 'Majestic Plural', but still a little shy in using it. "We had stepped out for a moment to take some air."

"And miscalculated your point of origin? Oh, We do that all the time in the beginning. It does improve though," Gabriel smiled again. "We noticed you on the ledge and We thought it best to rouse you before the Earthbounds did."

"Earthbounds?"

"Yes, Earthbounds are Beings who are still weighted by their choices and outcomes."

The two sat in silence for a while, and Angela, now Angie, realised Time had been slowed again, and that all outside their sphere had been caught in a moment of amber. Time had all but stopped. Gabriel began to chat, but small talk appeared to present more difficulties for him than Metaphor.

"We are en route to Lossingham to write up some notes for the next book. After that, We are seeking more understanding in the mountains. No doubt We will meet again." He then added, "There are some interesting articles in this edition." He tapped the paper like a magician, "We recommend you read them." Then rising from the chair he turned to leave. "Oh, We almost forgot, We made a small present to amuse you."

Then tipping his hat, he placed an envelope on the table then left. Now, perhaps it was the strong sunlight, but the curious thing was Mr. Messenger looked as though he was floating, about seven centimetres above the pavement as he moved away. After he turned a corner and disappeared out of sight,

Angie regained her composure. She opened up the paper and began scanning for what might concern her.

On the second page an article leapt from the paper, entitled,

'Exclusive Interview' "I had to be lost to find myself'

Mackenzie Davis, the multi-billionaire heiress who had mysteriously disappeared, causing her family to undertake a worldwide search, had reappeared some years later with complete amnesia as to where she had been, or what had happened to her. There had been talk of ransoms and terrorists, but all had drawn a blank. The only clue was she had been found wandering by a street urchin, who despite his own troubles had taken the ghostly Mackenzie to a local police station for help. Before her disappearance she had been known as a global business woman, and one who chose to remain as anonymous as it was possible for the super rich, which of course she was. But super rich people always raise curiosity, especially those involved in dubious empires, overlooking the need of a moral compass. Now apparently she was back and changed, desiring nothing more than to create value in the wider world. The article went further in describing how Mackenzie Davis had just completed establishing the newly formed Casimir Foundation promoting Education and Health for peoples in Third World countries.

"It is an excellent endeavour," Ms Davis said, "we can still satisfy our voracious business drive, by the need to deal with governments and other related organisations. We can use our intuitive skills to cut through, shall we say, obstacles, not just for ourselves We must stress, but on behalf of others who may not have the voice of education."

Ms Davis went onto outline her plans to eradicate the Rubbish Mountains which are in growing evidence in urban India. Firstly, Mackenzie described the development of recycling projects to encourage light industry, followed by cultural exchanges for children living there, and finally, transformation of the sites by building health centres and planting orchards of mango trees, known to be a spiritually significant tree in India. When asked about the meaning behind the name 'the Casimir Foundation', Ms Davis enigmatically replied; "It is a force which describes how the Universe works. It gets down into the makeup of life, of atoms and subatomic particles. By using fluctuations in energy fields, in the space between objects, an object could theoretically levitate: much like a gecko can walk across a ceiling. We have come to realise we have but a short stay on Planet Earth and if we have the means, surely We would want to elevate our lives, not just for ourselves, but for others too?"

For a Western woman, this is a monumental task and initiative to deliver, but Mackenzie Davis seems driven by a confounding sense of the power of compassion married with the hard-focussed stare of someone reminiscent of a World Stateswoman. "Compassion can move mountains. Once we engage with the concept, it becomes easier to transmit, and over time, We come to understand, We are all responsible for making life a more valuable experience."

When the pace of Time had resumed and the curvaceous Catherine had returned to Angie's sunlit corner, she found a slightly dumbstruck woman smiling a beaming smile. Angie was taking something out from the envelope.

"What is this you have?" Catherine asked, placing more coffee and cognac in front of her new friend. "Let me see."

"Oh, a friend made this for me," Angie replied thoughtfully, turning the strings attached to a small circle of card. "It's called a thaumatrope. It comes from Old Greek, meaning wonder turner. It has a different picture on either side, but when you spin the card like this, the pictures merge and they become one."

She twisted the toy between her hands, and as she pulled on both strings it began to spin. The image that pulsed was of a winged woman – an angel. When it fell still, Catherine picked up the card to inspect it.

"A woman on one side, and an angel on the other," she mused, "hmm, perhaps this might be you and me, eh?"

"Oh Catherine," Angie smiled back her new and quite lovely companion, "you have no idea, but if you have the heart to try, what do dreams know of boundaries?"

"That was a quote yes? Amelia Earhart?" Catherine squeezed Angie's hand. "Oh I do love adventurous women! Tell me, might you have time to stay for some supper?"

"We certainly will," Angie held on to Catherine's hand, the pair looking somewhat akin to the cover illustration of a romantic novel. *"Now is the time to begin."*

The Being Gabriel was talking to himself as he turned the corner from the Cafe L'Oiseau Du Nuit.

"It is so important to be in the moment, so as to listen out for the details. Those tiny but important things hiding in plain sight."

He had been advised more than once to try not to interfere, for by making a choice he would make an outcome and he would have to accept responsibility for it. Already he was sensing his own outcomes approaching as a result of his original meeting with the Being Angela. Every day, the impending outcome was making its arrival known, in little flickering strobe-micro-seconds, neutral yet ominous. It gnawed at his belly like an undigested fish, twisting and squirming for attention. Even as a new angelical, he knew to become closer in understanding simply meant a process of living and learning, much like another evolved Being he had once met who had said,

We have to continually be jumping off cliffs and developing our wings on the way down.

Now beyond the town, Gabriel had reached the outcrop of purple-black rocks, thrusting out from the lavender field landscape. Cicadas burred in the early evening haze. Hovering like a dragonfly, he gently rose to the rock summit, still debating with himself as he did, to whether or not he had made the wisest choice.

It is so difficult to trust and not to judge. We shall try not to interfere again.

When at last he had reached the ridge shelf he looked about him. He could discern through the flickering light, different phases of Time peculiar to this place, and for a moment, those Times could perceive him. A lone painter pushed back a straw brimmed hat to check what he was seeing, only for what he saw to vanish seconds later. Gabriel was slowing time, and focussing as he did so, in the Now, he suddenly threw himself forward from the rock's edge. Instead of falling to untold injury or worse, his previously unseen wings became outspread and visible, pulling him into a void suspended in midair. Black crows flew up, startled by the vision, while a local farmer, cycling up a nearby dusty track, his mouth watering for his tardy dejeuner, continued home, oblivious to the spectacle of the leaping man behind him. Gabriel's last audible words dissolved along with his physical body into the golden sunlit evening.

"We did say 'articles', did We not? We did suggest she read them?"

The breeze was picking up outside the L'Oiseau Du Nuit Cafe. The two newly acquainted women had retired to the apartment upstairs. All was quiet but for the sounds of mellow music and occasional reels of silvery laughter from the pair. The cafe had closed unusually early that evening, and was still not cleared of all the coffee cups.

"I'll fetch them in later," smiled Catherine, "and you can help me."

The wind was turning, blustering like a herald to something coming, shaking the canopies and parasols lining the street and fluttering open another page of the newspaper which lay discarded on Angela's corner table.

Page seven. Science page. 'D.N.A. BREAKTHROUGH IN HISTORICAL CRIME.'

'A major breakthrough in the refinement of D.N.A. analysis has seen a group of doctors from Lossingham team up with the genetics giant Magnadavistock International. The global MI organisation was initially contacted by Lossingham medics, concerning a patient with an unusual genetic condition, dubbed "Icarus". The hope was that some link could be established with the DNA of similar patients around the world, leading to greater medical understanding. The initial areas of contact between the two organisations have now expanded to include the acclaimed DNA Capture Programme, which allows unsolved historical crimes to be re-opened and solved. Within the programme, a significant local historical murder case is being explored.The infamous 'Shelled Body' murder has lain unsolved for over two decades, but with the exchange of D.N.A. information, and the application of cutting edge techniques, a new strand of the investigation has opened up. Police have provided access to stored D.N.A. samples, including a blood sample not matching that of the victim, extracted from fabric found at the crime scene. Magnadavistock International, the subject of intense scrutiny over its ethical practices in recent years appears to be making strong public relations attempts to change its image. The D.N.A. Capture programme may enhance and invigorate their global profile as a conscientious organisation, keen to distance themselves from previous accusations of scientific storm trooping.

A Police spokesperson confirmed they are encouraged by the breakthrough, and are working with Interpol to widen their net. Their spokesperson could not confirm whether or not an arrest was imminent.

Lossingham Hospital's Medical Director has stated,

"The most impressive aspect of this genetic pooling of resources is how, despite initially thinking of ourselves as but small participants in our input we now realise how we are all deeply connected with each other, whether by the world-wide-web or by our mutual genetic codes."

Up in the small apartment, the two women basked in a golden glow, quite unaware of anything beyond each other. Below their window, a gust of wind tore underneath the abandoned newspaper, lifting the pages from the table up into concealed hands of air, and away the stories flew.

Deborah Sanderson is a multidisciplinary contemporary artist. Her work begins always with the written word. Her creative roots have grown far and deep from the rich soil of film-making, sculpture, painting and performance art. Her visual alchemy transforms colour, texture and imagination into her intriguing debut novel 'The Wonder Turner'.

Deborah lives near Glasgow, Scotland, and spends much of her time working with oils, graphite and sculptural mediums, including mud. Deborah is insistent the abundant use of turpentine in her studio has not influenced the fantastical elements in her written work.

Deborah's visual art can be found at

https://www.facebook.com/DeborahSandersonArt.